No Time For Tears

by Janice M. Turner

PIRAAS PUBLISHING LLC
PO BOX 3093
ALEXANDRIA, VA 22302

Turner, Janice M.

   No Time For Tears/Janice M. Turner

   1. Fiction 2. Thriller 3. Suspense

ISBN: 978-0-9767408-7-2
Library of Congress Control Number: 2009940310

INTRODUCTION

One in every three women knows their perpetrator; one in every three women has been beaten, coerced into sex, or otherwise abused in her lifetime. Hold onto your daughters for dear life. Talk to your sons about their choices…and pray they don't become the perpetrator of any heinous crime.

Innocent women are being stalked; many are raped and brutalized. Let there be no doubt, someone will be victimized, leaving yet another woman scared and scarred for the rest of her life.

Acknowledgements

I would like to personally say thank you to everyone who supported me in the writing of this book. First and foremost are my siblings who braved the moments...vividly and candidly with love; to Dennis, at PIRAAS Publishing who saw the potential within this journey and reached out believing our accomplishment would be something priceless; to Lisa Morris, Janice Holly and Beverly Fleiss, in our perseverance, we each discovered a professionalism and personal conviction that bonded us; J. Elmore, you are truly an inspiration, a very gifted storyteller, and someone who saw in-between the lines with great insight; and to you Keith, for the long hours, dedicated service and constant professionalism you have exhibited, truly you are my right hand.

ON A PERSONAL NOTE, AS REPORTED BY UCSC RAPE PREVENTION EDUCATION

- AROUND THE WORLD AT LEAST 1 IN 3 WOMEN HAS BEEN BEATEN, COERCED INTO SEX, OR OTHERWISE ABUSED IN HER LIFETIME. (JOHN HOPKINS SCHOOL OF PUBLIC HEALTH 2000)

Again, thank you for all of your patience, understanding and commitments to excellence, but more so, thank you for the evolving friendships that go beyond our business.

PROFESSIONALLY,

JANICE M. TURNER

The Story Line

When the reality of misplaced alliances becomes the subject for an investigation, panic ensues among the collegiate community of Taft University. The disturbing report of a fourth victim found battered nearly to unconsciousness has left the community more fearful.

The what...any woman within the reach of the assailant.

The who, at this moment cannot be answered.

The where... in the darkened shadows of the night amongst the moonlight.

Once again, there are no witnesses. The only evidence is the tormented victim of a heinous crime and the distorted recollection of a living nightmare.

Welcome to the maze of secrets and corruption among friends; the jealousy and animosity between brothers; and attraction fueled by unbridled passion among strangers. Eavesdrop on the dialogue that befriends the hidden agendas among them. Discover old alliances that expose a past each of them sought to remain silent. This is a story of desperation among friends, unfulfilled desires between lovers, and a series of violent events that allow… "No Time For Tears"

Chapter 1

"Are you sure she's coming?" Marty felt nervous as he strained his eyes to see the jogging trail. It was dusk, almost fully dark now, and they'd been waiting there for the girl for an hour. He looked down at his feet and kicked at a cigarette butt that was just winking out, the ashes having reached the filter. Marty had to get his mind off the trail, off of the possibility that he may not get what he'd come here for. He counted the butts at his feet, including the one he'd just finished. Five. He'd smoked five cigarettes while they waited here.

He should probably pick them up before he left. Marty leaned over, gathered the butts together with his feet, and made sure the last was out before he took them into his hands. They left an ashy, gray trail on his fingertips, and he could smell them already turning stale.

"Here, pocket these, would you?" He handed them to the big man next to him, who took them with a grunt and shoved them in his shirt pocket, saying nothing. His eyes were fixed on the path.

"Don't throw any of your own onto the ground," Marty cautioned him, and he nodded.

"I ain't smoking today anyways," he said, turning his eyes to Marty and then away again.

Marty glanced over at his companion, taking in his heavy brow and sweeping pompadour of black hair. Geez, it looked like the guy still used a vat of hair grease to style it; his bulk and his hair made him look like a cross between an ape and a throwback to the 1950's. *Or a Neanderthal,* he thought dismissively, looking again at the man's profile. He was staring off into space, ignoring Marty and looking idiotic, as usual. Maybe he was slightly retarded or something; borderline.

Why the hell did he hook up with Kirby anyway? He could have done things better himself.

"I'm going to take off," Marty said, abruptly standing to prove his point and pocketing his cigarettes. "She's not coming. And I've wasted too much time here."

For a moment, Kirby didn't move, and the expression on his face stayed stonily silent. Then without warning, his hand shot out, grabbed Marty's forearm, pulled him back down again.

"She's coming," his tone was even but held a tinge of something menacing, dangerous. "I smell her," he threw back his head and chuckled lightly, the sound of a man disturbed. What he said was weird, or would be to a layperson anyway, but Marty was used to him by now. What Kirby said *was* weird, but it excited Marty, too. He felt the hairs on his arm raise and grow with anticipation. But he kept his cool demeanor.

"How do you know?" he demanded, a slight hint of annoyance creeping into his voice. He fought to hold it down and stay in control. "You told me she doesn't always come. You told me sometimes she takes an evening off."

Kirby clicked his tongue on the roof of his mouth as if to say Marty was nothing short of an inexperienced asshole. While it was true he *was* inexperienced, this being his first such endeavor in fact, he was still a hell of a lot smarter than Kirby, the fucking fry cook or whatever it was he did when he wasn't with Marty. Marty ate people like Kirby for breakfast. As far as he was concerned, Kirby was the blue collar guy happy to do the dirty work so his master could enjoy the fruits of his labor.

"I told you how I know," Kirby sneered, lifting one meaty finger and pointing down the jogging trail.

Marty's eyes jerked to attention. He squinted again as he tried to take in the dusky outskirts of the path.

There she was. Marty felt his breathe hitch back, but just for a second.

Get it together, he told himself, and his breathing returned, calm and uniform.

She was jogging at a nice clip, and Marty had only a minute, maybe two, to take her in and imagine how it would be. Then she would be past them and he would have to think on his feet.

She was slender and athletic. That much he could tell even from this distance and in the darkening light. She had light hair, just as he'd wanted, pulled tight in a long ponytail at the back of her head. He couldn't make out her features, but Kirby had promised she was naturally lovely and built like a colt with long legs, a slim waist, and small, firm,

9

round breasts. Kirby had been watching her for Marty for weeks now, learning everything about her except for her name. That was unnecessary.

She *was* fast; the girl was almost slipping past them even before Marty could entirely gather his courage. He allowed himself one quick glance at her ass, imagining himself sliding into her, no; *slamming* into her from behind.

"I smell your sticky cunt," Kirby sneered, as her feet pounded the pavement in front of them, and Marty froze.

That idiot! That fucking idiot! What if she heard him?

The sound of her feet faded with her form. Her legs pumped along as she headed onward toward the more forested part of the park.

It didn't seem as if she heard him. Marty felt himself relax, and he rose quickly to his feet.

"Go get 'em, tiger," Kirby said, as he leaned back against the park bench they had been sitting on, his own cigarette glued to his bottom lip while his hands draped lazily over the back of the seat. "That's what they say on the commercial. For cereal. With the tiger," Kirby said distractedly. "I like that cereal."

Marty shot him a look of disgust, but otherwise ignored the commentary. He had work to do. As did Kirby.

"Be watchful," Marty hissed back over his shoulder, hoping he could trust the big man with the stupid leer on his face and that he understood what watchful meant. "I mean, keep an eye out for anyone."

10

Kirby nodded, waving him away, and Marty went. It was time.

His ass was sore from sitting so long, but he broke into a light jog himself, trying not to alert her of his presence. He ran along the grassy side of the pavement so she wouldn't hear his approach; unlike most of the joggers he'd noticed, this girl did not wear an IPOD. He reached into his pocket, pulled the mask from its depths and pushed it down over his face. Adrenalin began coursing through him almost immediately – the anticipation of what he was about to do. What he had dreamed of and planned on doing for months surged through him, driving him forward like an athlete himself. His penis pushed forward, too, making a tent of his sweatpants. He could feel it throbbing with every step he took.

The promise of what was to come was magic. He closed the gap between them with ease.

Marty caught her by the ponytail and yanked her head back at the moment she entered the part of the path that ran along the tree line. He couldn't have planned it any better. This whole area was grassy, shaded, and private enough to do what needed to be done to this uppity bitch. She was a college student, that much he knew, a track star who worked part time in the library. She dated some big man on campus, a football or basketball player, maybe lacrosse, he wasn't sure which. This was the type of woman who would never give Marty a passing glance, never mind

11

give herself to him. This was the type of woman who turned her nose up at the likes of him, regardless of his accomplishments and how far he had come.

Now Marty was going to show her who she should have been watching out for all along.

He had her hair in his hand, and he wrapped it around his fingers, twisting his wrist to hold it firm. Then he pulled her backward with one quick, forceful jerk. She didn't fall as he expected she would, but she stumbled and cried out in pain. Things were happening too fast for him to be sure, but he could imagine the look on her face as the string of events that were about to unfold began to dawn on her and her fear took over. His loins ached; there was no other way to describe the part of his body in which he felt this pulsing expectation. Marty had never felt so strong and in control in all of his life.

She spun around to face him, striking out blindly with her hands. She had no way of knowing exactly what the hell was going on. She wasn't completely panicked yet, but almost…..

She'll know what she's facing when she sees me, he though, a leer creeping its way across his face. His breath filled the mask and sounded like the heavy panting of a dog just back from a particularly lively car chase.

And she did. Marty could see her taking in the form of the man before her, still hanging onto her ponytail, which was now a knotted, twisted mass caught between his fingers. Her brain registered the danger quickly, and she began struggling immediately, scratching Marty down his arm and drawing a welling trail of blood as she kicked him sharply in the shin. The contact sent pain rolling down his leg, and he took a step back.

Don't back up. You're in control! He warned himself, stepping forward again despite the lingering burn.

This was something Marty had thought he'd be ready for, but she took him by surprise. Everything was unfolding quickly, and both of them were depending on their own instincts in the struggle. She must have noticed his excitement, which seemed to be growing by the minute, and she kicked at his penis so quickly, Marty could feel the rush of the air against his left hand. He just managed to sideswipe that little bit of nastiness before she made contact. She was stronger than he had expected, and the shock, fear, and fury on her face turned her features ugly.

Dammit, she wasn't as pretty as he hoped; she was masculine really, hard and muscular, angular and thin. He could feel the hard knot of muscles in her thighs as she kicked out. This close up, he could see the twisted mass of them in her forearms as well.

Dammit, Kirby, he breathed silently, feeling his anger rise at the girl, at his companion, at the time consuming annoyance of her fighting him. Somewhere his description of what he wanted in a woman had crossed wires in Kirby's mind.

13

Are you surprised? He asked himself and he could feel his rage growing, his face burning hot beneath the mask. There was a pulsing beat in his temples, and if he could see himself at that moment, he knew the veins in his neck and forehead would be standing in base relief.

She screamed then, and it was loud and shrill, shattering the air around them and driving Marty into action. He threw his body at her full force, knocking the wind out of her and knocking the scream out of her with it. They rolled together down a short hill, his hand still in her hair and picking up speed as they went. Old beer cans and paper wrappers whizzed by. Something sticky got caught in her hair and swept along with her toward the bottom, and Marty felt the slight temptation to pick it out. He didn't want her sullied that way. She landed half sitting on her side, and he plunged into her, all gangly elbows and knees and stiff penis jutting into her body.

As soon as they landed, his hand came back, and he smacked her with such force that he lost the grip on her hair. She fell back then, but not on the soft cushion of grass. She fell and cracked her head against the very end corner of the pavement before the jogging trail turned into soil. She lay there, stunned and unmoving, and Marty was left stupidly on his knees with a handful of blonde hairs clinging to his fingers.

"FUCKING BITCH!" He roared as he looked down at her, completely lost in his fury. It didn't matter if his voice carried all the way across town. This shit was going to go down the way Marty wanted it to, had planned for it to. "DON'T YOU PASS OUT ON ME! YOU WILL BE PRESENT FOR THIS!"

He slapped her across the cheek hard, leaving a red shadow of his hand imprinted there and bringing tears to her eyes. And then he was on her. Even as she began yelling and kicking again, he had ripped her pants down to her ankles, wrapping her feet in the material and letting it hinder her movements.

He pulled his own down, not even giving himself a chance to take her in with his eyes. It was too dark anyway.

"Shut up," he said, feeling a calm take over him as he leaned close. He looked straight into her face as he pinned her arms to her sides. "Shut up or I'll shut you up."

That sounded stupid, even to his own ears, but it was too late to back up and do it again. He had wanted this to be executed to perfection. But it was getting messy.

Marty resisted the urge to stand there in front of her and let her get a good look at his penis, to have the luxury of watching as he shoved it into her mouth and forced it down her throat, but instead he dropped himself on top of her, pulled her legs apart, and forced his finger into her asshole.

She started crying then, really crying, snorting back snot, and begging him to please stop.

"I have," her breath came out like a ragged hiccup. "I have..." Marty's impatience grew. He slapped her again, and a fine spray of saliva and nasal discharge flew up and splattered his forehead. He wiped it away, but kept his eyes locked on her face.

"I HAVE MY PERIOD!" she finally managed, spitting each word out as if it tasted like dirt. "I have my period." She collapsed into tears, almost hysterical now. Marty reached down and felt the string of the tampon between her legs as he smelled the light stench of it now. He hadn't wanted her sullied; she was to be clean, fresh, and almost virginal, if that was even possible in this day and age. He brought his fingers to his nose, searching for her scent, but all he could smell was menstrual blood now.

The crying had pissed him off, but this thing about her period almost made him go limp. He had to slap her and call her names just to keep himself going. He pushed his mouth against hers, smashing her lips against her teeth and splitting the skin there, tasting her blood.

Only then, as he slapped her and pinched her nipples, could he pound himself into her. He lifted her hips off the ground with each maniacal thrust. The thought of the tampon pushed deeply inside her now made him elated.

The bitch deserved it, he thought as he felt his climax rise all too quickly. He hoped it hurt and hoped that she was dying inside.

He humped furiously against her. She grunted and groaned, but she stopped yelling at least. He bit her breasts, her neck, and one nipple until he felt more salty blood rush against his tongue. After that, it was over, quicker than he had hoped. Marty found himself listening to her whimpering and crying as he lay unsatisfied on top of her, the last bit of his patience peeling away like bad paint in a steamy room.

This was no good, he told himself. *It hadn't been enough.*

"Be quiet," he hissed, lifting his leg and kneeing her in the vagina. She moaned, and a new spurt of tears burst from her eyes. They were closed, her eyes, squeezed tightly against the tears, and she needed to be looking at him even if she couldn't see who he was. His mask, the one he had fashioned himself of latex in the heat of his garage over the last months had remained perfectly in place; the eye holes allowed him to retain his clear vision, and the nose and mouth holes allowed him to breathe and speak throughout the entire event. *Kirby may need one now, too*, he thought, and his heart twisted for a moment as he remembered his companion on the hill. *What if he had forgotten to watch? What if he had wandered away somewhere?* A light flutter of panic took off in his chest. Marty squeezed it away as he concentrated on the woman under him.

"Open your eyes, pussy," he said as he tried to force them open with his fingers. She squeezed them tighter against his fingers, and a new

17

wave of rage rolled over him. He considered poking one right out of the socket, and even positioned his thumb to do so, but she let out a fresh wail and a jolt beneath him that made him all too aware that time was running thin. He needed to finish this thing.

Finish it, learn from it, and make it better next time.

Abruptly, Marty took the girl by the front of her scalp, his lip lifting in a curl of utter distaste. The unexpected quickness of his movement made her eyes fly open and her mouth snap shut.

Good, that's more like it, he thought, as he pounded the back of her head again and again into the corner of the pavement. Blood trickled down behind her, pooling beneath her tangled blonde ponytail and turning it rusty brown. Her eyes rolled back into her head. Marty pounded, his penis raging again, until her body shuddered involuntarily beneath him, and until he was sure she wasn't going to call out or plead to anyone again. Standing up, he kicked her bare leg, right above the knee. It fell back into place, all gaunt muscle and toned thigh.

"Bitch," he muttered again. "That's what you get."

Reaching down, he took his memento, running the crotch of her underpants through the puddle of blood beneath her head. Then he took her by the hair one last time, pulled her off the edge of the trail and dropped her still form just inside the woods. Someone might find her in an hour, or maybe it wouldn't be for a day or two. He didn't care. He wasn't even entirely sure that she was alive.

"Something to remember you by," he told her softly as he left her. He stared down at the already drying panties in his hand. Marty pocketed the garment and headed back toward the park bench and Kirby, toward whatever and whoever would come after. He found himself exhilarated, breaking into a full run as soon as he pulled the mask off his face and cleared the first bend.

Chapter 2

Exhilarated. That was definitely the word for how Diane felt. Although it was outside of her nature entirely, she wanted to jump up and down, shout to the heavens, and celebrate with all her might. Instead, she stood quietly alone in the elevator, swallowing her excitement, and smoothing her navy skirt down around her thighs. She'd chosen the outfit with care, painstakingly ironing every crease out of the material last night while she practiced her responses over and over again, even watching her face in the mirror to make sure she didn't grimace or make any uncomely faces as she did so.

And it had all been worth it. All of the time she had put into preparation for this moment had been worth it. Just landing an interview with Hazleton and Horowitz was a dream in itself. Now she was working for them, and junior or not, she was ready. Monday would come, and she would walk into her own office, her own file drawer of cases, and the beginning of a life her parents could only have imagined for her in their wildest dreams. She couldn't even begin to guess the amount of hours she had put into her studies and the amount of fun she'd missed out on to get here. But none of that mattered now. She'd reached her destination.

"I did it Mama," she whispered, peeking upwards at the ceiling of the elevator, but speaking to the heavens way beyond it. "I did it, Daddy."

Normally when she spoke to her parents, her heart ached and tears started, the kind that nothing could hold back. Today though, her pride and happiness blanched any anguish. Diane hoped her mom and dad could feel the warmth of it, wherever they were. She wouldn't let herself remember or relive things today. This was a day for jubilation.

She stepped off the elevator, and before she even reached the exit to the street and the busy city beyond it, she had her cell phone out. She stopped for a second to privately admire the marble columns, the carved wood, and architectural details of the old restored building, which were polished to a fine, shining bronze. *I belong here now*, she thought, still amazed at the truth in that statement. An hour and a half earlier she had passed through this entryway a wide-eyed, hopeful graduate of Taft University Law School. She returned as an attorney. Diane Harper, Attorney at Law. It rolled off her tongue like velvet.

Ninety minutes, she marveled to herself. That's all it took to make a dream a reality and change a future. It could have been all it took to crush one, too.

Diane hadn't even told anyone about the interview. Not Stephanie, not Ruby, not her friends at the apartment building or anyone else she knew. If she failed, and she had been just as certain of that as she had been at succeeding, she wanted to mourn in private, apart from their well-intentioned gestures at trying to make her feel better.

But she hadn't failed. She had won. And because she had won, she planned to keep a promise to herself that she made a long time ago.

21

She flipped open the cell phone, ducked into her car, and shut the door to all of the outside noises in this central business part of town: beeping horns, clattering feet, people chattering away on their own cell phones and to each other. She'd get used to all the noise soon enough and would take the subway here with all the other worker bees, but today, she had needed peace and privacy right up until the moment she stepped into that interview. So she'd driven over, paying a small fortune just to park. But as part of her preparation for this moment, the fee and the quiet were well worth it, especially because of what she was about to do now. There was the number, glaring up right in front of her from the cell phone screen.

"Dial it already," she said aloud to herself, as she watched her fingers hover over the number pads, seeing them shake just slightly in anticipation. Nervousness was more like it. Fear.

"Face it, you're terrified," she said out loud again, but the sound of her voice gave her a little courage, and she plugged in the numbers quickly, before she could think about it anymore.

If she didn't call him now, she never would.

The phone rang, and she closed her eyes, silently willing him to answer one moment and then will him not to the next. If she got his answering machine, she would hang up. That was it. If he wasn't there, if he didn't answer, she would take it as a sign that this was a bad idea. She'd hang up, go about her new life, and forget him.

Two rings, three. They sounded so loud in her ear, and her heart beat unnervingly fast. Maybe he recognized her number. Maybe he had caller ID. He could be avoiding her, just as she had done to him for so long. Her finger poised over the hang up button. *One more ring and…*

"Hello?"

Shit!

Diane coughed, unable to find her voice.

"Yes? Hello?" He sounded curious.

Jesus, say something! You just spent an hour and a half selling yourself to two senior law partners at the biggest firm in the city, and you can't even say hello to a man. What the hell is wrong with you? Get a grip of yourself, girl!

She was afraid she would choke, but she didn't. Her voice came out clear and smooth, almost professional. Very, very cool. For the second time today, she felt a surge of pride in herself.

"Mark? It's Diane Harper," she said, exhaling on the last consonant as she lobbed the ball back into his court.

Silence on his end. She twisted the bottom of her suit jacket in her index finger, disturbing the perfect crease that had been there. Her hands were sweating against the receiver.

"Diane?" he finally countered. "Wow. I'm sorry, I just wasn't expecting…"

"Yes, I know." She cut him off. *Dammit, uncool!* But it was done, so she kept rambling forward… "Um… surprise!" she finished, glancing at

23

herself in the rear view mirror and giving herself a look of admonishment. *Stupid! Stupid! Stupid!*

"Yes, it **is** a surprise," he agreed.

She thought of Mark's face then too, and she imagined a look of puzzlement playing at the edges of his lips. How she longed to feel them on her again.

"To what do I owe this honor?"

She heard the puzzlement in his voice and knew she had his look pegged. Diane couldn't help but smile herself at the game. It was too bad she couldn't just say what she wanted, or rather, how much she wanted him. How she was sorry she had to put him off for so long, but that her career, *her self-preservation* had to come first. She wished she could say those things because she wasn't even sure she could play this game of love, sex, or whatever it was. But she plunged ahead anyway. She'd give it her best shot.

"Well, I was wondering if you'd be interested in dinner," she said, pushing the desire from her voice.

"Dinner?" His voice remained cool, collected, uninterested even. "When?"

How dare he, she thought. He wanted her as much as she wanted him, she knew it. Why couldn't he just say the things he'd said before? Why couldn't he make this easy on her now? Didn't he realize the amount of courage it had taken for her to call him?

"When? Oh... tonight," she said, sounding firm and nonchalant. "I was hoping for tonight. You see, I got this new job and I wanted to celebrate and well, I just thought of you and thought you might need a break from the hospital and... it should be fun..." She trailed off. She wasn't going to beg him, for God's sake.

"Hmm, let me check my schedule." He laughed then, and the tension slid from her shoulders. She almost dropped the phone. "You know I'd love to join you for dinner," he said, suddenly serious. "I'd love to join you for just about anything in fact," he said, his voice turning gruff.

Diane felt a sudden nervousness, but fought the urge to call off the date entirely. She'd been doing that for far too long. She looked in the mirror again. Her cheeks were flushed, and a light sweat had broken out across her brow.

"So?" she managed. "When are you free?"

"Now," he said. "Portofinos?"

Diane turned over the engine. "I know the place." She thought of the little Italian place near the hospital. Of course Mark would know it. "I'm on my way then."

This was exactly how she'd hoped it would happen.

"You're going to dinner in a business suit!" Diane chastised herself as she drove, shaking her head. How romantic is that? At a stoplight she checked her hair and applied a thin line of sheer, red gloss to her lips. She would be the first to criticize a woman for applying her makeup while driving, and yet here she was doing that very same thing. Diane shrugged off the light tinge of guilt she felt for breaking her own rule. This was a special occasion.

How often did she go out on a date? How often was she the person who asked someone else out on a date?

She hadn't seen Mark for three months. Diane hadn't meant to keep track, but she found herself doing it anyway, continually pushing him to the back of her mind and then doing nothing to stop him when he crept back up to the forefront of her thoughts. What had started as an overwhelming burst of desire, a fling, had started to feel like maybe it could become more.

Their last date had just been for coffee. Diane had agreed to meet only because she'd needed a break from studying for the Maryland Bar and only because she figured coffee was innocent. There would be no alcohol to lull her into Mark's arms (she still blamed wine for the last time she'd allowed this), no nearby bedroom to distract them into thinking that is where they would, or should, end the date. No, it was coffee in the afternoon at a busy café, far from campus and far from the places they normally frequented. Safe, simple, and undaunting.

It *was* coffee and all they did was talk - right through the sexual static that ran between them. It clung to them so heavily that she feared if their hands met, sparks would actually jump from them both. Yet still they were able to carry on a conversation from the moment she arrived to find him smiling broadly at a private corner table. He'd kissed her chastely on the cheek as if they were old friends as opposed to hopeful lovers, and she'd appreciated that small gesture. To her it meant he was looking for more than a romp in the bedroom himself. That was important.

So they'd talked and managed to learn a little about one another, to test that side of the relationship. It held. And then he said it, that absurd statement that still made her grin from ear to ear when she thought of what it had really meant.

"I love coffee," he'd told her, as the waitress delivered their order, "In fact, I drink quite a lot of it." Mark sounded like a conspirator trying to bag a partner in crime. The corner of his mouth turned up in that crooked smile she was growing so fond of seeing, and he had winked at her.

"I like coffee, too," she'd said, bewildered but figuring she may as well play along. "I like tea better, though," she said, gesturing to her mug and flicking the tea bag gently so that it fluttered back against the cup like a dying moth.

"I like my coffee with a lot of sugar," he said. "And a lot of cream."

The conversation was taking a decidedly unusual turn, and she hadn't been sure of what to say to this. Instead she'd just smiled and nodded her head a little to acknowledge him. He smiled back, beamed, rather, and his hand reached for the glass sugar jar, but stopped right before he reached it.

"Oh, wait. When can I see you again?" he asked, really throwing her for a loop then as he switched gears so abruptly.

27

Her mind swam. *What did that have to do with anything? She'd just gotten here for Pete's sake! Maybe this guy was a bit much for her, pushing his luck like that. Maybe he wanted only one thing after all.*

"I thought I was clear," she stammered, as she felt her face heat up. "I'm just not ready for anything serious. I have some professional goals to reach before I can commit to a relationship. I'm sorry, but that's just the reality of my life right now." She crossed her hands over her chest to cover the tasteful amount of cleavage she was showing. She had argued with herself passionately about it when she had dressed earlier.

Looks like the outfit was a mistake, she told herself as she felt disappointment start to settle low in her stomach. She wanted this man so badly she ached, but not if he wasn't the person she thought he might be. That was too big of a risk. She had to be sure.

"I was afraid of that answer," he said, shaking his head slowly from side to side. His smile faded fast from his lips and his eyes. "I was expecting it, but dreading it, too." The hand that had been headed for the sugar suddenly grabbed the salt shaker and vigorously began salting his coffee.

She gasped. "What on earth are you doing?"

Mark had looked at her, right in her eyes, as he covered her hand with his own. Both of them felt the jolt of longing as he did so. "I love cream and sugar in my coffee," he repeated. "But if you won't see me, I need something to remind me of what I am missing. I'll salt my coffee and

28

drink it black. Every cup, every day, until you agree to see me again."

She'd made him drink it that way too, and if he were to be believed, he'd done it for the past three months. Diane loved the gesture and yearned to give herself to him, but held firm. School first, she'd promised her parents and herself. Then she'd fulfill her personal needs: her needs as a woman.

That time is now, finally she told herself as she pushed the gas pedal a little harder than she normally might, navigating her way through the least busy side streets. She found the restaurant entrance along one of the back alleys which faced the hospital's emergency room.

Mark was already there, standing by the door to his old yellow Jeep, and she had to stop herself from rushing to him. She managed to gracefully exit her car without showing too much leg. When she reached him, she handed him a large coffee. "Extra cream, extra sugar," she told him, trying to mask the flood of feelings she felt as he leaned against the door frame, casual and collected.

"Well, I'll be damned. All I brought is flowers," he said, handing her a spray of color. There were tulips and roses and tiger lilies, all bunched together. She took them without really looking at them, their eyes glued together in that moment. Mark broke the gaze, looked her up and down, and let his eyes drink her in. She could feel his desire burning as hotly as her own, but he kept himself together. Diane let her own eyes linger over the length of him. He wore a shirt and tie, pressed khakis, and a pair of slightly worn, bright green sneakers that spoke to his sense of humor.

29

At six feet, three inches with broad shoulders and a slim, yet muscular body, Mark more closely resembled a basketball player than a young doctor. He had curly, sandy hair that Diane wanted to run her fingers through, full, suggestive lips, and sexy grey eyes that made her think of hot nights and cool sheets.

The only thing less than perfect about Mark was his slightly askew nose. Diane thought it lent character to his face and a kindness to his overall appearance. She loved his nose best of all.

"Aren't you looking lovely?" He smiled as he ran the back of his hand gently down the side of her face, and Diane melted. "And so business-like as well," he teased. Mark always seemed to have a smile on his face and was eternally positive. For all of her pessimism and worry, he was a perfect complement to her. "Congratulations on your job, by the way. *Very* impressive."

"Not as impressive as those shoes," she teased back, shaking her head.

"I'm flattered you noticed. A guy has got to have a way to stand out in a crowd." He took the coffee from her hand and leaned over to kiss her, his face so close that she could smell his sweet breath and see the light blue flecks dancing in his eyes.

"May I?" He said softly, his free arm curling around her tiny waist.

She couldn't fight it anymore. And what did a little kiss hurt anyway?

"Please do," she said as she shut her eyes and let his lips brush lightly against hers. They were moist and soft, and she felt as if she were tumbling forward as she kissed him back. She parted her lips, accepted his tongue, which flickered tentatively over her own, and leaned forward into him.

The kiss was over far too quickly.

"That's the best thing that's happened to me all day." His lips curled into another famous, crooked smile and he took a huge swig of coffee. "God that's good! I was just about to invest in a lifetime supply of salt."

Diane couldn't hold back a laugh as she let the joy of being with him take hold of her heart. It felt right and comfortable being with him like this.

"My shift's at eleven," he told her as they walked over to his Jeep, his arm protectively around her waist. It felt to Diane as if they were a real couple with a history, and she hoped Mark felt that, too. "But I think that gives us a few good hours to catch up on the past. Let's see, how long has it been now?" He checked his watch, teasing her again.

"Three months," she answered begrudgingly. He was really going to make her pay for this, she could tell. And still her heart was light and hopeful.

"Three very long months of salty coffee and lonely evenings." He shuddered theatrically as he led her toward the door of Portofino's. "Have they really come to an end?"

She giggled a schoolgirl's laugh. *Ugh how embarrassing.* But it felt good all the same. "Maybe," she said, holding his gaze for a minute.

"God, I hope so." He stopped her at the entrance, kissed her once more longingly on the lips and led the way to dinner.

Chapter 3

The roar of the ambulance sirens alerted the hospital staff that another patient would be entering their doors within minutes; but it did not prepare them for the horror the patient had encountered hours ago and was still living. You could hear the woman screaming before she was even pushed through the automatic doors of the emergency room. Her shrieks were so piercing, they caused a momentary silence to fall over the hospital as everyone inside paused. The waiting room, which was filled to capacity, fell silent. No one even coughed. The waiting patients looked silently at each other, wondering what could cause the type of anguish they could hear in the woman's voice. Some of their eyes betrayed fear, others compassion. Most of them immediately felt relief. Whatever illness or injury had brought them there was not comparable to that of this new patient. Whatever this woman had endured, it was horrendous.

The Emergency Room staff had received a call only moments earlier telling them to expect the woman and warning them that she was on the verge of hysteria. However, no one was completely prepared for how intense and overwhelming her condition would be. "Oh my God, this is going to be bad," one of the nurses mouthed to her co-worker.

They rushed into action. Some of the staff was already beginning to set up the room to accommodate their new patient. Tubes and crash carts were flung into position. They needed to be ready for every possibility.

33

Mark Lawson was in the locker room after just having completed a 12-hour shift. He was exhausted, having opted to spend the prior evening reacquainting himself with someone who might just be the woman of his dreams instead of sleeping right up until his shift began. He had the feeling he made the right choice, though. His whole body was electric when he thought of her. Everything he did and imagined doing with her – going to the movies, washing the car, falling asleep. He'd never considered such things when dealing with a woman before.

Diane Harper. She'd gotten him good. He still found it hard to believe that she'd called him and he'd finally managed to find a crack in the shell she'd built around herself. He glanced in the mirror over his locker to see if he looked as tired as he felt. *Go home and get some sleep, man.*

He wanted to see her again. As soon as possible.

But exhaustion was closing in, filling up the little spaces of energy that he had left. Mark yawned loudly. The only thing that kept him going was pure adrenalin, and he didn't know if that was because of his excitement over Diane or the insane pace he'd had to keep at the hospital over the entire length of his shift. This was the busiest day he had ever experienced in the emergency room at University Hospital, and it had kept his mind and heart occupied. No sense over-thinking this thing with Diane. They just needed to let things happen naturally.

Easier said than done, of course.

As he slammed his locker shut, he heard a commotion erupt from the general vicinity of the hospital entrance. It was so loud, he could hear it clearly through the walls and two doors that adjoined the locker area to the hospital proper. It sounded as if a frightened and wounded animal had been let loose in the halls. Concerned, Mark acted entirely on instinct and went into overdrive. Still in his work scrubs, he turned back immediately and ran down the hallway, full throttle toward the noise.

Mark caught up to the gurney as it turned into the ER exam room. He could see legs and arms flailing off the side of the gurney as the woman continued to scream over the din of the medical personnel and their equipment. By the time the woman reached their area, they were prepared for anything. Her screams continued, still bordering on animalistic. They echoed off the walls as she was rushed toward the waiting medical team.

"Trauma Room Three", the nurse directed. "Be prepared with a sedative!" Dr. Ostrado, the ER Chief warned. "We won't be able get an assessment started without it." One of the nurses appeared next to him, syringe at the ready.

She was thrashing wildly, and Mark could see her head was caked in dried blood. Her clothes were torn from her body, now half covered by the blanket the paramedics must have provided. He jumped into action, helping three nurses and another doctor to secure her arms and legs in order to administer the sedative. In moments she quieted, and Mark turned to Dr. Ostrado to see if he should remain to help the team.

"Dr. Lawson, I appreciate your commitment, but I think we have this under control," he said, as one of the nurses was finally able to secure an IV drip. "Take the opportunity to go home and refresh yourself. There will be plenty for you to do here later tonight," he finished firmly. Mark knew he was right, as a fresh wave of exhaustion threatened to take over his body. And yet, Mark couldn't tear his thoughts from the screaming woman.

What he suspected she had endured was quickly confirmed. As Mark walked away, he overheard a female EMS worker talking to one of the staff. "She was found at Sainted Mother Cemetery. Apparent rape victim, Doctor. By the condition of her, it's possible she'd been lying there since last night. She was unconscious when we arrived, but as soon as we stabilized her in the van, she started to panic. It was impossible to get her IV'ed during the ride. She was fighting harder than anyone I've ever dealt with. I thought I might break my arm trying to strap her to the gurney." Her voice and the voice of the doctor faded as Mark passed through the swinging doors.

Another rape near the campus? He thought to himself. How many had there been now? Three? No, four. There had been four victims over the course of the past 6 months, and the first had been beaten into a coma, where she remained.

All of the victims had been treated at University Hospital, and all of them had been attractive female students in their early twenties. Other than that, the girls all had differences. One was athletic and blonde, another buxom and dark-haired, and a third was a library aide, quiet and shy, a girl that not many on campus really knew. Now there was this fourth victim, nameless for now, but traumatized beyond words, her entire life changed in moments by such a vile act. It made Mark feel sick in his heart and soul.

The police had been reserved in their comments up until now, not down playing the situation, but careful not to put out misinformation that would generate even more alarm in the city. They had indicated that there were two rapists working together, and this news was sending shock waves of fear throughout the campus and the community. Being raped by one man was frightening enough, but knowing two men were working as a team was sickening. And no one knew where they would strike next. Although all of the victims were students at Taft University, none of them were attacked on the campus in the heart of downtown.

With serial rapists on the loose and targeting students, perhaps following them, getting to know their movements, their schedules, the women at Taft and the people who loved them were becoming increasingly worried. Women were traveling in groups, staying out of desolate areas, and growing eyes in the back of their heads. Paranoia was rampant, and with good reason.

As he thought all of this through, Mark felt compelled to stay and started to turn back, but thought better of it. He was beyond tired, potentially dangerous to patients if he stayed awake any longer. He made his way into the now relatively quiet ER nursing desk area, lost in thought.

"Hi, Dr. Lawson," he looked up to see one of the nurses, a friendly young woman named Leah, smiling and waving in his direction. She was a beautiful Hispanic girl with gleaming black hair and eyes to match. Many on the hospital staff loved her. She was a local girl, having grown up in the city, and she knew how to talk to the patients and make them feel at ease. Leah was full figured and youthful and always wore an almost startling mouthful of red lipstick. Despite her good reputation around the ER, to Mark, Leah gave off the air of trouble with a capital "T."

Ever since she'd started to work on this shift, she'd made it a point to show she was interested in him. As lovely and sexy as she was, she simply wasn't Mark's type, and he had managed to thwart her attempts to get to know him better. He always kept Diane in the back of his mind, even over the many months that she hadn't given him any signs of encouragement. Mark had made mistakes with women before, some of which he was still paying for. But he wasn't about to make those mistakes with Diane Harper.

"Hello, Leah." He smiled softly, not wanting to encourage her attention.

"Crazy night, huh?" she said, pointing toward the doors where their newest patient had been wheeled minutes earlier.

"Yes, very intense," he said, as he searched deep within his last energy source to creatively cut this conversation short without appearing rude. He didn't want to date Leah, but he didn't want a reputation around the hospital as an unfriendly asshole. He planned to be working with these people for years to come, and he wanted it to be on good terms. Following his instincts, he couldn't shake the thought that Leah appeared the type that might start rumors if she was dissatisfied about anything and for any reason.

"Want to grab a cup of coffee? I'm almost on break." She flashed a blinding white smile that was showcased by her lipstick. *How did she get it to stay on all night?* Mark's thoughts wandered briefly. Leah was thrusting out her breasts and tugging on her tight uniform while she ran her hands down the side of her hips, displaying all the signs that she would allow him to have her whenever he wanted. There had been a time in his past when he would have taken her up on the offer. He would have had her moaning with her legs up in the air in one of the empty hospital beds within minutes. But things had changed since his young college days, and now he had a new set of priorities and plans. Unfortunately, they didn't include one night stands with his co-worker, or anyone else, for that matter.

Should he tell her he was involved? Was he involved? Diane's face flashed before his eyes. She was a goddess of impossible beauty in his opinion, with her rich caramel skin, full breasts and hips, and hazel eyes dusted with gold. She was smart, together, and graceful in every way. In Mark's eyes, Diane was perfect.

But it wasn't time to tell the world about her and potentially damage the growth of this still tenuous bond they shared. If he told Leah about Diane, Mark had a feeling it was just a matter of time before the whole hospital would know. And beyond that, with the hospital's affiliation to Taft University, maybe Diane would hear she was Mark's girlfriend before she even agreed to it herself. *No*, Mark thought, *that would not go over well with a woman like Diane.*

"Thanks, Miss Sanchez," he said gently as he tread carefully, "but I've been here over twelve hours already and I'm exhausted. I think I am just going to head on home."

She looked disappointed, and her smile fell immediately into a frown. "Some other time then?" she sounded hopeful. Mark pretended not to hear her and beat a graceful exit toward the hospital doors.

This was one of the rare times where it felt good to feel the cold air against his skin. Mark's night had been anything but quiet. He'd been placed in charge of three broken bones, a woman involved in a hit and run accident, and a 15-year-old gunshot victim. They'd come in, one after the other, and he'd been running from room to room for the past several hours. It would feel good to get home and put his feet up, clear his head, and re-fuel.

"What type of person makes it a point to brutalize women?" he wondered, thinking back to the damaged girl on the gurney. Mark pulled the collar of his jacket up over his neck. It was almost spring, but the weather hadn't wanted to turn warmer yet. It was downright cold out here, but he thought the chill he was feeling might have more to do with the victim he just witnessed rather than the temperature of the air. He was anxious to get home.

Home for Mark was a few miles outside of the university. He'd wanted to stay in the city but still have a neighborhood feel, and he'd found that in this little cottage with white and brown trim, just on the fringe of downtown. The house had belonged to an elderly woman before him who had decided that pink walls and carpeting were the order of the day. Mark had spent the better part of a month repainting and pulling up carpet. As a bonus, he had been delighted to find beautiful hardwood floors underneath and ended up leaving them be. Mark had always been good with his hands and opted to do all the work himself. It had been good, hard manual labor, and he felt good doing it. It kept his mind off other things at the time anyway. Things that had changed his world.

As he pulled up the driveway, it hit him how dark and quiet it was coming home to an empty house like this. He felt a momentary longing to fill it up with a beautiful wife and a group of boisterous, happy children. *Someday you will*, he told himself, and Diane danced behind his eyes for the umpteenth time that day. For now, what he needed were those small, everyday comforts in life - a full stomach, a clean body, and a warm bed.

One day at a time, he told himself. *Take one day at a time.*

Chapter 4

There was so much activity in the Java House that Mark started to turn around and leave. Last night had been brutally busy at the hospital and had ended disconcertingly with the arrival of the latest rape victim. The Java was abuzz with news of the attack. Mark could hear people talking as he passed through the crowd.

"I heard he tortured her first and then raped her," whispered one student at the table next to front door. Her face had the look of a frightened doe caught in the headlights of an oncoming car. "I keep thinking about how scared she must have been, knowing that she was all alone and had no way to defend herself." She shivered as her friend touched her hand and tried to reassure her, but it was obvious that her friend felt the same angst.

At another table nearby, Mark overheard more talk - less fearful but a lot angrier. "What kind of animal would attack someone and then leave them for dead? These guys are fucking maniacs. I hope they tear off their balls when they catch them," hissed a woman to her boyfriend. He, in an effort to bring down the level of tension, made a comic display of protecting his crotch. Even though they both laughed at his antics, it was obvious that the laughter sprang more from nervous tension than humor.

Mark couldn't stand to hear anymore, so he surged forward with a group of rowdy freshmen. Exhausted as he had felt, he'd found himself unable to sleep after work, his mind drifting back again and again to the date he'd had with Diane earlier the previous evening. They'd talked a lot, and for the first time he saw Diane without her guard up. He saw into her hopes and dreams for the future, and maybe even glimpsed her heart and the feelings (he was starting to believe) that she had for him. She'd had a few glasses of wine, and whether she felt giddy from that or from landing her new job, he wasn't sure, but she'd been open, natural, and talkative. Mark found himself hoping that part of Diane's giddiness was because of being with him, but he didn't want to jump to conclusions or get over-excited before it was time. He just knew that he'd felt complete pleasure in watching her, the way she curled the edge of her hair around her finger, the way her face showed so much emotion when she spoke, and the way her suit hugged her curves in all the right places.

It had been a lovely evening. But they'd left the future open, and Mark was struggling with what that meant. Diane wanted to take things slow and easy. Mark wanted to jump right in. But of course he'd agreed with taking things one day at a time. He would do just about anything to win her heart. So he hadn't called her today, He didn't want to spoil his promise by moving too fast.

Mark pulled his thoughts back to the here and now. Stay at Java and have a coffee and sandwich before his shift or go somewhere quieter? He stood there a minute and surveyed the place.

It was standing room only in Java House, the most popular café near the campus. Java was an ideal meeting place for students, staff and professionals between classes or work to relax with a cup of coffee, tea or hot chocolate. Java House wasn't a modern place with high-powered espresso machines, bells, whistles and bursts of steam so loud they could make a person jump. It didn't boast thirty different varieties of coffee beans and coffee-based drinks. If you wanted that, you went to the coffee boutiques positioned on every other corner in town. This was an old style coffee house, cozy and warm, that had some of the best coffee in town, and it was a home away from home for hundreds of patrons who regularly frequented the place. In fact, the name Java House was probably the most "modern" thing about the whole place.

Just stay, his inner voice told him, and Mark decided to listen to it for once. Wherever else he might go would be just as busy on a Friday night, so he may as well deal with the crowds here. So he did stay and ordered a turkey on rye, soup, and coffee. He carried the tray over his head while he cut through the crowd, managing not to spill a drop.

He found a seat at a corner table near the kitchen door (*beggars can't be choosers,* he told himself, sniffing away the smell of fried onions and grease that overpowered his senses). He settled in with his I-POD and a novel he'd been meaning to start but never quite got around to. He saw a few people he knew: a couple guys, a phlebotomist and X-ray tech, he thought he knew from the hospital's basketball team. They all played in a local adult league on Saturday afternoons, and they stopped to say hello, the three of them agreeing to go for a beer after the game the next day. Mark liked the team and all the people on it; it provided him with a good way to get his exercise, meet people, and indulge in a healthy dose of competition, the last of which was certainly one of his weaknesses. Mark liked to win, and when he didn't, well, he'd been known to balk.

He glanced around the room again. *Was that Jasmine Aromark from first year biology? She hadn't changed a bit.* It would have been good to catch up, to see where life had led her beyond biology class, but he needed some alone time, what his mother always called "me time". *Time to lose the outside world for a bit.* He flipped on his music, adjusted the volume just over the din around him, and lost himself in the music in his ears and the words on the page before him.

Why on earth does Stephanie insist we meet at the busiest times in the busiest places? Diane asked herself as she jostled her way through the front door of Java. She was slightly annoyed at herself – after all, she should have known what the Java House would be like on a Friday night, but mostly, she was excited about seeing her best friend. She had a lot to tell her, and lately it seemed, they hadn't had enough time to catch up. Diane chose not to think about all she had been hiding from Stephanie - on purpose - namely the interview and job at Hazelton and Horwitz.

Oh, and then there was that little thing about Mark Lawson. Although Stephanie knew Mark, their connection lacked any friendly overtures, and Diane wasn't sure if she was ready to mention his name, let alone the time she had shared alone with him.

She couldn't get her mind off Mark. She had barely stopped thinking of him since he passionately kissed her good night in the parking lot of Portifino's the night before. He had let his hands linger lightly on her hips as he gently pressed his pelvis against her. Mark had given her just a taste of what she was longing for, and then he'd pulled away, seeing her safely into her car before he headed across the alley to begin his shift in the ER.

She had tried to play it cool most of the evening, afraid to appear too anxious. She even convinced him that this relationship was something they shouldn't rush into full force. If only she could convince herself of that. Even now, in the middle of all of these people, she felt his presence somehow. She felt something trembling, tingling, deep inside herself.

Get out of my head for a minute, Mark Lawson. I have too much to think about besides falling in love with you!

He wouldn't budge, and she felt that shiver again, as if he were right there, touching her arm.

Like a brand new job starting Monday, she told herself as she tried to shake him. Mark, the memory of his eyes, his kiss, his arm around her, or whatever the hell it was that was sending shooting sparks up and down her body right now, was stubborn as a mule. She sighed. If he didn't call her this weekend, she might come out of her skin.

Diane stopped and scanned the crowd. People were everywhere. They danced by the juke box, talked at tables, and stood in line to place their orders at the counter. Waitresses glided through the crowd, navigating expertly through bobbing heads and moving bodies. *Amazing*, Diane thought as she watched them. *I would never make it as a waitress. I'd be fired my first day on the job.*

She didn't see Stephanie anywhere, but decided that as soon as she found her, she would suggest they leave. *May as well get some tea and find a place where I can see through this crowd better.* Diane joined the line at the counter, grabbed a campus paper and reading it while she waited.

Another Business School Student Brutally Raped

Oakmont police have confirmed a fourth rape victim found last night. The Taft University Business School student, whose name has not been released, was found brutally attacked at Sainted Mother Cemetery in the Jackson Hills section of the City. It is reported that she managed to crawl from the rape scene, collapsing at the gated entrance to the cemetery. She was admitted to University Hospital early this morning. Police have not said if the student is the latest victim of the so-called "Coed Rapists" who have plagued the metropolitan area for the last six months. Her current condition is unknown.

The first known victim of the recent string of attacks was released today to the custody of her parents. The victim was taken September 14th to University Hospital's Trauma Center, where she remained in a coma for several months. The woman's mother, Abigail Howard, says her daughter sustained significant head injuries and remembers little of the attack. University Medical staff was unavailable for comment.

Sandy Howard, 24, had been jogging when she was attacked by what is believed to be two white males. Found at the crime scene were the victim's clothing, identified by her family, as well as a dime sized piece of latex material believed to belong to a pair of gloves or a mask of some sort.

Officers are asking that all women remain aware of their surroundings, travel in pairs or groups, and avoid secluded areas. They are also asking that citizens with any information related to this crime contact the following

hotline which has been set
up specifically with regard to
recent rape cases: 1-800-425-
9000.

Diane felt her heart twist as she finished the article. She'd made
a promise to herself when she took the state attorney's oath to uphold the
law, and that was to protect and represent victims, people like these poor
women whose very lives had been ripped apart by the heartless bastards
who pursued and raped them. She felt a renewed sense of vengeance stir
inside of her. If there was anything she could to help these women and their
families, she was more than ready to do it.

"May I help you?" She came back to earth.

Oh, God, it was the damn owner. Diane recognized him instantly,
and as usual, he made her skin crawl. The owner of Java was working the
counter. The little man by the name of Goodwin always flirted with the
female patrons in a very unsettling way. Everyone knew he was a pompous
freak who treated his employees, and sometimes his customers, without
much respect. He was a man small in stature but big in ego, and he always
made Diane feel like he could see right through her clothing. She almost
turned away, thinking that a cup of tea wasn't worth his scrutiny. But then
she remembered the woman in the article, and she felt a twinge of anger
prickle its way up her back. *Women shouldn't have to be intimidated by a*

man, she thought. *So, let him look.* Diane would look right back, straight in his eyes. She followed the person in front of her and continued to make her way forward in line.

As she suspected with her past experience with Goodwin, tonight was no different. After she placed her order, Diane handed him money and he made a point of touching her hand as he took it. She stared at him hard, pursing her lips into a line of disgust and briefly even letting her mind wonder if he was one of the men plaguing the campus. Diane could feel her skin crawl.

"I'd appreciate you keeping your hands to yourself," she told him, staring him down as she called him on his game.

He pretended not to know what she was talking about. "I'm sorry, sweetheart, did I do something to offend?" His smile was broad, and as she turned, she saw him, out of the corner of her eye, blow her a kiss as she walked away.

"Asshole," she hissed, as she restrained herself from turning back and really letting him have it. Men like that would never understand how to treat a woman. Trying to explain otherwise and threaten him into behaving, would only be futile. As if to prove that point, she heard him laughing behind her, and she could feel his eyes on her back as she made her way through the crowd. She tried to lose herself in the throng of bodies so he couldn't see her anymore as she hoped to find a seat as far away from the counter as possible.

Mark saw her the moment she stepped away from the counter. Something had pulled his eyes from his book. It was a little niggling feeling that made the hairs on his arms stand up. Diane was here; he felt her.

He watched her as she paid the counter man and almost came out of his chair when he saw the way the man looked at her. The man stared at her lecherously, eyeing her breasts as he handed her the change and made it a point to caress the back of her hand. *I'm going to kill that asshole*, he thought, surprised at the vehemence in his heart.

You're in love, man. He shook the thought away. That was crazy. He was just getting to know her. But he couldn't keep his eyes off of her. She was on the other side of the room, but he kept track of her movements as she slipped in and out of his vision. The sway of her hips was hypnotic. She finally found a chair at a table about 20 feet away from him. He stared as Diane took off her coat and scarf, revealing a bulky turtleneck sweater. She must have been warm because she even removed her turtleneck, exposing a shear blouse that clung tantalizingly to her generous, firm breasts and her well-placed curves.

Mark moaned aloud, hoping that no one would hear him. Unconsciously he licked his lips. He imagined tracing her nipples through the thin material of her blouse and gathering her breasts into his hands as he bent to kiss her ample lips. He kept his eyes on her as she settled herself into her seat. He glanced over at the counter to make sure the greasy guy who took her order wasn't keeping his eyes on her as well.

He had to go over and see her. To hell with taking it easy. He needed to tell her how he felt **now**. He started to gather his things as he prepared to go to her. But he stopped in his tracks as soon as he saw Stephanie Kramer headed in Diane's direction. *Dammit*, he thought, as he sat back down, wanting to hide his head.

"Diane!" Stephanie was pushing her way toward her, late as usual, but that was to be expected. Diane looked up and waved, feeling a warmth rush over her at the sight of her best friend. They'd been close for years now, living together in the sorority house before Stephanie had taken time off from her studies. She had surprised everyone when she announced she was engaged.

"Hey, Steph. What's up girl?" Diane rose, embracing her friend as soon as she reached the table. "It's so good to see you!"

"No kidding! We've been like two ships in the night lately!" Stephanie hugged her, then pulled off a woolen hat and scarf that virtually covered her entire face. She brushed at her short, dark hair to get rid of hat head and to bring it to some semblance of order.

As if it was the first time she'd ever seen her, Diane was still in awe of Stephanie's beauty. Stephanie was what some people would call a Nubian princess with her ebony skin and tightly coiled hair. Her complexion was flawless and as smooth as a porcelain doll. She had a generous mouth which was shaped in a perfect bow. Her eyes were huge, slightly slanted, and so dark they appeared almost black. She was tall and slim, with a voluptuous body. Simply put, she was exquisite. And much to the chagrin of most men on campus, she was married.

"Can you even see in that hat?" Diane asked cheerfully. "And that scarf must be six feet long," said Diane as she laughed.

"Please, I can't believe it's March already and still this damn cold," Stephanie complained. "Anyway, I should be at the library studying. But I like hanging out with you a lot more." Stephanie was in her last year at Taft Law and was struggling through, to put it lightly. She needed to get in all the study time she could.

Diane chuckled. "You'll finish this semester, I'll help you as much as I can. Tonight even."

"I'm so cold and tired I don't even think I can handle the library tonight. There's so much tension in the air, the quiet would probably take me over the edge," Stephanie was good about making excuses to keep from studying, but she was right. It was certainly tense around campus, especially among the female population.

Stephanie's mood suddenly brightened. "Let's grab a drink. The books will be here tomorrow. And this place is a madhouse. How are we supposed to talk with all this noise around us?" Stephanie smiled. Diane replied, "I was wondering what on earth possessed you to choose Java tonight!"

"Come on then. Let's blow this joint and trade the coffee and tea for something that will really warm us up. I even have Paul's blessing to skip the library tonight.

Diane frowned at the mention of Paul's name. If anyone put pressure on Stephanie to keep up with law school, it was her husband. Paul was older than Stephanie, an executive accountant on the fast track, and he was all business. He expected the same of Stephanie.

Knowing Stephanie as well as she did, Diane still didn't understand how such a free spirit could marry such a straight-laced person. It was certainly a case of opposites attracting. That made her think of Mark again, and she felt the goose bumps rising on her arms. Diane rubbed them away as she tried to purge him from her thoughts. This time was for her and Stephanie. And Stephanie for one, was clearly in the mood to party.

"When was the last time you let loose and had fun? Oh, I forgot. For you that would be never," Stephanie teased, goading Diane into doing whatever she wanted.

"Never is a long time. I just don't go out very often. But a drink sounds like a good idea. And I have a lot to tell you, girl, so get ready. Let's go, before I change my mind."

"Oh, don't leave me hanging! We'll talk on the way!" Grabbing their things, they made a dash for the door. And ran right into Mark.

Diane's breath caught in her throat at the sight of him. *No wonder she kept getting goose bumps and tingles. He must have been here all along.*

55

"Mark!" she said, unable to keep the light tremor out of her voice and a blush from creeping into her cheeks. Fate was pushing them together; she could feel it.

"Diane!" He smiled broadly as he refrained from taking her in his arms right there. It was Stephanie that was holding him back. She stood there, arms across her chest and shooting him a look of disdain so fierce it made his face grow hot.

"Hi Stephanie," he nodded briefly at her as he kept his heart rate in check. Mark was in a precarious position, but it was one he knew he would eventually have to confront. If he wanted things to move forward with Diane, he would have to face her friends, one way or another.

If only Stephanie could keep her mouth shut.

"Mark," she acknowledged, pursing her lips as if she'd just sucked on a lemon. She opened her mouth again, and Mark held his breath. His eyes darted from Stephanie to Diane, who seemed puzzled and uncomfortable by Stephanie's scorn. She twisted her hair around her finger, a gesture Mark was becoming familiar with seeing when Diane was nervous. Before Stephanie could say a word, Diane interrupted. "We are just getting ready to go for a drink, Mark. Would you like to join us?"

"I'd like that," he said, as he glanced quickly at Stephanie, who shook her head back and forth just out of Diane's view.

Mark cleared his throat. "Unfortunately, I'm headed to the hospital. My shift starts in a couple of hours." he said, looking at his watch.

Diane looked disappointed, hurt maybe, and Mark hoped he wasn't blowing his chances with her already. Before Stephanie could say or do anything to dissuade him, he added, "But let's take a definite rain check— sometime soon." He held Diane's eyes. He wanted to tell her he'd call her tomorrow but Stephanie was tapping her foot, looking as if she was ready to claw his eyes from his head.

Don't push your luck, he thought, excusing himself. He let his hand brush down Diane's arm as he passed. He hoped she understood that he wasn't trying to avoid her.

Shut up, Stephanie. Don't rat me out.

Diane's eyes followed Mark as he left the Java House, and Stephanie could barely contain herself. "Bad idea," she said shaking her head. "Don't get involved with him, Diane."

"What are you talking about?" Diane asked, spinning abruptly on her heels to face her friend. She felt a flutter of panic in her chest. Was it that obvious she was interested in Mark?

"He's a player," Stephanie sneered. "He's only looking for one thing, for God's sake." She stared back at Diane, refusing to back down and shaking her head back and forth. "And I would know. I dated Steve for more than two years," she finished.

Ah, Steve Lawson. Diane had never met Steve, but she certainly knew who he was. Mark's wayward brother was a bit of a campus legend himself. *Of course that had to be bothering her.*

His relationship with Stephanie had ended before Diane had met her, but as far as Diane could tell it had been a tangled mess of he said/she said nonsense fraught by ugly rumors of violence and cheating.

"You see this scar?" Stephanie had told her one night not long after they'd met. She had pulled back her hair to show Diane a spindly cross of white tissue at the corner of her forehead. "That's the work of Steve Lawson." It had been a dramatic, unexpected declaration, and Diane had been shocked that her feisty little friend had stayed with a man who would inflict that kind of damage on his girlfriend.

Exactly one of the reasons she had yet to mention Mark to Stephanie at all.

"Give me some credit, Steph," she said softly, not wanting to spend the evening arguing. "Do you honestly think I can be so easily persuaded?"

"I know if anyone's going to do it, it would be Mark. He's a master at manipulating women. And believe you me, when he gets what he wants, he's going to move on."

He wants your virginity, Diane told herself. It was a revelation she had been unwilling to admit might be true before. It felt like a hard slap in the face. *He wants your virginity.*

And then he's going to leave you.

Stephanie's words stung. This realization stung even worse. She tried to push it aside, but it lingered, poking at her conscience. Diane felt the lovely evening with Stephanie and the lovely evening the night before

58

with Mark crumble away. But she stood her ground.

"That's extremely insulting," she said. Diane and Stephanie both stood there not speaking, letting the noise of the Java close in around them. Their eyes locked, and the air felt stifling.

"I'm sorry," Stephanie finally said. "I know you can handle yourself. But I don't trust that family, and I don't want you to get hurt. Like I did. Even the smart girls get burned, Diane," Stephanie's eyes welled with tears, but she kept on talking through them. "It's just that I love you," she opened her arms for a hug. "Forgive?"

Diane felt herself melt at Stephanie's vulnerability. "Only if you promise to trust my judgment. I'm a lawyer! It's in my nature to sniff out the bad guys." She smiled a little, hoping it would dry Stephanie's tears.

Stephanie sniffed and brightened. She never stayed angry for long. That wasn't in **her** nature. "I could really use that drink you mentioned," she said. "Ruby's?"

"Definitely."

Chapter 5

The two of them left the warmth of the Java House to face the cold night air. It had gotten colder since they had been inside, and the sky had that frosty look of snow.

"I'll drive," Diane suggested.

"I don't know, Diane. The Mercedes has heated seats." Stephanie giggled, rubbing her bottom in jest. The recent disagreement between them faded a bit with their laughter. Diane's car, a 12-year-old powder blue Audi, sat at the corner of the lot. Diane had earned the money for it by working two jobs her junior year, and she refused to give it up. It was like a trustworthy and steady old friend. Diane had even picked up the habit of lovingly referring to it as a classic. She had named it "Classy Sassy".

"All those fancy gadgets are just one more thing you can count on breaking!" Diane said. "My girl's got two knobs, and she's never given me a minute's worth of trouble!" She protested.

"Yeah, the on and off knob! Sassy is about as reliable as a Tonka truck. Let's take the Mercedes. At least we know the heater will have warmed up before we get to Ruby's!" Stephanie snorted, and Diane figured she'd let her win this one. Relationships were give and take. She could laugh later when the Mercedes was in the shop for something silly.

The engine purred to life, and just as Stephanie promised, a rush of toasty, warm air puffed across Diane's face within minutes. Ruby's was located just outside of the campus nightlife fringe, which made it generally inconvenient for the party kids and perfect for those who just needed a nice, quiet evening out.

"So start talking, sister," Stephanie said. "Spill all your secrets to your best friend, Stephanie!" She made her voice sound like a commercial for a television psychic.

Diane didn't need to be asked twice. "I got a job!" She blurted.

"A job! Congratulations! Where?" Stephanie sounded almost as excited as Diane although she was personally less than enthralled with the idea of working herself.

"You'll never believe this, but Hazleton and Horowitz. I start on Monday."

"You are kidding me! YOUR DREAM JOB! Oh my God, Diane, that's fantastic!" She grabbed Diane's hand and gave it a firm squeeze. "I'm so happy for you!"

"Thanks, thanks!" Diane felt a momentary twinge of guilt about not sharing the news with her friend sooner. And for having shared it with Mark first. AND for keeping Mark a secret from Stephanie.

Were they growing apart? She wondered, appalled at the idea of letting her friendship with Stephanie slip away for a man - or anything. She changed the subject, not wanting to dwell on that possibility.

"Speaking of work, how is Paul doing at the firm now? Still top dog?" Diane poked fun.

"Oh, please, he has a stick up his ass the size of Iowa right now! If only I could loosen him up a bit, we could have more time to work on making a baby happen by the time I graduate this spring," Stephanie answered. After the way she had grown up, in the inner city, practically in the streets, Stephanie wanted it all—a family, a career (eventually), a house with the white picket fence. And she wasn't willing or patient enough to wait until the timing was mutually agreeable. Her marriage was in trouble now. It had been two months since she stopped taking her birth control pills, and still she wasn't pregnant. Stephanie knew time wasn't on her side.

"How many employers do you think are going to hire a woman fresh out of law school with a bun in the oven?" Diane asked. She knew having a baby to save a marriage, or even to save your own self within an unhappy marriage was never a good plan. Not to mention that since graduation, Diane had spent a great deal of her own time tutoring Stephanie so that she would be ready for the bar exam. Stephanie certainly needed the help, between her own indifference and the year she had taken off after she got married.

This was another sore point between the girls. It frustrated Diane when Stephanie told her she didn't really care about school or practicing law. She steeled herself for Stephanie's response. *Here it comes: the wrath of Stephanie*. And she was right.

"Who cares?" Stephanie shot back, quickly becoming defensive, even while knowing her friend just had her best interests at heart. "I want to live my life my way, Diane. I won't wait to make up for all the things I didn't have. We have enough money without my earning a salary. So who cares if I have to wait a year or two to jump on the career train? Right now, I want a baby more than I want a career." Stephanie was in denial, even to herself, that the reason she wanted the baby was to distract from the real problems she faced with Paul.

Can you imagine Stephanie trying to care for a baby? Diane felt mean just thinking it. But it was, at least partially, hard to contemplate.

Diane said nothing, and another stony silence passed between them. They were almost to Ruby's when Stephanie relented. "I'm sorry, Diane, but…" Diane tuned her out, halfheartedly accepting the apology as she said, "Let's just move on and enjoy the rest of the evening." Easier said than done.

*We **are** growing apart. They'd just had their third disagreement in one evening.* Diane felt her heart drop into her stomach. She changed the subject again, but she couldn't shake the annoyance she felt at being the one who had to do all the forgiving in this friendship. In her opinion, Stephanie was being exceedingly selfish right now.

And then they were at Ruby's. Diane felt the tenseness in her shoulders relax a bit. Ruby was really a person and not just the name of some faceless joint. It never failed that she was on duty even though she owned the place. She always stood behind the bar and watched over things like a mother hen. She'd watched over Diane and Stephanie, too, back

63

when they were still undergraduates and both of them needed a strong, mother figure in their lives. It seemed like it had been forever since they'd all been together, and even though Diane had just talked to Ruby on the phone last week, she was anxious for a big dose of nurturing. It would be good for her soul.

Ruby, a full-figured buxom woman, was complicated and had a knack for doing exactly the opposite of what society would expect from someone so strong-willed. She'd lost her husband to alcohol, and yet her whole life revolved around a bar. She had no children of her own, yet she instinctively knew exactly how to take care of others. She seemed born to be a mother. Those incongruities made her special, and Stephanie and Diane loved Ruby for who she was, without judgment. She gave them advice and hugs as often as they needed them, and what was maybe most telling, she would protect them with her life.

On this particular evening, Ruby's was less than half full when they arrived. Like always, Ruby held court behind the bar. She was in the middle of a deep conversation with a tall, bearded man neither woman recognized. She noticed their arrival and immediately left her post to welcome them with hugs and kisses.

"Well, well, well, look what the cat dragged in," she teased, as soon as they were finished exchanging embraces.

"Ruby, we missed you!"

"Tell me everything that's going on in your lives," she said, as she sat down with them in the nearest booth. "Howard can take care of the drink orders for now." She gestured to her bartender, a morose, older gentleman with a hunchback who shuffled when he walked. He made his way over to the table with two cocktail glasses full of pink, bubbly liquid.

"House specials for the only two sweethearts in the whole joint," he told them, making a grand gesture of laying out napkins and presenting them with the cocktails. Howard managed a smile and a wink and then shuffled back to finish doling out brimming mugs of cold beer and dishes of peanuts to the regulars.

"I'm going to insist he retire soon," Ruby said, a soft sadness inching into her voice. "He's just too old to be on his feet all night." She shook her head. "I don't know where I'll find anyone to take his place, though."

Howard had been working the bar long before Ruby took over the place. He belonged there. Ruby looked for a second as if she may start sobbing, but she brightened again. "Enough of that, now. Tell me everything, ladies." She clasped their hands, one of theirs in each of her own, and sat back to listen.

Stephanie and Diane filled her in, allowing her to lavish them with praise and attention. Stephanie made it out to look as if there was no question she'd be finished with school this semester, and Diane let the potential lie sit between them without correcting her. Ruby practically beamed at hearing all of their news, and she insisted on taking them out to dinner later in the week to celebrate Diane's job and Stephanie's upcoming graduation.

"Where is everybody tonight? The place is so quiet," Stephanie asked, sipping up the last of her drink.

"Oh, everybody is checking out that new sports bar, Bases Loaded. It has all these big screen televisions with every game on. The younger crowd who used to come here to make time go there now, have beer, and cheer for their team. Seems like a waste of time to me," Ruby explained. "But don't you worry. They'll come back. They always do."

"They'd be stupid not to," Stephanie said, and Diane quickly agreed. "For now, Ruby's is for the mature, sophisticated crowd."

"Oh, honey, let me get you another drink before you look around and really see the crowd that hangs out here." Ruby broke into a rough laugh and bustled away. She returned to the bar, brought them both a fresh cocktail, and excused herself again. She told them she was sending Howard home for the night. His feet were swollen, and she wanted to give him a break since he refused to sit while on duty.

"Don't either of you dare leave this bar before stopping to kiss me good-bye," she warned, as she shook her finger in their faces.

"Of course we will," they promised, watching her walk back to her customers.

"STEPHANIE!" A loud voice caused them both to jump. Stephanie turned and tried to put on a happy face to greet whoever was yelling to her. "Oh, Leah, hi!" she said, as she saw the raven-haired girl bounce over to her.

"What the hell are you doing here?" Leah leaned down to kiss her cheek, leaving a red, lip stain against her lovely skin. "I haven't seen you in ages!"

Stephanie glanced at Diane. Diane was annoyed at the interruption of their evening by this female she didn't know, but she forced a smile. She thought she noticed a flicker of unspoken apology in Stephanie's eyes. It wasn't Stephanie's fault, Diane reminded herself.

"We're just having a drink and chilling out. Ruby is a personal friend of ours." Stephanie said.

"Tonight is my night off," Leah began. "And believe it or not, my drunk friend over there," Leah pointed toward a girl slumped on the corner, "is dating one of the guys who comes in here a lot. He must be 50 years old! I told her it's ridiculous, but she has a thing for older men. She says he can outlast any 20-year- old by an hour!" Stephanie and Leah laughed, but Diane only smiled.

"Leah, this is my best friend, Diane. Diane, Leah. We used to cheer together on the Taft squad as undergraduates," she said. "Diane and I were in law school together, but she beat me to the punch. She is a new attorney with Hazelton and Horowitz now," Stephanie told Leah.

"Impressive!" Leah smiled, holding out her hand in greeting. Both girls traded niceties, and Leah must have taken it as approval for her to join them, because she plunked herself down in the booth and settled right in.

"Thank God you showed up. I am bored out of my mind!! I didn't

67

know I was walking into a bar full of half bald, very drunk, middle-aged men!" She laughed again, a loud, shrill sound.

Stephanie shot Diane a look, and this time there was no doubt about it - she was definitely saying she was sorry. It was obvious that she didn't want Leah's company any more than Diane did. Diane just shrugged, although she knew she would now have to suffer through a myriad of cheerleading gossip. She barely listened as Leah and Stephanie wondered if one of the girls they knew from the squad was sleeping around and about how someone else who was failing chemistry was no doubt servicing the professor. They droned on and on, and Diane found herself leaning into the red leather of the seat, the effects of this second drink causing her to slump a little. She turned her thoughts to her upcoming job. What would it be like to walk in that first day and sit at her own desk in her own office?

Will they ever stop gossiping? She thought, as she turned her attention to the other patrons spread sparsely throughout the bar area. But then she heard something that brought her attention squarely back on Stephanie and Leah.

"Oh, I forgot to tell you! I'm working with your completely hot Dr. Lawson now at University." Leah took a sip from her cocktail and smirked as if she and Stephanie shared a most delicious secret.

What the hell did she mean by saying he was "Stephanie's" Dr. Lawson? Diane leaned forward, completely alert. An electric current of nervous tension passed between her and Stephanie. Something was definitely not right about that statement.

Leah continued unaware, looking straight at Stephanie, "Girl, I can't believe you didn't jump on that gravy train when you had the chance," Leah said, shaking her head and flipping her hair at the same time. "I hope you're not mad, but I am going for it," she announced. Grabbing Stephanie's hand, and leaning forward, she asked, "Is he as hot out of his clothes as he is in them?"

Diane was taken aback. She looked straight at Stephanie for an explanation, but directed her question to Leah instead.

"What do you mean? How would she know?" she asked letting her eyes bore into Stephanie.

"Oh, you know, girl." Leah slapped Diane lightly on the hand as if that was the silliest question she had ever heard.

"No, I don't know," Diane answered, pulling her hand back as if Leah's touch had burned. "Enlighten me." She looked back and forth from Leah to Stephanie, demanding an explanation with the fire in her eyes. Stephanie looked like she wanted to fall through the floor and gladly knock on hell's door.

Leah just looked amused. "Why are you so interested?" Leah asked, suddenly turning defensive. "Please tell me you aren't sleeping with the dear doctor yourself?" She gave Diane the once over, took in her shiny, straight, dark hair, her long lashes and lean frame, clearly judging the competition.

"Leah, I'd rather tell her…" Stephanie began, but Leah was already on a roll.

"Okay, I'll tell you then." Leah looked contemptuous. "Stephanie and Mark got it on, and then they got caught naked together by her boyfriend, Steve. Who happens to be Mark's brother. Mark and his brother got into a huge fight, I mean knock-down drag-out, beat the shit out of each other fight, and now they're estranged. It's old news. Everybody knows about it." Leah rushed through the story, looking pleased to have shattered whatever interest Diane held in Mark.

Diane felt sick. "You had an affair with Mark?" Diane demanded, as she turned back to Stephanie. "Why didn't you tell me?"

"It wasn't a long-term affair, Diane. I mean, I wanted it to be an affair," Stephanie was flustered. "But it happened for all the wrong reasons. You have to understand, my relationship with Steve was so confusing. He was always traveling with the team. And I was just looking for comfort," she tried to explain.

Diane was beyond livid at this news. All this time she had believed that Stephanie and Mark were barely acquaintances.

"So you balled his brother? What kind of person are you?" Diane's voice rose, and she was shocked at her own vulgarity. "How could you not mention this? For God's sake you just had the perfect opportunity this evening!"

Leah looked shocked herself. "You didn't hear about the blowout

70

with Steve and Mark? Jesus, it was all over campus! You must live under a rock," she snickered. Then she frowned as she remembered Diane had a romantic interest in him, "By the way, I have dibs on Dr. Lawson."

For a moment, Diane looked like she didn't know whom to smack first. "Look bitch, get back over there with your drunken friend, before I smack your ass under this table," she spat furiously. Leah looked surprised, opened her mouth as if to argue, and then snapped it shut as the fury in Diane's face made her think better of it.

Stephanie was wild with sorrow, or else she would have been shocked to hear Diane speak so heatedly as well. Diane was always a lady, always controlled.

Stephanie struggled with her words, desperately trying to fix things. "I am so sorry. I didn't know how to tell you," she stammered. "You know you are my best friend. It's just…"

"How many times do you think a friend should have to apologize to another friend in one night, Stephanie? You are a selfish, inconsiderate, conceited bitch. Our friendship is just an afterthought to you!" Stephanie began to protest, but Diane cut her off immediately.

"I can't believe you would sink this low. How could you lie to me about this?" Her tears started then, as much as she tried to hold them back. A fresh wave of anger came over her as she realized how much she cared and how little it appeared that Stephanie did.

"This is crazy. I can't believe you didn't know about it. You're best

71

friends?" Leah only added insult to injury. Finally she found the good sense to know when enough was enough. "I better let you two work this out." She rose, but neither woman even acknowledged her. Leah beat a hasty retreat back to her friend's table, daring to cast a quick glance over her shoulder only once.

Stephanie began crying. "I know how bad this looks, but please forgive me, Diane. I didn't think it would matter after all this time. But Mark is an asshole. He used me! He isn't worth us fighting over, isn't worth hurting our friendship over," she said. "Please, please listen to me."

Diane snorted with disgust. "Friendship," she sputtered. "Bullshit!"

"Diane, please…" Stephanie continued.

"I have to go," Diane said, standing up and knocking over her drink. Stephanie stood and tried to stop her from leaving. She wanted to make things right, but she just wasn't sure how.

Diane held up her hand as if to ward off a blow. She wiped at the spill and sputtered, "I can't even look at you right now!"

Stephanie went on autopilot herself as she tried to mop up the spilled drink with her cocktail napkin and figure out what to do. Diane had never talked to her like that.

"Diane, come back!" she yelled across the bar, and heads turned to look at her.

Diane ignored her, crossing the bar in what seemed like three steps, her long legs carrying her quickly away.

72

"You don't have a ride home!" Stephanie called out again. "Let me at least drive you back to your car!"

The door slammed shut before Stephanie could even leave her seat. She glanced at Ruby, who looked completely puzzled and concerned. She and Stephanie both dashed to the door after Diane, pulled it open, and called out into the night air from the sidewalk. Where the hell had she gone so fast? The streetlights were swallowed in darkness just ten feet ahead. Diane was nowhere.

They both stared into the night, and then Ruby took Stephanie by the arm. "Come back inside, honey. Let's try to get her on the cell phone."

When they came back in, only a few heads lifted at the sound of the door. When they saw the argument was over, wasn't going to come to blows or intensify any further, those that had been curious quickly lost interest. They moved back to their own conversations or hookups or whatever had drawn them there.

"Let me get that," said Ruby, as she came over with a bar towel and cleaned up the spilled drink. She patted Stephanie on the arm. "Now, now, stop your crying. All friends get into it sometimes. Why don't you call her and see if she wants to talk it over?"

"You don't understand. I've kept a terrible secret from her." Stephanie's nose was dripping. Ruby gathered her up in her arms, letting Stephanie cry on her shoulder but saying nothing further. Ruby never pried, and she wasn't about to start now. For that, Stephanie was grateful.

73

Maybe Ruby was right, she thought as her tears subsided. The initial shock was bad, but as soon as Diane realized that the affair wasn't a real affair and that the feelings between her and Mark were lost to the past, she would be rational about this. Turning to Ruby again, she added hopefully, "Do you really think she will?"

"Of course she will," Ruby reassured her, patting her hand. "You'll patch things up good as new by tomorrow."

Stephanie sat there for a few more minutes, still stunned, until Leah, realizing the threat of bodily harm from Diane was over, returned.

"What the hell is up with your friend?" she asked. "She's a fucking psycho." Stephanie glared at her, not responding. "I mean, who does she think she is, threatening me like that?"

Stephanie sighed, "Look, Leah, fuck off," she said quietly, with no venom in her voice, just sadness. "You obviously don't understand the situation, and I am sure as hell not going to explain it to you."

Stephanie pulled her cell phone out of her pocketbook, dismissing Leah, who smirked and shook her head to herself.

Stephanie tried in vain to get Diane on the phone, and as Leah left the bar with her friend, she heard Leah's voice expressing her excitement about the prospect of telling Dr. Lawson all about this little exchange firsthand.

Chapter 6

The night was so cold, Diane's tears felt like they were freezing to her eyelids. It didn't matter though; the heat from her anger would melt them away. She felt betrayed. Betrayed and pissed off, and that was an understatement. Diane was practically running down the street, she was so full of furious energy. It kept the cold air at bay but it couldn't clear the storm of emotions she felt inside.

She felt her Blackberry vibrate in her pocket. Surely it was Stephanie calling to find her and patch things up. She almost threw the damn thing in the gutter and would have loved to hear the shatter of plastic against the cold concrete. But her practical nature told her that having to pay for a new one was a punishment she didn't deserve. After all, it wasn't she who had done anything wrong. She hadn't slept with the man her best friend was falling for and then failed to tell her about it! She wasn't the one faking her happiness to the world, trying to get pregnant behind her husband's back! She hadn't skated her way through law school, relying on other people to take care of her. What else was Stephanie hiding?

Diane's heart ached, and her head was beginning to pound along with her footsteps, but still she kept walking. She thought of how they'd come to be friends in the first place. Stephanie had pledged Diane's sorority six years ago, and they had gotten along from the first moment they had met. Both of them were without parents to guide them, and both of them were strong, black women who were on scholarship (Stephanie for cheerleading and Diane for academics). They were both interested in physical fitness, and they were both pre-law.

And both of them were beautiful. Beautiful women, Diane had learned, had trouble making girlfriends. She didn't know if other women were intimidated or jealous or simply afraid to talk to her, but she'd never had a lot of girlfriends, and Stephanie admitted that neither had she. Between them, they found an instant chemistry from the start, almost becoming inseparable. Over time, they formed a bond that Diane had believed was unbreakable. It was one she had thought would surpass graduation and continue throughout their lives. Now Diane thought maybe Stephanie had just been using her.

She tried to remember the circumstances of Stephanie's late pledge. Stephanie told her then that she had just broken up with her boyfriend, who was a star of the Taft Titan's basketball team. Stephanie had said that he hit her and she had broken it off and joined the sorority to start anew. Then she'd shown her the scar on her forehead. *Steve's work*, she'd called it. *Was that even true?* Diane wondered.

Stephanie had simply failed to mention that the reason they broke up was due to her screwing her boyfriend's brother, the very man Diane had considering giving herself to completely.

Stephanie didn't know that. Not until tonight, Diane reasoned. But what bothered Diane, deep down, was the knowledge that Stephanie would sleep with her boyfriend's brother, sacrifice her moral fiber, and lie like she had. Not just about Mark, but about a lot of things. To Diane. To her own husband. Diane couldn't shake the feeling that Stephanie was not the person she thought she was.

It was simply unforgivable. Diane muttered to herself, lengthening her stride. How could she look at Stephanie, knowing she had been intimate with the man she loved? How could she feel the same toward Mark? Diane felt as if her entire world had just blown up before her.

She walked on, and her pace seemed to quicken with every block. She was oblivious to where she was headed or how far she'd gone. The cold air was clearing her head a bit now. The anger she felt was still ripe but she was feeling more rational. Diane needed to get the real story of their relationship. From **both** of them. She paused. Yes, she needed to hear everything, no matter how badly it hurt, dammit. Diane couldn't carry on a relationship with either one of them unless she knew the truth.

She checked her phone. Three new messages, all from Stephanie. *Diane come back, please*! The first one read. Then in screaming capitals, *I AM SORRY*! And the last one: *You have my keys*!

"Shit", Diane said aloud, fishing in her pocket. Stephanie had given her the car keys right before they entered Ruby's.

"You're the designated driver," she'd said, plunking them in Diane's palm. Diane had taken them, trusting herself to stop at two drinks much more than she would have trusted Stephanie to do the same.

77

What time was it anyway? Diane was stunned to see that over an hour had passed since she stormed from Ruby's. She felt a little ashamed in the wake of it, making a scene like she had. It was completely out of character for her to react that way.

Mark. That's what had really set her off. It had been the thought of her best friend being touched, kissed, *loved*, by Mark. That was the worst of it. A small sound escaped from her, and she pushed the image of them together from her mind.

Home was that way, back the way she had come. So was Ruby's. It wouldn't hurt to stop in, see if Stephanie had gotten a ride home and at least apologize to Ruby for her behavior. She steeled herself, took in a deep breath, and began to retrace her steps. She passed one of the off-campus fraternities where a group of unruly college guys with a keg beckoned to her to come inside, whistling and cat calling.

"Thanks, but no thanks," she said to herself, walking past quickly and leaving their voices and laughter echoing behind her.

What had she been thinking wandering off alone at night? Hadn't the police been warning women of this very thing?

She almost turned around again as she thought about asking one of the frat boys to escort her back to Ruby's might not be such a bad idea. At least she wouldn't be walking alone.

You can call a cab, she reasoned. But by the time it got here, she could be safe and warm back at the bar, too. On Friday nights, the cab fare somehow seemed to double, and the wait for a driver was just as bad.

She stopped on her heels for a moment to get her bearing and decide. While it seemed so unfair that a woman had to be afraid to walk alone at night in this world, it didn't change the fact that she suddenly felt frightened. Diane decided to cross the street. The lights were brighter there, and it looked like a few of the restaurants were still open. Ruby's was only a few more blocks, ten at most. She'd make it there and then never do something as stupid as this again.

The rest of the walk was well lit, and she started to feel comfortable again. She passed a couple snuggled closely together as they walked, and her heart jumped painfully as she remembered again what had driven her out here in the first place. She shook her head. *Truth first, tears later*, she told herself. Maybe there wouldn't be as much to cry about as she feared. Maybe this adversity would make her friendship stronger and her feelings for Mark a solid reality.

Her steps echoed off the pavement. They sounded loud, like heartbeats pounding. Since she passed the couple in love, she hadn't seen anyone else. Looking ahead there was only one part of the street that looked dark. It was near the alley, the one that ran along the back of that Chinese place with the greasy egg rolls that had made her sick last year. Once she passed that, she'd almost be back at Ruby's. She hurried on, head up and aware of her surroundings.

At first she thought she imagined the noise. It was a soft rustle like sheets when someone turns gently in their sleep. A cat in the alley maybe, rummaging in the trash? *Don't eat the egg rolls!* She thought, trying to use humor as a shield, but it fell short. Something made the hairs stand up on the back of her neck.

"Shit, shit, shit…" she began to chant as she realized the sound was not imaginary. There was something in the alley, and it sounded much larger than any cat she'd ever seen. As if to answer in the affirmative, she heard moaning, a sound that would emblazon itself on her memory for all time.

It was definitely a person making that sound. A drunk perhaps, moaning in his sleep? Whoever it was sounded as if they were in pain. The moaning stopped intermittently and then mixed with what sounded like whimpers and crying. Diane stopped in mid step and cocked her head to the side to get her bearings on the sound. It was very dark back there, too dark to see from the street. She forgot her fear; her whole being was ready to help whoever was making that noise. Diane turned down the alleyway.

Chapter 7

Stephanie had another drink as she furiously texted Diane, tapping her foot in expectation of a reply, even an angry one. Some of the other patrons were looking at her, and she felt uncomfortable and embarrassed. She had half expected the response she had gotten from Diane, but not coupled with such fury, and it stunned her at first. Now she wasn't sure what to do. Leave the bar and search for Diane? Or stay here and drink herself into oblivion and forget the evening's events until she had to deal with them tomorrow?

Surely Ruby would have good, solid advice and a strong shoulder to lean on, not to mention a healthy dose of pink house specials if she stayed. With three drinks in her now, she was starting to feel spiteful and sorry for herself.

Diane completely overreacted, she decided. *She was making more of this than there actually was.* The idea of Diane and Mark, together, in love, rubbed her the wrong way. *What makes Mark think Diane was any better than me?* Stephanie asked herself, letting the self-pity drape over her like a dark curtain. Mark had rejected *her,* and here he was falling all over himself to get Diane's attention.

And he had. The worst part, to Stephanie, was that Mark had Diane's undivided attention.

Her thoughts wandered back to the here and now, letting Mark and

Diane slip away for a minute. *Fuck them*, she thought, abruptly. *I have my own life to worry about.* Like finishing school. Like having a baby…

Paul, she thought, as she accepted another drink.

"You're not to drive," Ruby warned her, as she set it down. "We'll call Paul or I'll take you."

Stephanie nodded back at her in the affirmative, telling her she didn't have her car keys anyway, and slid down slightly in the booth. The cool, slick material of the seats felt soothing against her cheek, which was warm from the liquor, and she let her thoughts wander.

Had she ever felt for Paul what she had felt for Mark? For Steve? *Yes*, she decided, feeling the alcohol really take affect now. Yes, she had felt love and passion for him when they first met and all the way through their first year of marriage. He was commanding, rich, interesting, and educated. And hot. They used to have a sex life that blew her mind. Maybe she could breathe new life into that old passion. Maybe she could even make a baby. Tonight.

She glanced at the bar, making her decision on the spur of the moment. Ruby was distracted and busy with a very drunk, very obnoxious older gentleman with a long graying beard. "But I got more money, honey!" Stephanie could hear him saying loudly over the jukebox, and Ruby appeared to be telling him he'd had enough and he had to go. There was a hotel a few blocks down; it was a little bit sleazy and definitely known for one night stands, but what a better way to put a little excitement back into their failing love life? She'd get a room, call Paul from there and ask him to meet her.

Stephanie scribbled a note on an old receipt, leaving it with a twenty-dollar bill for Ruby:

> Going to meet Paul. I promise I am
> not driving. Call you tomorrow. Hugs &
> Kisses, Stephanie

And then she left, slipping out discreetly and welcoming the cold night air. "I'm coming for you, Paul," she whispered, smirking to herself. "So you had better be ready."

"Why don't you just shut the fuck up," Marty said, as Kirby droned on and on about moving down South and blowing this cold, crowded city. "I've had a shitty day and I am in a shitty mood, so I need some quiet." He didn't want to hear about Kirby's pitiful dreams for the future. He didn't want to share in that level of intimacy with the idiot.

That's what you get when you help someone get out of prison. They think you want to save their lives forever. They think you are interested in their futures. Marty felt his skin bristle at the thought of being friendly with Kirby for the rest of his life.

For tonight, Marty had hooked up with Kirby just for a drink or two, but mostly to relive last night. He wanted to talk about the woman in the park, wanted to remember how she looked and felt. Each one was

83

getting better, each more satisfying and yet, not quite enough. Seeing all those couples on the dance floor tonight had really pissed him off, made him feel queasy, even. Now Marty was about to come out of his skin. He felt electric shocks course down his arms; his energy level was that of a stampede of wild animals. He felt *enraged.*

"Why don't you calm the fuck down?" Kirby answered. "You don't gotta take everything so serious."

That last whiskey had been a mistake, Marty thought, feeling as if he could lose control at any moment. *Kirby was an imbecile.* And now he was trapped having to deal with him for God knew how long. At least as long as it took to convince him he should move down South, pronto. But right now, in this minute, talking to Kirby was like a punishment. He stopped short, leaving Kirby to walk ahead for a minute.

The girl just fell into his arms. She came out of nowhere, tripping on the sidewalk in front of him, almost knocking him backwards with the force of her weight.

"Ugh," she burst, quickly pulling herself back. "Sorry." She shook her head to get her bearings, and although it was dark on this part of the walk, Marty could see she was attractive and built. He could smell the alcohol on her breath, too. She had definitely been drinking. He turned his head from the woman and when he did, he caught sight of Kirby.

Kirby was turning around to see where he was. He'd gotten almost a block away before he even realized Marty was no longer beside him.

IDIOT, Marty thought and felt a fresh rush of anger course through him. At the same moment, he realized he was standing next to a very dark, very secluded alleyway, and that no one, except Kirby and this woman, were anywhere around. The woman was sitting on the ground, her head between her knees as if she was about to throw up.

When opportunity knocks, he thought, as he moved lightening-fast, *you damn well better answer.*

He took the woman around the neck and felt the surprise catch in her throat as his hands bore down, choking her airway. He dragged her, on her ass, into the alley.

WHAT THE HELL? One minute Stephanie had stumbled along the sidewalk, feeling sick as she came down on her rump, and the next she couldn't breathe. Her pulse surged, and her heart pounded like a set of drums in her chest. *WHAT THE HELL WAS GOING ON?*

Stephanie's knee smacked the pavement, making a splat as she landed in a standing pool of liquid. Whoever had been choking her had thrown her down on the ground, and the impact sent shock waves of pain up her leg. She cried out, but her voice merely crackled; the man had squeezed so hard that her throat felt bruised and tight. She took in a deep breath, trying to open it.

The man was there, standing over her, but he wasn't touching her anymore. Stephanie's eyes flew everywhere, her thoughts going in a hundred directions at once. *Where the fuck was she? How could she get past the man whose shadow stretched ominously along one side of the alley? It was so hard to fucking see!* The only light was from a single, dirty bulb hanging over the back door to a business… *Chen's China Palace!* It came to her at once. Stephanie knew where she was. That gave her a small comfort, and she started to rise to her feet. She couldn't get out of here on her knees.

The man pushed her back down. "Stay where you are, bitch. I need a blow job." His voice was cold and piercing, and his hands reached out and held her in place by one shoulder as she struggled against him to stand again. Stephanie found her voice. She started screaming.

The bitch was screaming now, at first startling Marty with the sudden outburst. Kirby found them then, rushing into the alley sounding panicked.

"Shut her the fuck up!" he warned, his voice the hiss of a snake. "There are people coming up the block!"

The woman must have heard this because Marty felt her take in another breath, apparently to scream again. She lashed out at him, clawing and slapping him, throwing herself back as she tried to get out of his grip.

He wanted her conscious, but he needed her quiet. Time was short. She was fighting too hard, all arms and legs bouncing off him. She knocked a can with her foot, and he heard it clatter down the alley, rolling onto the sidewalk beyond it. If someone walked by at that moment, surely they would look down here to see where a moving can had come from…

86

No time to plan this out. Marty broke her nose. *That should do it*, he thought, as he felt the bones smash under his palm. He hit her, hand open, driving the heel of his hand upwards, and a wash of warm blood coursed through his fingers and down his arm. *They didn't have much time*, he reminded himself again. This would have to be quick.

Marty's penis stiffened. The woman fell back, her legs and arms splayed apart. Her head bounced off the concrete. Then she lay still, stunned perhaps, but still conscious. He could hear her moaning deep in her throat. And then Kirby was next to him, pulling his buck knife from the band under his shorts.

"You'd better be fast," Marty sneered, knowing it was Kirby's turn, but wishing that he had been able to lose him back on the street now. The woman kicked out, missing them both, and then Kirby dropped to his knees with the knife as he started to work on her clothing.

The pain was horrific. Her nose throbbed and spurted, and her eyes swelled against the pressure. One of her cheeks felt numb. Stephanie wanted to sob, but nothing in her face was working. Frantically, she clawed at the pavement under her as she tried to get up and get away. Her nails made a scraping sound, and she felt one split and break as it snapped upwards. *GET UP, GET AWAY!* She told herself. But nothing would move except her hands; it was if she were made of stone.

She could hear shuffling above her, but she couldn't see anything.

87

Her eyes were swelling shut now. She lifted one leg and kicked out into the dark at whoever was standing there. She felt only air as her leg came dropping back down like dead weight, smacking the pavement and sending a shock wave through her bones. Her shoes slapped the pavement, echoing with a clacking sound off the building walls.

Her heels! They were still on her feet; she could feel them. Three-inch spikes at the end of her boots. Weapons. Stephanie imagined herself ramming one to the hilt into the eye socket of her attacker.

Suddenly he was there, ripping at her coat and yanking on her clothing. She heard it rip and part and felt the cold air sneak in, touching her skin. Stephanie panicked as she rolled back and forth spitting, hissing and kicking again. She made contact with someone (*Oh, God, there are two of them!* and already she knew who they must be), her shoe glancing off his leg. Something nicked the side of her breast, something sharp, and she felt a hot flash of sharp pain again and something wet drip down.

"Don't make me cut off your boobies," a voice said, deadly serious, ugly, and *venomous* and she cried out again. Tears, blood and fear made a sound all by themselves, she realized. "I'll take them home and feed them to my dog," the voice finished, as he slapped her now exposed breast, leaving a vicious sting behind. She felt hands everywhere between her legs and fingers inside of her, pinching and biting. Fear overwhelmed her as she was struck again and then again. Her legs were lifted into the air, completely exposing her bottom half. They spread her thighs and she let them, and all the while her brain screamed to fight on. She couldn't move though, could barely speak in words. Stephanie felt the tip of a penis push against her anus, and she began to cry.

"Oh God," she moaned. "Oh God, please……"

And then she fell silent, shutting off her brain.

Marty listened for any passersby, holding the woman's legs over her head as Kirby rammed himself violently in and out of her. She'd hit at him once, scratching his arm with the top of a ring she wore, and Marty angrily ripped it from her finger, propelling it wildly into the darkness and hearing it ping against the side of a large trash bin, lost forever. After that she fell quiet and submissive, and Marty felt his penis fall, too. By the time it was his turn, there would be no fight left in her, no reason to hurt her. *He* wanted to be the one to drive her into obedience. Marty found himself hating Kirby more and more with each thrust.

"Hurry up," he seethed. "Finish already."

Kirby ignored him, pounding away, his head back, a lusty leer of satisfaction in his face. Marty sucker-punched him under the chin, and Kirby's lidded eyes flew open, surprised.

"WHAT THE FUCK YOU DO THAT FOR?" Kirby asked loudly, grunting at the same time.

"HURRY UP, YOU STUPID BASTARD," he warned. "We've been here too long," Marty warned him, although the people Kirby had heard coming before never materialized, and he hadn't heard or seen a thing anywhere near this alley.

Kirby finished with one final lunge, shuddering and then letting the woman's legs fall hard onto the ground. She moaned again, low in her throat and Marty kicked her in the head, trying to get his erection back. His penis stayed flaccid.

Damn Kirby, he thought, reeling with outrage. *DAMN THIS BITCH!*

He fell on her then, unable to see anything but red. He tore at her with his hands, gouging skin, ripping hair, punching and biting. He took a nipple with his teeth, spit it out into the alley, and left a part of her bottom lip flapping open.

"Marty, you're killing her," Kirby pulled at the back of his shirt. "Get off her man! Don't kill nobody!"

Marty paused at the words and looked down at the battered figure under him. She looked nothing like the pretty drunk woman that had fallen in his arms a half an hour earlier. She was meat on a hook now. Marty felt avenged.

Just meat on a hook.

"Yeah, I'm done," he said, as he spit onto the woman and cleared his mouth of the rusty taste of her blood. He put his normal face on now, the one he showed to the rest of the world, and he felt the hateful creases smooth and the sneer fall from his lips to cover his teeth again.

"Let's go," he told Kirby. They left the alley together, neither of them looking back.

Chapter 8

Kirby was afraid. For the first time since he had met Marty, he saw a glimpse of something that made him shudder. Marty may have killed that woman. If Kirby hadn't been there, maybe he would have. *Maybe he did.* That would make Marty a murderer. Again.

Kirby's head swam. Marty had helped him once, that was sure. He'd saved him. Back then, Marty had been the good guy, and he only killed someone who was bad. This was different.

She ain't dead, he assured himself more than once during the ride and since Marty left him at his walk-up. *He just beat her real bad.* Neither man had said much on the way home. Marty was agitated and distracted, barking at him to shut up. After seeing how he bit that lady on the ground, Kirby did as he was told.

"Get the fuck out," Marty told him, barely stopping the Volvo to let him unlatch the door. Kirby had jumped to the curb as he watched Marty speed off until his tail lights winked away in the distance. You just couldn't trust people like that. People who did nice things and then turned mean. And *murderers* were likely to do anything. Kirby wanted nothing to get in the way of him leaving town this time.

If Marty kept acting like a lunatic, leaving would come sooner rather than later. No forwarding address, no good-byes. Kirby was out of here.

You should have checked her breathing or her pulse or something. Kirby was confused. *What if she was dead? Did that make him a killer, too?* He looked at the door to his walk-up. It was a shoddy, brick building sorely in need of a spruce up. He had a couple of cold beers in the fridge and half of a sub sandwich from the night before. Both were calling his name.

But the lady was calling his name, too. He'd just wanted sex from her. Since his Momma left him, he hadn't found anyone to love him. Girls didn't talk to Kirby, and he couldn't talk to them. His words got tangled whenever he tried, and then they pointed and laughed and called him stupid. The ladies that made you pay were mean and nasty, dirty and diseased.

So Kirby liked taking sex whenever he wanted it. He liked doing things to ladies that they wouldn't normally let him do: forbidden things. Sometimes you had to hit them a little, scare them so that they saw things your way. After you scare them enough, they usually listened and let you do the secret, bad things. But that was all he had wanted from her. He didn't want her to be dead.

Just go check. You can do it quick. His conscience goaded him. He took a step away from the building.

Marty will kill you if he finds out. Kirby paused. Marty **could** kill him. Probably, anyway. Even if Kirby was bigger, Marty was smarter. Marty could find a way to blame everything on him because Marty had money and brains and an important job helping people. Money and brains and jobs meant power.

Marty won't find out, he told himself, as he shook away his nerves. *I'll be real quiet and fast.* He had to know if the lady in the alley was breathing. If she wasn't, Kirby would blow town tonight and never come back.

Without thinking about it again, Kirby hot-footed it back uptown.

Diane circled back to where the sounds had come from. What she had heard sounded like someone weeping. It wasn't any animal. Now, she was absolutely positive. Someone was hurt.

She peered down the alleyway as she tried to make out shapes. Her ears were pricked to sound; her whole body was on high alert. There was a very small light source: a dim light bulb outside the back entrance to that Chinese place. Otherwise, she could just make out the bulky mass of a dumpster and a pile of trash bags.

Go back to Ruby's and call someone from there. Don't go down a fucking dark alley by yourself! she thought, finding herself halfway in the depths of the narrow passage even as she warned herself not to continue.

Is that a foot? Her heartbeat was furious and burning a hole in her chest. *Jesus, Mary, and Joseph, please if that is a foot, please let the person it is attached to be alive.* She wanted to rush forward, but she didn't. She felt as if she was walking in quicksand. The few steps she had taken were

94

shaky and arduous. She kicked something metal and it flew, pinging against the wall, making her jump and cry out.

The foot didn't move.

"Hello?" she said, quietly. Then with a rising, shaky voice, "Are you okay?"

Diane tried to swallow, but her mouth was drifting sand. It was definitely a foot, one that looked to be wearing a very high heel. A woman!

It took less than a second for her to realize what a woman might be doing lying in an alley at this time of night. SHE HAD TO CALL SOMEONE. NOW!

Diane was panicked and afraid to go any closer. She had envisioned herself kneeling beside the person, giving them first aid, comfort, something! But now that she was here, three feet from a body, she felt solidified. Her feet wouldn't move further in any direction.

The woman made a noise then, a movement that sounded like bone grating against bone. It was a dreadful sound she'd never heard before, but instinctively understood. Diane's hand flew to her handbag, frantically digging for the phone. *Why the hell hadn't she kept it in her pocket, within reach? Where the hell was it?* Her fingers met gum wrappers, pens, her checkbook, but her phone eluded her.

"I'm calling someone," she said to the woman, but her words just floated away in the air, meaningless. *You aren't doing anything!* She screamed at herself. *You're scavenging for your FUCKING phone! You're not helping anyone!*

She found it! Her hand closed around the cool egg shape of her cell phone and she yanked it out, dragging coins and some papers out with it, letting those fall to the ground, clinking and rustling away from her.

"I'm calling now!" she screeched at the figure, still unmoving and quiet again. Her fingers shook as she dialed, but at least she was dialing. She heard it ringing and she bounced up and down, willing the emergency operator to answer. "It's ringing," she said, loudly to the woman on the ground, and her voice echoed back to her.

C'mon! Answeransweranswer! She could barely breathe.

"What is your emergency?" *FINALLY!*

"I am in the alley," she stammered, for a moment not realizing that would mean little to anyone. "Behind the bad Chinese place," she continued.

What the hell are you saying?

WHAT WAS THE NAME OF THE BAD CHINESE PLACE? Her mind closed, and she scrabbled around there, unable to speak.

"Ma'am?"

"ARck..." a sound came from her throat.

"Ma'am? What is your emergency?" The voice was urgent, insistent.

"Ruby's," she sputtered then, the restaurant name lost in the recesses of her memories somewhere. "Ruby's is on Foster Ave!" Diane was shouting.

"Ma'am, where are you on Foster Avenue?"

"I'm in the alleyway on Foster Avenue!!" Diane felt like she was going to have a heart attack. Her throat was closing; her chest had a boulder on top. The world was swimming.

Without warning, from somewhere in her peripheral vision, a hand appeared. It came so fast that her palm stayed in position curled around the cell phone even as it went sailing onto the pavement, clattering into pieces. Diane's head slammed backwards as the hand came back forward, hitting her against her eye and filling her head with a blinding light. A second blow forced her to fall, and she instinctively curled into a ball to try to break the impact. But her arm and hip didn't cooperate. She felt the bone of her forearm break through the skin just as she was driven into unconsciousness. The lights that had flashed before her eyes dimmed and went completely black

Kirby was shocked to see the other woman standing there. He had almost been on her before he saw her at all. The light from her cell phone and the sound of her panicked voice drove him into action.

She was calling the cops! He hadn't meant to hit her so hard, but

SHE HAD BEEN CALLING THE COPS! Calling the cops meant no Florida, no freedom, no nothing.

He'd *had* to hit her.

Kirby had run before they could get there. Before he could tell if either one of them was dead or alive, he just grabbed a purse and some of the ladies' things from the ground and left. They would be his treasures. But he couldn't tell Momma about them.

He took the back way home, panting like a dog after he ran the first half mile. He lit a cigarette and walked the last three to clear his head.

He shouldn't have gone back there. He should have just left well enough alone.

He had the lady's pocketbook with her wallet inside, and he could find out who she was. He could watch the news and find out how she was doing. He could call the hospital and ask about her.

"What hospital, you idiot?" It was his mother's voice, bouncing around in his head, showing him the truth of things like she always enjoyed doing. She was his angel, looking down on him and helping him through the rough times. She *knew* about the purse and the rest of the things he had taken. Momma always seemed to find out. Kirby guessed she was looking down from heaven.

"I don't know," he answered out loud as he walked. "I don't know what hospital."

"That's cause you're a big, dumb fool!" She told him, and he could almost see her, hands on her hips, holding the paddle, preparing to give him a good ass whipping. "You did the bad thing again, didn't you?" She demanded. She sounded angry, furious.

There was no sense lying. She knew.

"Yes, Momma." Kirby hung his head and stood still, feeling like he might cry. He had done the bad secret things to another woman. *He just couldn't help himself!* He had broken his Momma's heart again. But she wasn't here anymore to help him stop himself.

She didn't say anything for a minute, and he stood there, shifting his weight from foot to foot and waiting for her scorn. When she finally spoke, it was searing.

"You burn up that purse and everything inside of it! And don't go calling no hospitals. What's done is done."

"Okay, Momma," he said, thinking he could burn the purse in a trash can down past the brewery. Or throw it in the water or something. He just wanted to peek inside and see who she was. Maybe she had some money in there. Stealing wasn't the same as killing. He knew that for sure.

You maybe are a murderer, though, his mind teased, and Kirby felt the sharp pain of remorse again. *I didn't mean to hit her that hard. I am so stupid!*

His mother always said he was a stupid, rotten, and a no good piece of shit. *Why did she ever even bother to bring him into this world?* That was her favorite thing to say. Kirby never did have an answer to that one. He still didn't.

Chapter 9

The Emergency Room at University Hospital ran like a well-oiled piece of machinery. When a call came in, everyone jumped into action, working side by side to help whoever needed their expertise. The medical team was the finest in the state, and it was an honor when Mark was accepted for his residency there. He'd stayed, of course, accepting a position in Emergency as soon as he finished his training. Mark loved the action and excitement of being in the heart of the hospital in what was usually the busiest time of the day. Most catastrophic cases in the area went to University Hospital's ER, which also boasted the best trauma team in the city. Mark loved even the routine aspects of the job, and tonight had been fairly routine. He even had time to keep up with his paperwork so he wouldn't have to stay after his shift to finish it. He had three hours left in his shift and then he could go home, sleep, and call Diane just as he had planned.

"Mark Lawson!" a friendly voice called to him, just as he grabbed a tray in the cafeteria.

Mark turned. "Dan the Man!" he smiled broadly as his old friend, Dan Travis, strode toward him, lab coat flapping behind him. He was a tall man, broad shouldered and wild haired. The young neurologist was brilliant to a fault.

Dan's curly, brown hair was spiked with early hints of gray and was his trademark feature. It bounced in unmannered spirals on top of his head, no matter how hard he tried to tame it. Most of the time, he just gave up and let it fall in whatever direction it chose. Tonight he looked like a mad scientist as he walked briskly toward Mark with a big, goofy grin on his face. It made Mark want to laugh out loud.

"Feel like a sharing a table?" Dan asked, and it felt like no time at all had passed since the men had sat down together, though surely it had been a year or more.

"I'd love the company," Mark answered.

"We wiped the floor with the Generals!" Dan was still an avid college basketball fan, although his personal days playing with the Titans had been anything but glorious. "You need to keep your eye on Jerry James, number 27. That kid's going pro!" He beamed as if Jerry was his own son.

"I miss the games," Mark sighed, as he reminisced about the days he went to see Steve run the court and Dan warm the bench for the Titans. Mark could almost hear the deafening sound of sneakers pounding and squeaking against the waxy gym floor and the stands of cheering, jumping people all around him. The excitement had been infectious. Maybe he should think about catching a game with Dan one of these days.

As if reading his mind, Dan laughed, saying, "Those were the days," as he punched Mark jovially in the arm. "And look at us now, nearing middle age for God's sake. I'm starting to resemble my Dad," He joked, pointing at the gray hairs in his crown. "I'm even thinking of asking Cindy to be my lawfully wedded wife," he said, referring to his long time girlfriend.

"Wow," Mark teased. "You ARE getting old!" He found his thoughts drifting to Diane again, though. Was there a future for the two of them? Mark was getting older, too. Most of his friends were settling down now, starting careers, and getting married.

Dan smirked sarcastically, and then his voice took on a more solemn tone. "It was like the end of an era when you and Steve couldn't fix the thing between you. Man, we all just got so serious after that." He shook his head as if he still couldn't believe it.

Mark frowned, thinking how true that was. Their whole group of friends had seemed to divide after Mark and Steve stopped being Mark and Steve, stopped being brothers. They broke into little subgroups and then all but disappeared from Mark's life. He'd stayed friendly with a few of those closest to him and let the others go. They belonged to a different time in his life. Dan was one of the few who remained, true to both Mark and Steve in a way only a real friend could pull off. For a moment, a look passed between them.

"Life has a way of shifting gears fast on a guy, doesn't it?" It still hurt to remember what happened between him and his brother.

"Yes," Dan answered. "I suppose things don't always turn out how we expect them to. It's funny I met up with you though, because I saw Steve the other day. He asked about you, but I wasn't sure what to tell him.

Maybe you should fill him in yourself. What do you say?" Dan was clearly making a fresh attempt at acting as an intermediary between them.

"You talked to Steve?" Mark asked hopefully, feeling his spirits brighten. *Steve had asked about him.* That was a step in the right direction.

"He's totally caught up in running that bar, but it seems like it may be pulling him out of his slump. I had a beer in there the other day, and the place is hopping. Just what the doctor ordered for Steve, if I do say so myself." He paused, smiling softly. "Don't put it off, Mark. You both have let this go on too long." Dan looked at him earnestly, and Mark knew he was right.

One of them needed to take the first step.

"I'll call him then," Mark promised, and he meant it this time.

"Good...."

Steve and Dan's beepers pulsed wildly on the table in front of them.

"Incoming," Dan said, checking the code. "Blue." He looked at Mark.

Code Blue meant imminent death. Whoever was being brought into the ER was in danger of dying at any moment. Both men raced to the ER.

Chapter 10

Stephanie heard the sound of an ambulance siren in the background of her thoughts somewhere. She wasn't sure if she was imagining it. Everything was so hazy. *Were they coming for her?*

She hoped so. She needed help. She couldn't see anything.

I'm blind, she thought, and tears formed under her swollen eyelids.

"I... don't... want to be blind!" The sound of her own voice was punctuated by wracking sobs. Something was wrong with her ribs, too, because it hurt to breathe.

When her tears broke, Stephanie wiggled her fingers, testing them. They worked. They moved when she told them to, and she carefully lifted them, letting them gently explore her face.

Mashed potatoes, was her first thought. It felt like someone had spread a plate of cold, lumpy mashed potatoes over her face. Nothing was even, and it felt wet. Her eyes were thick and bulbous under her fingertips.

Everything hurt. Her inner thighs, her vagina, her anus. All throbbed. All felt ripped and misshapen. *They had torn her apart.*

And she was cold. Freezing. Little bits of what had happened to her were fitting together like puzzle pieces. She could feel them clicking into place. Her hands started moving quickly as she felt herself everywhere. Waves of pain washed over her, making her grit her teeth.

Something was wrong with her right breast. The top of it was missing.

Her right nipple was missing! Stephanie's brain stopped registering her injuries then.

A light shone in her face, but she couldn't see who was behind it. Hands were touching her again, checking her pulse, putting things over her mouth and in her arm as they lifted her up. She wanted to push them away, but her hands had stopped working. Right after she stopped touching herself, trying to figure out what was wrong with her, her hands had stopped working, too.

She heard words.

Stabilize.

Raped.

Fractured.

Words that couldn't possibly belong to her.

"Are those mine?" she whispered, barely audible within the oxygen mask, but no one answered. "Are you talking about me?" She tried again, but only liquid bubbled from her mouth. It frothed over her ravaged lip and dribbled under the plastic face mask, onto her cheek. The spittle burned her face, and Stephanie thought she might not even have a face anymore.

Just let me die! If I don't have a face, I don't want to live anymore. Shockwaves of panic took over, and Stephanie yanked the mask off her face, startling whoever was working on her.

"Calm down. We're trying to help you." A voice trickled down from far away. Someone was holding her arms down, keeping her from fighting back.

NO DON'T HELP ME! LET ME DIE! She shook her head back and forth violently. *Didn't they understand that she couldn't live without lips, without a nose, without her eyes?*

She tried to cry again as she felt herself fall back into the blackness of unconsciousness. It was safer there, and she preferred the darkness to whatever waited for her in the light.

The emergency technicians who worked over Stephanie and Diane tried to push their shock away. The scene before them in the alleyway was gruesome.

"I've never seen anything like this." One of the techs choked back bile, his face an ashen circle. There were pieces of body parts missing from the woman before him. The crushed bones, crushed faces, and the blood mixed with feces that stained the ground were stunning. He couldn't help thinking of his wife and daughter. They were safe and sound at home. He'd just left them curled in bed together an hour ago at the start of his shift. But it could have been them lying here, bitten and ravaged, looking as if a pack of wild dogs had gone at them. The technician choked again as he leaned on the ground over the woman. Her loved ones would barely recognize her now, but he couldn't fix that. It was his job just to stop her bleeding and stabilize her heart rate, He had to get her to the hospital in one whole piece.

Someone, a police officer, was looking for the pieces of her that were missing. They shined a bright light around the alley as they searched for her nipple and her lip.

"Unresponsive," his colleague muttered, as he worked frantically over the second woman they'd found splayed out like a discarded rag doll next to the dumpster. "No breathing, no heart rate. She's not going to make it!" he yelled, as he turned up the oxygen he'd been trying to feed her. "I'm going to shock in the van NOW!" He was on his feet, launching the gurney into the back of the ambulance.

"Code Blue!" he called back over his shoulder at the driver. The alley was a blur of lights and frantic activity. "FUCKING CODE BLUE!" he said again, grabbing the paddles that could shock her heart back into life.

Curious bystanders had formed a circle at the entrance to the alleyway, and the police held them back and tried to keep a clear path for the ambulance. Everyone milled around, whispering and frightened, as they asked for more information than anyone was able to give them. A ripple of unease and anger hung over them all.

"GET OUT OF THE WAY!" The ambulance driver yelled at them

through his open window, turned on the siren, and pressed the pedal down flat. "THIS ISN'T A FREE SHOW!" He raced past them, the vehicle's shrieking tires burning rubber as he turned out of the alley. He forgot to look for traffic either way. The crowd surged forward again, trying to get a look down the dark alley as the police took over and started the tedious job of gathering evidence.

Paul had checked his watch a dozen times as he waited for Stephanie. He had finished his work around midnight, closed the last file and turned off his computer. She'd gone for a few drinks with Diane, but she should be home any minute. And Paul was ready to talk. He had a few things to discuss with Stephanie.

Paul hated being alone like this with nothing to do. He hated thinking. He needed action, and tonight, he was going to fix his marriage or end it. Paul knew that things between him and Stephanie were turning sour. They hadn't seen eye to eye on anything in months. They'd barely made love, and when they did, it was hard to feel anything for her. Sex had become mechanical, and they were both only going through the motions, fulfilling a physical need, but any emotional connection had been lost. It made him feel angry and resentful. Here he was working his ass off, trying to make a good life for them, a life they could be proud of. And what does Stephanie do?

Take time off. Get her hair done. Go to the gym. GO OUT FOR

DRINKS WITH DIANE! What the hell was he working for anyway?

Paul wasn't going to tolerate a frumpy, unemployed wife clinging at his boot straps while he was on his way up the corporate ladder. That would not do at all.

Paul snorted. And even better, now she wanted a baby. Stephanie wanted to sit on the couch, stuff her face with bon bons and grow fat with a child that she couldn't possibly take care of. He laughed again sardonically.

"Stephanie caring for an infant!" he said aloud. The very thought was laughable.

She hadn't told him she wanted a child. She hadn't told him that she wasn't taking her birth control pills anymore. But Paul knew Stephanie hadn't taken a birth control pill for at least three months. He knew this because he found her latest prescription shoved into the glove compartment of their car last week. The prescription had been written three months ago and hadn't been filled. Just to be sure, he had called the drug store. No refills had been issued to their account since last November.

It had been a nasty surprise finding the script. Paul hadn't been snooping; he had just wanted to take the car in to be detailed, He had pulled out a tangle of papers and wrappers that she had shoved into the glove box. She had snowed him, that's for sure. He would never have suspected Stephanie would stoop so low.

Paul imagined that conversation. Stephanie, eyes wide with innocence convincing him that her birth control method had failed. And him buying it, allowing her to sidestep right into the role she was playing all along. He never imagined this would be his life, his marriage.

Well, Paul wouldn't have it. Either Stephanie would see things his way tonight, or there was going to be no more Stephanie and Paul.

He didn't even know Stephanie anymore. The woman he knew had been a fighter, a sassy little fireball with ambition and striking beauty. More than a trophy wife. She was an equal.

The first time he'd met her at a college football game (his school against hers) he had been struck by the whole package. Her skin was the color of warm milk chocolate, and she had legs up to there, an ass that begged to be stroked, and a brassy attitude. Simply put, she turned him on. They'd come together like a thunderstorm rolling across a prairie, fast and furious. Companionship and sex and respect all rolled into one.

Maybe she was having an affair.

Stephanie was beautiful, desirable in every way. Maybe she had grown as bored and tired of Paul as he was of her.

Ridiculous, Paul concluded. He'd know it if she was.

Then where was she then? He checked his watch again and was surprised to see it was past three. Was she w*rapping those long, chocolate legs around some other poor, unsuspecting bastard? Turning you into a joke? A cuckold?* Paul seethed at the thought.

She was fucking another man. She had to be out with someone.
Stephanie may have liked to push the envelope, but her friend, Diane was

a stickler. If she was really with Diane, they would not be out so late. The bars weren't even open anymore.

The phone rang then, jangling in the hallway and Paul ran to it.

"Dammit, she better not have gotten picked up for drunk driving," he muttered, as he picked up the receiver. "Hello." his voice was agitated.

"Mr. Kramer?" A voice he didn't recognize.

Paul listened, incredulous. Stephanie was in the hospital.

"Why? What happened?" he demanded, as he forced his perceived sense of authority past any sense of alarm.

"The doctor will speak with you as soon as you arrive. It's important you get here as soon as possible," the nurse told him.

Paul hung up the phone and silently pulled on his coat. He was torn between anger and confusion. What the hell had Stephanie gotten herself into now? And what was it going to take for him to fix whatever mess she'd made?

Then, feeling guilty, Paul realized that his wife was hurt and hospitalized. *They didn't hospitalize people unless something significant had happened to them, did they?* He felt a twinge of fear for her, and an almost urgent need to get to the hospital. But as he climbed into his own car, Paul already decided what had probably happened.

Drinking and driving. She probably crashed the damn Mercedes.

He couldn't face her just yet. He didn't want to have to watch her crying and pleading with him to forgive her for her newest, stupid mistake.

He couldn't stomach that. Especially if she had been with another man, allowing him to touch her and taste her and have her.

Paul was still too agitated. He took the keys out of the ignition, went back inside, and poured himself a Scotch. He needed a drink himself before he faced Stephanie.

Stephanie was alone in her room now. She looked around through slatted eyes, unable to rest, unable to get comfortable. The swelling had subsided slightly, and she could see a bit now. *Thank God, thank God, she wasn't blind.*

Green walls, the smell of disinfectant, and the quiet beep of monitors attached to her arm made everything feel so damn real. She could hear her own heartbeat as it echoed back from the blood pressure machine. Blip, blip, blip. Every time she remembered a piece of what had happened, the sound of her heartbeat rushed forward, bouncing frantically off the walls.

It felt like a heavy wet towel was pressing against her mouth and nose, and just the effort of moving was enough to keep her still. The hospital staff had numbed her before they had sewn her up, (she was torn apart from vagina to anus, she heard one of them say, and she thought that couldn't possibly be true. That couldn't really have happened to her). But Stephanie could feel a jagged, insistent throbbing between her legs that wouldn't go away, and she knew it must be true. She was destroyed *down there.*

Why? Why had this happened to her?

113

She felt so dirty. And embarrassed. So devastated.

What did her face look like? She didn't want to know. She'd closed her ears to the sound of the doctors' and nurses' voices. She didn't want to hear, didn't want to hear how bad it was.

It's bad. It's horrible and you know it. You're ruined. She wasn't Stephanie anymore. She was empty and victimized.

Paul was coming because they had called him. She knew because the nurse had told her, but that seemed like a long time ago. *Where was he? What would he do when he saw her this way? What would he say?*

Stephanie knew what she wanted him to do and say. She wanted him to take her in his arms, to circle her with protection and love and promise her that she would get better. To tell her that she would be Stephanie again someday. She wanted him to do those things, but she didn't think he would. Stephanie thought Paul would be angry instead. He would be offended and fuming and demanding that the hospital and the police DO something about this mess.

Who would fix her?

She felt very afraid and very alone in the world. Stephanie didn't miss her mother, but this was the time in a girl's life that she really needed the comfort of having a mother by her side. And she supposed that she had earned the right, in the wake of what had happened to her, to feel just a little bit sorry for herself.

Ruby would come. Diane would, too. But first the hospital had had to call Paul because Paul was her *husband*. So he would be there first.

Diane! She had forgotten that Diane was so angry with her. Maybe now, maybe now Diane would forgive her. It was a terrible reason to wish back a friend, but wouldn't Diane feel sorry for her, lying here like this, battered and bloodied and practically dead?

She shifted uneasily in the bed. Sure Diane would come. She was mad, but she wasn't unreasonable.

Stephanie couldn't stop herself from thinking. Everything was so confusing, so out of control. *WHY THE HELL HAD THIS HAPPENED TO HER?*

She started crying, big wracking sobs that made her heart rate beep so erratically across the machine that a nurse came running in. She was a good nurse. She didn't try to tell Stephanie to calm down or lie to her about everything being okay. The nurse checked her vitals and put something in her IV that immediately sent a wave of peace through Stephanie's being. *She was a good nurse*, Stephanie thought again, until a new understanding, a scary one, pushed its way in.

She could have a disease. What if she got all fixed up and then she ended up having a disease? Paul would leave then, that was certain. If Stephanie's face got fixed, if her crotch healed over, if Paul could *stomach* looking at her, he might stay. But if she had a disease that he could catch, Paul would want a divorce. *Would she stay with him if he would never look or act or be the same? Would she stay if he had a disease that could kill her,*

115

too?

That should have made Stephanie cry again, but her eyes stayed amazingly dry, and her heartbeat even. The medication the nurse had given her took the edge off everything. She'd have to ask for more of it. Stephanie strained to see the IV bag. If she could see the name of the medication, she could request it later. But everything was blurry, and her eyes were feeling heavy. She had held them open for long enough now.

Where was Paul anyway? What was keeping him? Didn't he know what had happened?

Didn't he care?

Her mind felt fuzzy, but clear, too. Stephanie forced herself to face the truth. She might deny the truth later, but for this moment, she was going to look at reality.

And then she was going to sleep.

She was a rape victim. Twenty-four hours ago she was a struggling student with a shaky marriage and an uncertain future. But twenty-four hours ago she was all in one piece, too, a beautiful young woman who could have done anything she wanted.

Now she was damaged goods. Her face was crushed, and part of it was missing. Her nipple was missing, too. And she would never have children. No one needed to tell her that she would never be able to experience a child growing inside of her. Her insides were jelly.

Stephanie was a rape victim. And just about everything she used to be had been stolen from her.

Tomorrow she was going to be interviewed by two detectives who specialized in cases such as hers: rape cases. They were going to ask her all sorts of questions about what had happened to her, and she was going to have to remember the terrible, embarrassing things that would leave her feeling ashamed and filthy.

It felt so unfair. She had to wait for everything now. Wait for Paul, for his reaction to this chaos, and wait to see if she could be fixed. She even had to wait for some sense of salvation. She didn't have anyone to talk to about it right now except herself and God. Maybe that was okay.

God, please let me come through this, she prayed, as she drifted off to a restless sleep, still waiting.

Chapter 11

There she was.

The woman he loved.

She might be dying. She might even be dead.

Diane Harper had flat-lined just prior to being propelled through the swinging doors of Trauma Room One. Now there was a stand of bodies encircling her, all working on bringing her back to this world or letting her move painlessly into the next one. She hung in the balance between becoming a medical miracle or a lost soul. This kind of moment either built doctors' egos or crushed them.

Mark couldn't see much of anything. Diane's bloodied, crushed head and twisted leg was the last glimpse of her he had gotten. One of her eyes had looked much larger than the other, and that was a bad sign. Seeing her eyes that way was like a hard blow to his midsection, and he had leaned against the wall in order to remain standing. It meant she was grievously injured.

"I know her," he'd muttered simply, unable to think of another way to respond to what he was seeing, and the rest of the team had pushed him aside. You don't try to heal people you know. That was the ethical code in any hospital, with any medical team. Mark felt the threat of tears behind his eyes and the hot burn of his rushed dinner rising in the back of his throat, but he held them both at bay. The world grew patterned for a minute, and

Mark bit his tongue, forcing himself back.

He had to stay here and see her life signs return. He blinked twice and held his ground.

Dan. Mark could see his wild cloud of hair fighting to escape the binding ties of the surgical mask tied haphazardly behind his ears. He wasn't the only neurologist there, though, and Mark knew something had to be wrong with Diane's brain. They had her heart working again; he could hear its tenuous pulsing on the monitor. It was fluttering now, dangerously close to stopping again, but Mark could almost feel it gaining a normal rhythm by the second.

What was a heart without a brain to free it? He couldn't imagine Diane that way. Mark stared at her foot, lying sharply at an angle.

That wasn't Diane! That couldn't be Diane.

Mark tried to console himself. *If Dan was working on her, everything would be okay.*

Mark wished he could really believe that.

"If you're going to cheat...cheat death." That's what his mother told him the day he was suspended for cheating on his spelling test. Sixth grade, Riverside Middle School. He'd never done it again. He'd never even really thought of it again until now.

"Cheat," he whispered to Diane. "Cheat death, cheat damage, cheat all of it." He closed his eyes and willed it to happen.

But the only thing that happened was Dan and the rest of the team whizzing past him and shouting to clear Operation Room 9. Mark got one last look at Diane, grossly distorted, tangled, and broken. She was a blur, nothing like herself.

Operation Room 9. Mark wouldn't follow them there. That's where they'd have to shave off her beautiful hair, open up her head with a saw, and poke around her mind, trying to fix the scrambled remnants of her being. Long after they left, Mark stayed in the hallway outside of Trauma Room One, still trying to recover from the shock in his belly. The hall had been strangely quiet, aside from the ghosts of what had just happened, which whispered fears and worries into his mind. The aftermath of trauma was a silent, lonely place for the ones who got left behind.

She was going to die. NO! She was being cared for by the best trauma team in the state, in the country. They wouldn't allow it.

She would be a vegetable then. Lost to the world. That was more likely. Doctors were humans, not gods, and Mark knew it in the depths of his heart. They might not be able to mend the delicate folds and fibers and make them work like they used to.

"Please bring her back," he said aloud, closing his eyes and swallowing hard.

"Dr. Lawson?" His eyes flew open. It was Leah Sanchez. She looked at him sympathetically, and he knew she had heard him. She had to have noticed that his eyes were red. Mark just stared at her.

"I know you knew her," she said softly. "I'm so sorry." The sincere tone in her words touched him.

He smiled dimly. "Thank you. Thank you, Ms. Sanchez." Mark lowered his eyes, unable to look at her anymore and afraid to cry in front of her.

But no one knew yet. No one knew he loved Diane. How did Leah know? Mark was confused. *What did she know?*

She nodded, lightly touched his hand, and said what he had been longing to hear all along from someone other than his own doubting conscience, "She's going to be okay."

Say it out loud. Say it loud and it will be true. Mark's voice cracked. "Yes, she IS going to be okay." For a second he almost felt joy. His fears lifted briefly from his shoulder. He felt Leah's hand under his chin as she pulled his face up to look at her, and he let her. He found himself staring squarely into her large, dark eyes. They were soft and warm, with long and luxurious eyelashes. Mark didn't know how she knew, but Leah realized he loved Diane Harper. He'd found a friend in the midst of his turmoil, someone who could share a little of his worry. It was completely unexpected.

"Of course she is. She's at University!" Leah moved forward, put her arms around him, and comforted him. For a moment it felt awkward, and then Mark let himself lean against her. He could feel her heartbeat strong and even against his own chest. It reminded him of living, of life, and it consoled him.

"Let me make it all better." Leah's breath tickled his ear and raised the hairs on his arms. He felt her lips against his ear and the soft dance of her tongue over his earlobe. His own heart rate doubled as he felt her gently push up against him, testing the waters.

Oh God! Oh no! Leah was making a pass at him! Mark yanked himself free in one quick jerk.

"Ms. Sanchez! Please!" Mark held her at arm's length, staring at her incredulously. He didn't say anything more. Leah looked hurt, as if she'd been slapped across the face, but it was clear she understood. There would be no relationship between her and Mark Lawson. Leah's expression changed immediately from compassionate to vengeful.

"Idiot!" she hissed. "She's a vegetable for God's sake!"

"You've overstepped your bounds," he warned, taking the hit and standing firm against it.

Diane was not a vegetable, she was not a vegetable!

"She doesn't have any interest in you anyway!" she spit back. "I saw her last night, and she knows all about Stephanie Kramer. She hates you!" Leah stood back and looked at him. "And you just threw away your best chance at a VERY good thing." She crossed her arms haughtily across her chest as she stared him down, waiting to see how much hurt she had inflicted with her words.

"What? Where? What the hell happened?" he demanded. Each comment Leah made pinged off of him like a stoning. "Tell me everything!"

his anger was at the surface now, and he grabbed Leah by the forearms, holding her in place. She wriggled, trying to get away.

"Take your hands off me. I'll have you suspended!" Her threats weren't hollow. Mark had been right to be wary of Leah before. She was trouble. It followed her like a tail on an errant kite. She caused it, and she reveled in it. And now she meant to throw a handful in his direction. *How had he allowed this woman to hold him?*

He dropped his arms, but not his animosity. Her threat was meaningless for the moment. All that mattered right now was to find out what she knew about Diane.

"Tell me what happened last night!" He held her with his eyes, and she took a step back.

"Go ask the fucking detectives," she said, pointing blindly down the hall. "Maybe they can fill you in on Stephanie and your precious little attorney."

Mark spun on his heel, looking down the hall where she had motioned. He almost expected to see a figure in a long overcoat come walking out of the shadows. His mind and heart sent garbled signals. Half-truths and emotions flooded him. Mark thought he might be going insane. His vision closed in around him like a tunnel.

Stephanie? WHAT HAD HAPPENED TO STEPHANIE? WHAT WAS GOING ON HERE?

When he was able to clear his head again, his cheeks wet and hot.

Leah was gone, and another nurse passed by with a medication cart, looking at him strangely.

"Detectives?" he managed, and her look changed to sullen comprehension.

"They're in family waiting, just down the next hallway," she said, avoiding his eyes and continuing on her way to whomever she was due to medicate.

"Thank you," he said gruffly, heading briskly in the opposite direction.

Chapter 12

Ruby Claire sat down with a steaming mug of fresh coffee and a bitch of a headache, which she hoped the caffeine would be able to cure. It had been one hell of a night. It had started with the argument between Diane and Stephanie. *What on earth had possessed them to scrap like that?* Ruby hadn't asked Stephanie, hoping that she would give up her secrets of her own volition. Instead, she'd slipped out of the bar, leaving some half-assed note about meeting Paul and promising not to drive. Ruby had checked, and her car was still in the lot, so that much was true. Then she'd tried both Stephanie and Diane's cell phones more than once, getting only voicemail.

It made her uneasy, but not frightened. Diane and Stephanie were both stubborn as mules, in fact, almost as stubborn and set in their ways as Ruby herself. But as soon as it was light out, Ruby would check on both girls. In person.

Ruby sighed and let the aroma of the coffee waft over her. A good barkeep always had a fresh pot going. She'd gone through a couple of pots over the course of the evening, between herself and the patrons. It must have been a full moon last night because everyone she'd come across was all out of sorts. Howard had felt ill, and half the bar was in a cantankerous mood, drinking far too much more than any of them should have. She'd run from one part of the bar to the other, trying to put out fires, sober up customers, and console crying women for more than half of the night. God help her, but Ruby felt like she might need a change in professions here soon.

She'd finally closed up shop at 2:30, and here she sat, too wired to sleep, too tired to think. "I am getting way too old for this," she said feeling the bones in her knees pop as she eased into the same booth that Stephanie and Diane had been sitting in earlier. "That's the sound of too many hours on my feet," she yawned.

The bar was the only thing she had left of her husband, Joe Claire. But it wasn't out of some deep love that she kept it up. The bastard drank hard every day of his life and right along with his patrons, some of whom still came in every night to knock back a few and relive the past. Although a lot of people on the outside wouldn't understand it, Ruby felt an odd comfort in talking about Joe and remembering him with the old timers who spent all of their free hours in the dark here with her. It was like they were in their own world, a safe cocoon. Not much changed here at Ruby's from day to day or year to year.

So Ruby talked about Joe and missed him along with his buddies, even though he had beat the shit out of her on a regular basis, and even though Joe had often made a fool of himself, stumbling over the bar and spouting nonsense to anyone who would listen. Those things were easy to talk about, or laugh about sometimes, because they weren't happening anymore. Ruby found it wasn't that difficult to turn a bad old memory into a better one. So even though Joe had died in her arms at the age of 45, yellowed and shriveled from the very thing that had been his livelihood and provided him a sanctuary, she tried to find some good in what they'd had, to understand it better. She'd decided that alcohol made a tumultuous suitor, undeniably tempting and dispassionate all at once.

Ruby never touched a drop. But she watched over the ones that did.

Coffee sure isn't going to help you sleep, she scolded herself, as she took a big slurp out of the cup anyway. Such was Ruby's life. Everything fell to either side of her in opposites, but she evened it all out. That was what the good Lord had put her on the earth to do, she guessed.

"Ruby! It's Jimmy Baker!" The banging on her door made her jump, driving her out of her seat.

Dammit, she thought, settling back down again. On any other night when she was feeling lonely she may have let him in, taken a clean glass from behind the bar and filled it up for him, free of charge. But not tonight. She was done fixing up people's lives with beers and whiskeys, for this day at least.

"Go home, Jimmy. You've had plenty, and I'm too tired to talk to you!" she hollered back from her booth.

"I don't want no beers, Ruby," he yelled back through the heavy wooden door. "But there's a whole lot of cops down at the end of the block. Peoples saying there was another one of them rapes right here on Foster!"

His voice was insistent and frightened. "I wanted to make sure you were safe."

Ruby's heart immediately flipped over. *A rape here on Foster Avenue?* Her thoughts immediately flew to Stephanie and Diane. She unlocked the door and let Jimmy in. His face was a white circle in the moonlight, and worry outlined the red rims lining his eyes.

"Are you sure that's what they said?" She came out on the stoop and peered down the block where indeed a jumble of flashing lights and a surging mass of people had congregated. She **had** heard sirens earlier when she was wiping the bar down.

"Yep, but I can't get close in, you know. The cops are keepin' everyone back, and they're not sayin' nothing. You want to walk down?"

Ruby looked down the street again. It looked like a mob scene. A news van went rustling past just as she ducked back inside again.

"Wait a minute," she said to Jimmy, and he followed her inside, plunking himself down on his favorite bar stool and watching her silently.

Ruby grabbed the phone from behind the bar and stretched the cord as far as it would go with her nervous pacing. *Stephanie first*, she thought.

That child was hardly ever without her cell phone.

Ruby's fingers shook as she punched in the numbers.

But the phone rang. And rang. And rang. And then the voicemail picked up, telling Ruby she had reached Stephanie and to kindly leave a message. Ruby tapped her foot, waiting for the beep.

"Stephanie this is Ruby. I am half sick out of my mind trying to find out if you got home all right. There are a dozen cops down at the end of my street and I need to know where you are. Call me as soon as you get this." She felt a glimmer of frenzy rise in her throat as she cut the connection and immediately began dialing Diane.

"Who you calling, Ruby? Don't you want to know what's going on down there?" Jimmy asked. His eyes looked clearer than before, and he was more alert.

"Shh," she warned him, putting her finger up to her lips. "Just one more minute."

More ringing. Ruby's head pounded with it.

Pick it up girl!

Two more rings went by. Ruby was counting. That made five and no answer yet. No voicemail. Nothing.

Ruby hung up her phone.

"Let's go see what the hell is going on down there," she said, fear and worry lining her brow and making her insides cold. *No sense putting off the inevitable.* Ruby put on her coat, braced herself for what she might find, and followed Jimmy down Foster Avenue.

Chapter 13

Mark stopped just outside the door of the private family waiting area. He could hear voices murmuring inside. This couldn't be happening. He couldn't actually be going in to talk to detectives about a vicious attack on Diane and, presumably, Stephanie Kramer as well. *He just saw them headed out for a drink for God's sake!* They were alive and well. And now... they certainly weren't well.

Should he knock? Or should he just walk in? Mark stood there, surprised to see his hand shaking as he lifted it to the knob. Then, changing his mind, he rapped his knuckles against the wooden door. The sound was dull and hollow and it made the situation seem far too real.

"Yes?" It was a female voice, beckoning him inside. Mark felt himself hesitate one last second. After that, he would have to accept the fact that the woman he loved, and the woman he hated, had been victims of an almost inconceivable crime. He saw himself turn the doorknob as if from afar, and then he was inside. There was no going back now.

The atmosphere in the room was stagnant, and Mark gulped air. In spite of the cold outside, it was hot, heavy, and sticky, all the qualities that make an uncomfortable, humid summer's day, and he immediately felt sweat break out across his brow. There were two plain-clothes detectives in the room, a man and a woman, and they both shot quizzical, almost annoyed stares in his direction.

The woman sat perched on the edge of a chair that looked as if it had seen a host of bodies come and go. It must have absorbed a million tears during its time here. The vinyl was cracked and ancient, and it crackled when she moved. But the woman who sat there, Sheryl Avery, looked fresh and energetic, and certainly too young to be a detective. Her unlined face and curly, brown hair betrayed a seasoned veteran. Her eyes were big and brown, and a smile danced in them, even though her expression lay puzzled and concerned across her face. Mark warmed to her immediately.

Jim Pranther stood at attention, a tall skinny man with a sour, pinched face. He was a white man, with chalky white skin, freckles and red hair. His pants hung loosely around his legs, and the ends of his shirt had pulled out of the trousers, giving him a slightly unkempt experience. It looked as if he had rolled out of bed and rushed over here, forgetting to tuck in his shirt.

His eyes said differently, though; they were cunning and smart. Mark could tell this man was a seasoned old vet, and he felt an immediate respect for him. If Jim had walked out of a movie from the 1930's, Mark would have pegged him immediately as a gumshoe. It was obvious he meant business.

"My name is Dr. Mark Lawson." He paused very briefly, offering his hand, "I'm a... friend of Diane Harper and Stephanie Kramer," Mark swallowed hard at the use of the work friend to describe either woman. That wasn't entirely true.

This piqued Jim's interest. "I'm Jim Pranther, and this is my partner, Detective Sheryl Avery." The woman nodded in Mark's direction, holding out her hand. Jim motioned toward a seat and Mark sat down.

"How do you know the victims?" Sheryl asked.

Mark hesitated, and then spoke again, "I was romantically involved with both of them." Then, as he realized how that sounded, he added more. "At different times, of course."

He saw the slightest raise of Jim's eyebrows, but no other expression crossed his face or Sheryl's. "Can you expand on that a bit?" he asked.

"Stephanie and I had," *what the hell should he call it? An affair? A fling?* "A relationship," he decided, sounding firm. "A while ago. Almost three years."

"And Diane?" Jim was a straight shooter.

"Diane and I are involved now," Mark said simply. He didn't want to explain further. The details of what they were to each other were new and pristine. Mark didn't want to sully their relationship by trivializing it or trying to explain the depth of what he felt for her.

"When was the last time you spoke to either of them?" Jim pressed on, neither his face or voice betraying any emotion.

"Last night. I ran into them at the Java about 8 p.m." Mark glanced at Sheryl. She was writing notes in a small, black notebook, and the idea of where he was and what he was doing struck him again as so unreal. *Did officers still take handwritten notes in tiny detective notebooks in this day and age?*

Was he sure this was really happening?

Sheryl looked up, waiting for the sound of his voice to continue. "Go on, please. Tell us what they said. What was the extent of that interaction?" She smiled weakly, her pen poised over the paper again.

She's the good cop, Mark thought. *Didn't they say there was always one hard ass and one sweet, understanding cop when you were being interrogated?* Again he was struck at how alien all of this felt. How unbelievable it all sounded. Mark's stomach was a vat of acid.

"They were headed out for a drink. They asked me to join them."

"The woman you are seeing and the woman you used to see asked you out for a drink together?" Jim looked as if he couldn't quite believe that.

Mark felt flustered. How to explain the intricacies of their relationships?

"Yes," he answered. "Diane did the asking. Our relationship is new," he tried to explain. "Neither of the girls knew about my relationship with the other." *There, that ought to put things in a clearer light.*

"I see," Sheryl said.

"I don't think I do," Jim countered. "From what we've been hearing, Stephanie and Diane are best friends. Best friends share everything."

"It was a secret," Mark insisted. He felt like a child stamping his foot, insisting he knew something he didn't. Not really. Except for what Leah said just minutes earlier. That the truth *had* come out between

133

Stephanie and Diane.

"So you all went for a drink?" Sheryl asked.

"No. I couldn't." Mark replied.

"Too uncomfortable with the situation?" she sounded understanding.

"Well - it wouldn't have been comfortable to be with them both at the same time." Mark looked from Jim to Sheryl. "But I was due here at the hospital at 11, anyway."

"Did they say where they were headed?" Jim asked, tapping his finger lightly on the table in front of him and pushing the magazine pile that sat there askew.

Mark shook his head.

"Did you notice them speaking to anyone before they left?" Sheryl didn't lift her head from her note pad and continued writing while she spoke.

"I left before them. Like I said, it was awkward talking to the both of them, given the circumstances."

"How friendly are you with Ms. Kramer?" Jim's eyes were cold and penetrating.

Mark figured the detective knew he was holding back information. "We haven't spoken for about three years. Since we ended things."

"And you didn't see them talking to anyone else? Didn't notice anyone watching them? Didn't ask where they were headed?" Jim peppered him, not giving him time to answer.

"No... no." Mark shook his head. His face was hot again, and he imagined it looked red and flustered. He could hear a tremor in the back of his voice, and he was embarrassed. He had nothing to hide.

"The owner of the Java, he was staring at Diane, though. It made me angry, I almost said something to him." Mark hung his head. He sounded like an idiot. Then his head shot up. "What happened to Stephanie?" he asked, looking from one to the other. "What happened to Diane?" Mark had to know the truth, all of it.

"You work here in the hospital," Jim said. "Why don't you tell us what you know? What have you heard? Seen?"

"C'mon, Jim," Sheryl said. "Dr. Lawson came to us." She shot him a sympathetic stare, and Mark was sure now that she was playing the good cop.

"I only know Diane was a bloodied, broken mess." His breath hitched at the memory. "I wasn't able to work on either of them. I didn't even know Stephanie was here!" Mark broke down. "I was going to call Diane tonight… we were just starting out." Sobs wracked his body. Someone came over and patted him on the back, but he couldn't stop crying.

This was real. These things had really happened.

The detectives let him cry. The room was impossibly still, except for Mark's reverberating sobs. He cried until he couldn't breathe anymore in the stifling air.

When he got himself under control, Mark looked up, eyes rimmed red and burning. He realized he might look as if he were guilty. "Am I a suspect?" he asked, holding his breath.

"Should you be?" Jim raised his eyebrows.

"No!" Mark felt his temple begin to throb, as anger and shock rose to the surface of his thoughts.

Jim set his lips in a thin, hard line. "Tell us why not then."

Mark wanted to scream: *I'm a doctor for God's sake! I'm in love with Diane Harper!*

Jim waited and watched. "Come on. Let's make sure we have all of your story straight. Just for the record."

Mark told them everything he knew, starting at the beginning.

Chapter 14

Steve Lawson limped out of his office at the Bases Loaded Sports Bar. The bar was closed until five, and it was dark and quiet in the main bar area, but Steve liked to keep a television on for company whenever he was here alone. He had been catching up on the week's payroll when something on the television caught his attention. He thought he had heard the name Stephanie Kramer mentioned on the local news.

Was he imagining things? His knee had really been hurting lately, and he *had* taken a Percocet this morning. Maybe his mind was playing tricks on him. Steve stood in the doorway to his office, leaning against the frame to take some of the weight off his right leg.

You didn't imagine it – you heard her name, he told himself. Stephanie Kramer was a name he would never have missed and one that he would never forget. She'd been Stephanie Marshall back then, and she had belonged to him. Steve closed his eyes and listened intently to the television, waiting for the news lady to repeat any of what he had heard.

He was in Mark's bedroom again. A woman was in the bed with Mark, firm round ass cheeks quivering in the air as Mark thrust wildly into her like a battering ram. Her full hips were raised high as he took her from behind. "Take me! Harder!" she'd moaned loudly, and Mark had, pounding at her ferociously. Mark's penis moved in and out of her, balls

137

swinging back and forth with the effort, his muscular ass cheeks growing taut with each penetration.   He could hear Mark's balls slapping against, her and he had watched as the woman's fingers reached around to catch them, fondling them with her fingers, squeezing and kneading at them. Her long, pink nails stood out in startling contrast. Mark reached under her, grabbing wildly at her full breasts as she arched her back against him. Both of them had their eyes closed, and both of them were moaning loudly, ready to climax.

"I LOVE YOU, MARK," the woman had cried out as she came, and they'd both fallen together, embracing and kissing, loving one another.

Steve had known that ass, those fingers. He had known that voice. Just as he knew the name the anchorwoman had mentioned now. It had been his girlfriend, Stephanie with his brother, Mark. And to Steve, finding them together had marked the beginning of the end of everything he cared about in life.

He opened his eyes, shattering the memory. Steve wasn't surprised to feel tears in the corners there. He swallowed them away, keeping his eyes on the T.V. for now.

Why would Stephanie be on the local news? Steve felt a little dizzy and unsteady on his feet. *Damn this knee!*

"Police stated that both women were victims of two vicious attacks that are believed to have taken place within an hour of one another but in the same location," the anchor was saying. "Both women were found in an alleyway off Foster Avenue."

Steve flew to the television, feeling his knee protest by sending a wild shock of pain straight up his thigh. Ignoring it, he turned up the volume.

"One of the women, 24-year-old Stephanie Kramer of Oakmont, is reported to have been raped and beaten. The second woman, 25-year-old Diane Harper, also of Oakmont, is comatose. Both women were transported to University Hospital where they are being treated for their injuries. Police are asking that anyone with any information connected to these attacks contact them at…"

Steve's leg buckled under him, and the world went black.

"Steve? What the hell!" Steve's eyes fluttered open at his name. He was on the floor, and his knee was folded under him, screaming like a banshee. *What was he doing on the floor?*

It only took him a second to remember. *Stephanie.*

He looked up at the voice coming from above him. It was his partner, Gregory. The lights were on in the bar now ,and Gregory looked like a distorted black shadow. He was frowning, and the concern showed on his face.

"Are you all right?" he asked.

Steve's entire leg throbbed. He couldn't imagine trying to put any weight on it to get up. Instead, he held out his hand to Gregory. "I could use a hand up," he said, trying to smile but knowing it was more of a grimace. "My damn knee…" he tried to explain.

"Well, Jesus, I came in here, the T.V. was blaring, and all the lights were out. I flip on the overheads and there you were just fucking lying right here on the floor. I thought you were dead!" Gregory pulled Steve gently to his feet and helped him into a chair. "What happened?"

"Man, my knee's been hurting all day. I guess I forgot to eat. Took some pain pills. And then the news." Steve paused, unsure how to proceed. "God, Greg, my ex-girlfriend was raped and beaten last night." Steve shook his head slowly back and forth. "I just can't believe it. I mean, I loved the girl. Before what happened *happened*, you know," he looked at Gregory, who nodded. "I was going to marry her..." His voice trailed off.

He had told Gregory about Stephanie, although he hadn't meant to. It had been the night they'd signed the loan papers on the bar, both of them sure they'd struck gold in a salt mine by buying the place. They'd gone out to celebrate, and one too many beers turned into one too many shots, and one too many shitty memories had snuck right up on him. Steve had told Gregory all about how Stephanie had an affair with his brother.

"I felt like I could have killed them both at the time. But you just think that. Something like this... I would never have wished something like this on her," Steve said, realizing that he never wanted to see Stephanie suffer, no matter what she had done to him. He might have wished her sadness and heartbreak, but *this*? No, his heart wasn't so black.

Steve was trying hard, too, not to cry in front of Gregory. Gregory was his business partner, not his best friend. And after that first mistaken confession, neither of them had talked personal stuff ever again.

"What goes around comes around, I guess. I'm sorry to hear it, though," Gregory said, clapping him on the shoulder and moving over to the bar to make sure things were stocked properly for the evening's clientele. Steve watched his back as he counted bottles, checked the beer taps, and opened the cash drawer.

It was, Steve guessed, an awkward tough guy's attempt to make him feel better, and he was able to smile slightly. Gregory most certainly could not be described as a tough guy. Gregory was older and seasoned, closing in on fifty. He was a smart businessman. He had marketed the hell out of Bases Loaded, and it had paid off, drawing crowds every night since it had opened. He almost always wore a tie, and he spoke softly with a slight hint of a lisp that never really materialized. His face was pockmarked with old acne scars, and his nose was thin and hooked, but his looks belied his huge confidence. If Gregory believed in anything, it was himself.

Steve admired him.

"Stick with me, kid, and you'll be a millionaire," Gregory had told him. As far-fetched as that may have sounded a few years ago, Steve was actually starting to believe it could happen.

"And now, folks, I am ready for the night to commence." Gregory had finished the prep work and was staring at Steve now. "Can I get you anything? A crutch, perhaps?" He smiled broadly as he held out a big shot of tequila. Steve shook his head no, and Gregory banged it back himself.

"How's the leg?"

Steve stretched his knee out slowly, hearing it click and pop, a familiar sound to him now when it came to his knee. The pain had fizzled to an aching burn, but it was nothing his brace and another Percocet couldn't cure.

"I'll live," he said, holding onto the bar to help himself get up.

"Good man," Gregory said. "Who's on shift tonight?"

Steve told him, spouting off a list of names he'd memorized from the schedule. It was another one of his job duties and, as Gregory told him, one of the most important parts of running a successful business. "Hire good people, train them well, and make sure you schedule the best ones for your hardest shifts," he told Steve. Saturday night was, by far, their hardest shift. And Steve was learning, slowly but surely. He hadn't wanted this life. It had almost killed him to give up ball, but this was his now. He had no choice but to roll with the punches now. Or give up entirely.

Steve lit a cigarette. *So much for being a star athlete.* Those days were long gone.

"I'm going to call the hospital," he said, unable to clear Stephanie from his mind. Her face swam before him, as it had the last time he had seen her. Startled, scared, her mouth curled into a large O of surprise. "We were going to tell you," she'd started to say, right before Steve had hauled back and punched her face, knocking her to the floor. He could still hear her crying as she lay crumpled there. He could still feel the remnants of hot

142

rage pulsing in his head right before he had turned on his brother.

Steve had hated Stephanie for a long time now, but the hate had transformed into something less sinister. It beat like some kind of mild, whimpering toothache he couldn't quite bring himself to go to the dentist to fix. *Time to face the dentist*, he thought, as he gingerly made his way back to his office so as not to aggravate his knee any further.

If Stephanie could have visitors, he would go see her. He'd already decided that much. What happened after that, well, would happen.

Was it too late for take-backs? He thought. *When do they expire?*

"If you don't quit smoking and taking pain pills, you're going to be in the hospital yourself," Gregory said.

Steve looked back at him. "I'm working on that," he said as he closed his office door.

Chapter 15

The door was shut, and the blinds were drawn in Room 421, Intensive Care. This was the second door today that he'd had to stop and contemplate before he entered the room beyond. What lay behind this, *Door Number 2,* was far worse than what he had faced in the Family Waiting Area. What lay behind this door was what was left of Diane.

Mark had spent over two hours talking with the detectives and telling them everything they wanted to know. Halfway through the interrogation, an orderly had come into the room and informed the detectives that Diane Harper was out of surgery, but comatose and that Stephanie Kramer would be available to speak with them very briefly, but within the hour. At that point Sheryl Avery left him alone with Jim Pranther. By the time Jim was done with him, Mark didn't know if he was still a suspect or not. At this point, he didn't think he really cared.

Mark did, however, have a general idea of what had happened to Diane and Stephanie. Not everything, but damn near enough.

"We'll be in touch," Jim had told him. "Stay close."

"I plan on it," Mark had said, grim-faced and starting to feel an anger creep into the parts of his heart that hurt the most. He could feel it coating all the pain over with a thick layer of fury. "You'll definitely be able to find me."

Who the hell had done this to Diane? And to Stephanie? What kind of sick, twisted animals were responsible for this? His adrenalin swelled, even though he was near complete mental and physical exhaustion. Mark felt murderous. He looked down and saw his hand gripping the doorknob. It had turned red with the effort. Mark let go and stood there a moment longer.

"Excuse me." A nurse swooped quietly past him, opening the door for him. His vision caught the edge of the bed, and his ears caught a gentle whoosh of the breathing machine. Then the door fell shut in front of him again.

The hallway was a church. Voices here never spoke above whispers. Disturbances were to be avoided at all costs. And all Mark felt like doing was screaming. He fought to control the urge, gripped the doorknob again, and felt it turn under his fingers.

The nurse didn't turn around when he entered. She was making a note of Diane's vital signs, checking that the IV lines were all working, and bustling about efficiently but almost silently.

Mark crept closer, and she spun on her heels, making him gasp. "Immediate family only," she said, nodding her head at the door as if to tell him to get his ass out of there, stat.

"I'm a doctor," he said, as he showed her his name tag. "Here at University. Dr. Lawson." She nodded again, apparently recognizing either his face or his name.

"How is she?" he asked, as he felt a lump rise in his throat. He pushed it down again.

She looked at him with an odd look on her face. "She's in a coma," she said, abruptly. She may as well have called him an idiot.

Mark came closer. He had to see her for himself. Now that he had completely entered the room, it was like he was encased in a bubble. There was no outside interference, save for the nurse, who looked as if she were about to leave. She gave him another strange look as if she didn't quite trust him with her charge, but she slipped quietly out of the room anyway, leaving him with Diane.

Just him and Diane.

"Diane," he whispered, as he moved forward to look at her. He could hear her heartbeat and the ventilator moving air into her lungs, but he needed to *see* that she was alive. He held his breath and stopped at the end of the hospital bed, averting his eyes from her face until he felt ready to really look at her.

He glanced over the length of her body, which was enshrouded under a sheet up to her breasts. Her arms were exposed, with her broken left forearm in a cast lying crookedly to one side of her body. It looked so uncomfortable, and Mark found himself trying to reposition it in at a less awkward angle. Her other arm was lying lax at her side, which gave it a posed look like a mannequin.

Diane looked so tiny and delicate. *She hadn't had a chance.*

146

Mark felt the breath hitch in his throat again. *Her poor, sweet arms.*

He moved slowly up the side of the bed, finally lifting his eyes to her face. He had tried to prepare himself, but the sight of her was shocking, and he took a step back as the room spun. There were angry purple and black bruises dotting the parts of her face he could see. Her hair was shaven on one side, and surgical clips like giant staples held the skin together there. The hair that remained was bundled beneath her, tangled and matted where the surgical staff had pushed it out of their way.

Her poor, sweet face. Her beautiful, silken hair.

"Oh, Diane," his voice broke from the agony of seeing her this way. Tears began to cascade down Mark's cheeks, although he was unaware of them. They puddled on the sheet by Diane's neck as he leaned down to gently stroke her cheek.

"I am so sorry I wasn't there to protect you," he told her.

Mark pulled the chair from the corner of the room over to the side of Diane's bed. He gingerly lifted her hand, avoiding the raw skin there, and clasped both of his own loosely around it. Hers was limp, but warm. The hand of someone living.

"I am so sorry," he said, as he brought his forehead down to the bed. "Please come back to me." His words flew away, lost in the room somewhere, empty and meaningless.

Diane may come back. The doctors may have fixed her brain enough that she would return, but she may never forgive him for what had happened with Stephanie. Mark may have lost Diane long before she'd ever been attacked, and maybe before she had ever met him.

He had to talk to Stephanie.

Chapter 16

He couldn't talk to Stephanie. He couldn't face her. Paul didn't feel ready to deal with this black cloud that had suddenly descended upon their world. God, he never saw something like this coming. He had never even considered it.

Not that anyone could have. But Paul was used to things going his way, or at least in the general direction of where he had intended. Nothing like this had ever happened to anyone he knew, let alone anyone in his family.

Why did this happen to him? And what the fuck was Stephanie thinking running around the city in the middle of the night?

Now that what had happened had begun to sink in (*his wife had been brutally raped! Another man had her and beat her and ruined her*), Paul realized this wasn't just a small annoyance he could push off to the side and deal with later. He couldn't fix it with an expensive lawyer and a good mechanic. This shit wouldn't go away anytime soon. This was going to require an endless amount of interviews with investigators, long term therapy sessions, restorative techniques. It meant having a wife that may never recover.

This meant never having children of his own.

No, there was no way Paul was ready for this. He might never be ready.

They'd shown him to her room, but they hadn't shown him in. Paul almost didn't go in at all. He didn't know what he would see, and he didn't want to see it. He didn't know what he would hear, and he didn't want to hear it either. But just leaving Stephanie a note or a bouquet of flowers seemed weak. And wrong.

Don't go in.

They tried to be gentle when they told him what had happened. They used polite doctor language - *sexual assault, trama, fracture, contusions* - until Paul finally told them not to mince words.

"Give it to me straight," he said, bracing himself for the truth. And they had. The doctors told him she was ravaged. There were parts of her torn and missing. She'd needed to be stitched from end to end. And her face was destroyed. Her beautiful, perfect face would never look the same, no matter what they did to repair the damage.

Paul had arrived at the hospital, the scotch still buzzing around in the back of his head and disappointment over his marriage still thrumming in his temples. He expected to find a wife with a broken leg and a car with a couple of nasty dents. What he'd found instead…

You have to go in.

She'd just been lying there, her face to the wall when he walked in. The lights were dim, but he could see her shape and the top of her head from the door. She was still, sleeping perhaps.

Sedated, not sleeping, he reminded himself. The doctor said she

150

was heavily sedated.

"She won't be able to carry on much of a conversation," the doctors warned him. "It's best you just quietly support her at this point. She needs time to heal."

"How much time?" Paul asked. He hoped they would keep her here for as long as possible. He needed time to think and sort all this out for himself.

"That's uncertain. She's been critically injured. And emotionally, there's no way to know yet, Mr. Kramer," The doctor told him blandly. "The police will have a 24-hour, armed guard outside of her room. She'll be safe here."

Police guard. That brought it all back home again. His wife was at the epicenter of an ongoing crime spree. Their lives would be under a microscope, prone to everything public.

Their world, *his* world, lay in ruins.

Paul took a deep breath, and she'd turned to face him. Either she heard Paul enter or had sensed someone there.

Here it comes. Paul swallowed hard, and it stuck in his throat like a shard of glass. His body tensed, and his bowels rumbled. *Here was the moment of truth.*

Her face was hidden, bandaged from just under her eyes, down to her chin. Paul couldn't *see* anything. But he *knew*. You don't cover someone's entire face with bandages if it isn't raw meat.

151

"Oh my God," he said, taking a staggering step backward. "Oh my God, Stephanie."

Tears shone in her eyes, but she didn't really cry. He could feel her breathing, heavy and thick through her nose, and it hurt to listen. Paul wanted to stick his fingers in his ears, to run from the room. To...

... fuck out of here!

But he stopped, trying to avert his eyes the way someone would try not to stare at a giant mole or a wandering eye on the face in front of them. Paul broke out into a sweat.

And still Stephanie remained silent, staring.

Paul looked everywhere but at his wife. He knew he should at least go to her, but he couldn't go. His knees were locked into place. He shoved his hands in his pocket, listening to his loose change jangle against the soft beeping of the medical machinery and the dull, raspy sounds issuing from the figure in the bed. Paul was reminded briefly of some old horror movie he had seen as a kid: The Mummy, shuffling toward some poor, helpless victim, breathing through the thick cloth wrapped around his face.

Stephanie was a monster.

Paul was the victim.

"It hurts," she said finally through the slit that was her mouth now. "It hurts so much," Stephanie's eyes burned holes into him, and he was forced to look at her. He let his eyes roam the landscape of her face, imagining what lay beneath.

What had the mummy been hiding under all that wrapping?

"Do you need more medication?" He asked softly, ready to push the call button for the nurse. A diversion would be good right now. Paul longed for another body in the room that could wedge itself between them.

He looked at Stephanie again. She *was* crying now, big round tears, one falling after another, tracing a crazy path down the bandages. A thin line of snot, sticky looking and streaked with blood, hung from one nostril. Paul felt himself move forward, take a tissue from the nightstand and handing it to her. He wanted to believe it was a kind gesture that had been born of his heart. But he just couldn't stand the look of it hanging there.

"Wipe your nose, Steph," he said, as he held down the gag reflex and let it burn in his throat.

She wiped, painstakingly, clumsily with her good arm, smearing the outside of the bandages a bit but getting most of the mess off her upper lip.

It was agonizing to watch her. Paul shifted nervously from foot to foot as he waited for her to finish. His stomach turned over. He grabbed the trash can so she could deposit the used tissue, fearing she would hand it to him instead.

"Here, put it in here," he said, holding it up so she could see. Her eyes were huge, dark, muddy clouds that followed him everywhere he went.

Leave me alone! He wanted to say. *Leave me alone and stop watching me.*

And then she did what he feared most. Stephanie had him standing

153

right next to the bed, and she trapped him with her gaze until all Paul could do was gaze back, desperate to think of something to say that would stop her staring and break the trance she held him under. The room was closing in on him and his voice wouldn't work. Slowly, laboriously, she held out her arms to him, asking for comfort.

Asking for him to hold her!

Oh God, please don't ask me to hold you!

Paul took a step back from the bed, still unable to break her gaze. "I can't," he started, begging her to release him. Her eyes filled again and she wiggled her fingers insistently as if to demand he come closer, to do his job as a husband.

"Come," she managed, her voice full of that blood-tinged phlegm. "Please."

Paul took another step back, then two more. His back touched the wall, and the door lay just along the edge of his peripheral vision. He reached out his hand and touched the knob. It felt cool in his hand, a welcome comfort. Real life, real hope, and fresh starts all lay just beyond it.

"I don't think I can deal with this."

There. He'd said it. The hardest part was over.

Chapter 17

It had been three days since Kirby had fled the alleyway. Marty had been furious with him when he found out he had gone back.

"What the fuck?" he had roared in his ear, and Kirby had held the phone at arm's length. "What the fuck is wrong with you? YOU DON'T EVER RETURN TO THE SCENE, YOU IDIOT!"

"I thought she was dead," Kirby had answered weakly. "Maybe that she was dead. You hit her real bad."

"So the fuck what?" There was poison in Marty's voice, and Kirby had been glad to be safe in his room, far from Marty for now. "If she was dead, she was dead. What were you going to do, fix her? Were you going to call the police, Kirby? "

That stumped him. "I don't know, Marty. I guess I could have called you to see what to do," Kirby said simply. And it was true. He *didn't* know why he had taken matters into his own hands. But it was okay now because the girls weren't dead. The news had said so.

"Don't you know you can trust me? After what we have been through?" Marty asked, trying to hide his fury.

This was the kind of shit that was going to get them busted.

"Yes," Kirby answered, thinking back on the day he met Marty. Those men had him cornered in the prison laundry. And then Marty had come.

"Don't you remember what I did for you?" Marty asked. "And you said, no, you *promised* your loyalty. Do you remember that, Kirby?"

Kirby did.

"You must never, ever do anything like this again." Marty's voice had grown firm and in control, almost as if he was scolding an errant child. "Kirby, you must promise that you will never… "

"I'm sorry, Marty," Kirby said.

"You'll have us both in jail!"

"I won't go back again," Kirby promised.

But he had crossed his fingers when he had promised. Since then, he had ridden his bike down Chestnut two times and seen that the police tape was still up. He could see it from the next block over through the gap between Sid's Smoke Shop and the Donut Box - a sunny yellow ribbon stretched tightly across the entrance to the alley. *Police Line Do Not Cross*, it read, and he chanted that quietly as he rode along.

"Police Line Do Not Cross. Police Line Do Not Cross," he hummed, as his feet circled the pedals. When Kirby grew tired of that, he added, "You're under arrest." "You're under arrest," until the chanting became a little song in his head.

Kirby knew how to be *sneaky*. His large physique and clumsy nature hid a stealthy spy. He was a people watcher. And he'd never been caught. Never.

Hadn't he been the one who found the women for Marty? Followed

156

them? Learned their habits? Listened to their conversations? Did all the
dirty work? He jumped off his bike, kicking a rock down the street with the
toe of his sneaker. Kirby watched it skid to a halt against the curb.

"Stupid Marty," he said.

Kirby entered his building, bouncing his bike up the stairs to his
apartment on the fourth floor. He knew he could pop a tire that way, but he
did it anyhow. Kirby liked the feel of the rubber tires rebounding against
the hard steps. It made a sound like a *boing. Boing, boing, boing.* The back
wheel-well scraped along behind it. Kirby smiled at the clatter.

"Hey you!"

Kirby almost dropped the bike. He spun around, and the back tire
slid down two stairs.

A woman stood on the landing between the second and third floor.
Her hair was red and wild, a frizzy mane, and her hands were on her hips.
She appeared to be in a nightgown. Kirby could see the outline of her
breasts, heavy and drooping; he could see the large, dark shadow of her
nipples through the fabric.

Just like his mother's breasts.

His mouth felt dry, and he licked his lips as he stared down at
her, meeting her eyes. They were green slits in her face, and they looked
annoyed. She was tapping her foot.

Kirby looked at her nipples again, but she didn't seem to notice.

"Knock it off, will ya?" she said, nodding in the direction of his bike. "I work nights." She started to turn and go back into her apartment. Her backside was broad, jiggling as she reached around to shut her door.

"What's your name?" he called down after her. Kirby didn't want her to go. He wanted her to stay and talk to him.

"Doris," she said, shooting him one last hard look. "Don't make any more noise, kid," she added, and in the light of her doorway, Kirby could see the lines in her face. She was older than she looked in the dank hallway.

"Hi, Doris," he said. "I won't make any more noise." Kirby smiled, shaky and hesitant.

"Yeah I bet you won't," she sneered. "If you don't want me putting in no complaints to the landlord, at least." She shut her door.

The smile fell from his face. *Bitch*, he thought. *Bitch bitch bitch bitch bitch! Just like his mother. Exactly like his mother.* Kirby wanted to punch his fist through the wall. He reared back, holding his bike with one hand.

Teasing with her big, hangin' titties. Hitting him. Sending him away.

Kirby shook away the memory. *That Doris was mean. Dangerous, maybe.*

Kirby couldn't chance complaints to the landlord. Not with the things he had in his apartment. He relaxed his fist, stretching the fingers back into position, and headed on up. He wanted to touch his things, to look through them and sort them again. That would make him forget all about

Doris and her ill-tempered threat.

Marty had tried to stay busy when he heard the news. He should have been feeling victorious, basking in the afterglow. But instead when the first reports had come out, he'd been surprised. When he and Kirby had left the alleyway in the early morning hours, they'd left one woman behind. Then the news reports said there were two women found in the alley. Marty had tried to act normal beneath the bundle of nervous energy that coursed through him as the news kept adding more and more insult to injury. He couldn't let anyone around him see that he was about to implode. The news reports droned on.

University escorts for students.

Help lines.

Angry mobs demanding answers.

And then the topping on the cake. *Kirby had RETURNED TO THE SCENE OF THE CRIME AND ATTACKED A SECOND WOMAN!*

What the hell was he thinking? The odds of that happening, of Kirby coming across a second woman in the dark, seedy alleyway off Foster Avenue had to be one in a million. And Marty knew about chances. He'd gambled enough in his lifetime to understand probability and improbability.

Marty should have been feeling like a celebrity. Instead, the odds were stacking up against him. He could feel the weight of all of it in his head like the pressure of an aneurysm that was just about to rupture.

So now here he sat, boxed in a corner, shutting the door against the bustle outside his doors, telling the others he was working. Marty pulled a bottle of good bourbon from the top drawer of his desk, drinking it straight from the top of the bottle. The liquid wasted no time tracing a burn trail down his throat and into his belly, clearing his head.

No doubt about it. Kirby was going to be a problem. He was a man-child with no reasoning skills, no rationale. He knew too damn much and it was just a matter of time before Kirby was going to make them front page news.

Marty closed his eyes against a vision of himself, shackled and shuffling as some hotshot local reporter snapped his photograph for the newspaper. He couldn't imagine himself in that position. Ever.

He sighed out loud, taking another swig from the bottle, "Fuck."

Kirby was going to screw up. Maybe he already had made mistakes, leaving them behind like a crumb trail to follow. The police just hadn't caught on yet. Marty needed to blow the crumbs away, scatter them to the winds.

Stupid cops.

But Kirby was even more brainless. And it was about time to get rid of him. Marty capped the lid on the liquor, feeling his sense of command returning.

He could send Kirby away, pay for his damn ticket to Florida or wherever the hell he wanted to go. Give him some money to just scat.

But he'd still *know*. He could still *talk*. Spill the beans. Fuck up Marty's world.

Dead people don't make mistakes, though. They don't rat out partners. They don't talk. Especially if they are never found.

Marty knew plenty about working with partners, too.

He felt himself able to breathe again. The air suddenly seemed to open up and he grabbed a big lungful.

The world made sense again.

And Kirby was better off dead.

Chapter 18

The world was a cruel dead place for Mark. For the past week and a half, nothing in it moved. Nothing in it changed. Diane lay in her coma and Stephanie lay in her bed, lightly sedated now but still mostly unresponsive. The only people with whom Stephanie had communicated, were the detectives; and even then, she'd offered little.

Stephanie *had* asked for Ruby. And Ruby had been sleeping there in a fold up cot the hospital had provided since day two. As far as the hospital staff was aware, Ruby was Stephanie's mother and they had allowed her almost unlimited visiting time. It seemed that Ruby was the only person that made Stephanie comfortable. When Ruby was there, Stephanie allowed them to change her bandages, clean her wounds, test the extent of her injuries and the pace at which they were healing. When Ruby wasn't there, they found Stephanie uncooperative, angry, and hostile; more likely to rip her own stitches out than to let them bind her skin back where it belonged.

Mark sat with Stephanie in the dim light of her room where they both stayed lost in their own thoughts, bathed in their own silence. This was his third visit to see her and she had yet to speak to him. Her eyes told him she was cognizant of his presence but nothing else. He hadn't seen a flicker of emotion, not even a spike of hatred, in those vacant brown eyes. As an old friend, an old *lover*, it bothered Mark to see them looking so spiritless. As a *doctor*, he felt helpless. He couldn't breathe life back into the cold emptiness that was Stephanie any more than he could breathe the spirit back into his beautiful Diane.

That's what Mark was thinking about when Stephanie finally spoke. Her voice was a shaky rattle, as if she hadn't used it in a decade.

"I wish I were dead," Stephanie said staring straight at the wall, refusing to look at Mark. "Just go away. Please." There was no emotion in her voice; it was flat and distant.

He knew she was devastated, knew she meant what she said about wanting to die, but he tried to convince her otherwise.

"Things seem bad now, really bad," he kept his voice soft.

She made a sound in her throat, sarcastic and scathing but her voice was gaining strength. She must have been waiting to say the things she was thinking aloud. Saying them out loud lent them power.

"Seem bad?" she said, her voice flat again almost immediately. "Ask the cop outside if I can borrow his gun. I only need it for a second." She grimaced and her teeth showed through the ripped opening of her bandages like the sneer of a hyena.

Stephanie had run out of tears. Sometime in between Paul's fleeing her room - *where the hell had he gone? When was he coming back?* - and her being informed that Diane had been attacked within an hour of herself and was lying in a coma on the floor above her, Stephanie had stopped feeling anything but occasional bouts of rage. And she'd stopped wishing for anything except an end to all of this.

163

Whatever thin, fragile hope for repair that might have existed had been brushed away like a hand through a spider web. The spider had spent hours spinning it and the big bad hand of fate had taken a millisecond to wipe it out.

Stephanie hated everything and everyone.

"What can I do? What can I do to help you through this?" Mark asked her. "Put the past aside. Let me help you." Mark soothed.

Stephanie let her eyes fall on him. Mark saw a flicker of emotion pass through them before they turned steely again. "Just get out of my room."

He sat there anyway, letting the quiet close in around them. Stephanie didn't move or say anything for a long time. But she didn't yell or spew hate at him either. She just lay there alternately looking at the wall and the ceiling.

Sometimes, just the presence of another person was enough. Even someone you didn't like anymore.

"Is Diane going to survive?" she finally spoke.

"I don't know," he answered. The words, the truth in them, crushed his heart.

"It's my fault she was there." She said bluntly.

"No."

Stephanie leaned over, spitting into a cup on her side tray. A thin line of dark, bloody mucus, remained anchored at the corner of her mouth.

"Okay. All right. Sure," she looked at him again. Another flicker, more painful than the first.

"I'm sorry for what happened between us, Stephanie. It was wrong. We were both wrong. But that doesn't make us horrible people. It doesn't make you a horrible person. You don't deserve what happened to you."

Silence again. She was thinking. Mark could see her mind processing his words. Deciding if she should believe them. Or reject them.

She ended up doing neither.

"Do you love her?" she asked.

"Yes," he answered.

"What are you doing here sitting with me then? You should be sitting with Diane." There wasn't hope in what she asked. Stephanie knew he wasn't there because he loved her. That was so long ago; left discarded somewhere in the dusty remains of *Stephanie's Life Before*. She no longer lived there.

"I'm here now to ask you to forgive me. And to see if there is anything I can do to help an old friend that was dealt a very, very rotten hand."

Stephanie closed her eyes. When she opened them again, she looked sad, but still empty.

"You're here to ask my blessing. You feel guilty loving Diane after what you did to me. And after what's happened to me now." It was a statement. And it was as close to truth as anything.

"Yes," he said. "Yes, basically."

"So cut all the old friend bullshit then."

"It's cut."

"Great so long as we're being honest. But it hurts to talk, Mark. If you hadn't noticed, I am missing part of my face. So I am going to make this short and sweet. You are free to love Diane as hard and long as you want to. I forgive you. That chapter of your life is officially closed."

It stung, but it felt liberating to hear her say the words.

"I thought I loved you, Steph. I thought I did, I swear it." Mark stood up, laying his hand over hers, squeezing it lightly. "I pray that you heal." He considered leaning over and kissing the top of her head but he saw the light sheen of tears in her eyes and he didn't want to make her cry. Not any more.

"Can I visit you again?" he asked her.

She shook her head, pulling the blanket up to her face. "Not for a while." She told him, closing her eyes, dismissing him the only way she could.

"Okay, okay. I'll give you some time. I'll see you, Stephanie, whenever you're ready." She heard the whoosh of the door knew that he had gone.

"Maybe. If I'm still here." She answered, letting the darkness of pain and the light relief of the tranquilizers lull her away.

Diane was floating in darkness, bobbing up and down on gentle waves. It was quiet and warm and relaxing, a little cocoon all her own. Sometimes, she could hear things in the distance. Voices and occasionally what sounded like chaos. She had felt hands and other things touching her, moving her body around. But all of that activity was so far away and she liked the quiet here so much, she didn't have the energy to move toward the sounds.

And her parents were here. That was the best part of all. It was so comforting to hear their voices after all this time! She couldn't see them, but she could hear them. They told her how much they loved her and how proud they were of her.

If only she could see them. *It wasn't time*, they had said and she had been trying to figure out what that meant. When would it be time? She had been waiting so long already.

It had been eight years since her parents had passed. Eight years of not having their guiding hands on her shoulders. Eight years of not having anywhere to go for Thanksgiving or Christmas or whenever she just needed the comforts of home. Eight years of talking to the ceiling, hoping and praying they could hear her. And now she knew they had. She could hear them, too!

So she wasn't leaving this place. She told them that in no uncertain terms. She'd stay here with them and listen to them and wait until she could see them again. It was nice here. And she was so very tired.

Chapter 19

"I told you to get rid of that, boy!" It was his Momma again, shouting at him from over in the corner somewhere.

Kirby put his fingers in his ears and squeezed his eyes shut. He was a young boy again, rolling the corners of the magazine over in his hand, trying to hide it before she would see.

She *had* told him to dispose of it and he'd tried. He really had. Kirby chucked it into the big metal bin behind their apartment, racing up the back stairs before it could call him back; shutting the door to his room, closing his eyes, poking his fingers into his ears, trying to forget it. But it was a boomerang, circling over his head and he'd returned to the trash bin, climbing in and sorting through a soggy mass of wet garbage to retrieve the book. It had *smelled* in there and things had squished between his bare toes but he kept on digging until it showed itself like the flash of gold through a chunk of rock.

His secret prize.

He'd been smart enough to remove his shoes before climbing in there, smart enough to know his Momma would notice if his sneakers were dirty from the remnants of their neighbors' trash. But he hadn't been smart enough to remember the shoes. It was too exciting to see the magazine again, to feel it against the palm of his hand, to know what was *inside* when he would open up the pages. He'd left the shoes by the dumpster. And

Kirby supposed that's where Momma had found them - right before she found *him* with the dirty naked girl book she'd warned him about.

Momma was so smart. He could never, ever fool her.

That was the last thing he remembered thinking before he was on the ground. Momma had smacked him hard across the face, knocking him back and dropping him to his knees. Kirby's nose spat blood like an angry cat, his eyes teared from pain and shame and fear. A cold flutter of dire expectation crawled up his stomach; shriveled his groin.

Momma was smart. And she was strong. And she was mad. A deadly combination.

"I'm sorry, Momma…." He started to plead, holding his hands up to protect his face. *Her* face was huge, veined, purple and bulging. She had the magazine in her hand, had rolled it into a long thin cylinder. She used it to deliver blows to the back of his head and neck, his hands, his thighs. Kirby curled into a ball on the floor, tucking his head under, letting his tears fall onto the floor underneath him.

"DON"T YOU COIL UP ON ME. SNAKE! STAND UP AND TAKE THIS LIKE A MAN!" She yelled, leaning over him so her face was next to his ear. Kirby could smell her breath, sour from her fury. He could feel the thin spray of spittle across the side of his face. He stayed folded.

"C'mon little man," she taunted, her voice low now, tickling his ears. "You want to look at this filth like a grown man but you don't want to TAKE YOUR LICKS LIKE ONE!" Her hands pummeled the back of his neck, his buttocks, his back. Everywhere she could reach.

And then she was ripping at his clothes, yanking him off the floor like a soft cloth doll, tossing whatever she could get off him aside. He heard the rip of material, felt his shirt being pulled from the back.

"MOMMA, NO!" he wailed, hitting his forehead against the floor, banging it up and down. Kirby had no choice. He had to hurt himself. He had been so bad.

"THIS IS THE DEVIL'S BOOK!" she roared, stopping him from thumping his own head by pulling him up by the back of his hair. She stood him on his feet and spun his body around so he was facing her. Kirby covered himself, his hands crossed over his genitals, leaving his face open to whatever assault she had in store for him, even if it was just from her eyes.

"This is the devil's book," she repeated. "And we have got to cleanse your body to get rid of the impurity that is on you now." Her black hair, showing gray, was standing on end like a used Brillo pad and she was breathing hard, panting, her chest heaving up and down. But there were tears in her eyes, too and she was no longer screaming, no long hitting him with her hands or the rolled up magazine.

She still had the book but it was folded in two now, crushed and ruined. His throat clenched at the sight of it.

He had hurt his Momma. Hurt her by looking at the girlie book. Kirby was supposed to *love* his Momma. And he had loved the naked ladies

171

instead. He hung his head in shame.

He was a bad, bad boy. Why did she ever bring him into this world?

She left him standing there, trembling slightly and staring at the floor. *What would happen now?* Kirby looked around. His clothes were strewn across the room, the scraps of one of his shirt sleeves clinging stubbornly to the hairs on his arm. He blew the strings away like blowing out birthday candles and watched them float in the hazy light, watched as they dropped into his carpet and blended into the fibers. Then he just stood there, trying not to think of his nakedness - s*o different from the girls in the book* - and trying not to miss *them.*

Kirby could hear the tub water running and then his mother was standing at his bedroom door again. She wiped her damp hands along the sides of her cotton gown.

"Everything is going to be okay as soon as we get you clean," she said resolutely, gesturing for him to follow her to the bathroom. Kirby followed, dragging his toes along the carpet, dreading the hot water, the scrubbing cloth, his red, raw skin that would be burning when this was all said and done.

But what had to be done, had to be done. Kirby entered the bright, fluorescent light of their bathroom and steeled himself for the inevitable.

Momma was going to cleanse him.

Kirby opened his eyes. The only sound in the apartment was his own breathing and the dripping faucet in the bathroom pinching out lazy drops of water every few seconds. His Momma wasn't there, not even her voice. And instead of the magazine cradled in his hands, he had his new prizes spread out before him in a straight line across the floor. It looked as if he was just ready to begin a game of solitaire. Here they were, gleaming little treasures, and there was no one that could take them away from him.

The lip-gloss smelled like cherries and he liked to pull off the little plastic cap and hold it to his nose, taking a big whiff of the waxy stick inside. *Soooo good.* He tried it on, too, rubbing it lightly across his lips and then letting his tongue flick across afterwards, testing to see if it tasted as good as it smelled. It didn't, but that was okay. *She* had used it to soften her lips and it was almost like she was kissing him when he smoothed it out over his own. It gave him little tingles inside. Kirby thought the lip-gloss might be his very favorite thing in the purse.

He had already thrown out the tissues and smashed the cell phone into a thousand pieces with his mother's old hammer. But he kept all the change he found in the bottom, stacking it up on his dresser, the biggest coins on the bottom, without counting any of it. Change confused him. It made no sense that the littlest coins were worth more than some of the bigger ones. And they were all almost the same color, except for the pennies which were the only coins he knew for sure were equal to ONE. If only coins had numbers on them like the paper dollars did. But as it was, he could never keep them straight. It just hurt his head to bother.

173

Kirby ran his finger over the wallet, lifting it up to smell the leather. He'd found forty-three dollars inside but he hadn't decided how to spend it yet. He was saving it for something special, maybe even a present for *her*. A present for her would have to be perfect.

She was perfect. He picked up the little plastic card with her picture and address on the front. Her driver's license.

Stephanie Kramer. She looked like a princess. No, better than a princess. A *queen*.

And better than the girls in his book had been, too. She was more than just a picture. Stephanie was a real, live girl.

Kirby looked around the room. "Momma?" he asked tentatively.

No answer; nothing. Just the faucet. Just his own respiration.

Drip. Drip. Drip.

Inhale. Exhale. Inhale. Exhale.

Kirby brought the picture closer to his face, staring into Stephanie's eyes.

"I love you," he whispered, kissing the picture.

Drip. Inhale. Drip. Exhale. Kirby stared into Stephanie's eyes.

"I told you to get rid of that purse, boy." Momma!

He dropped the license. It landed face down on the floor. Momma *was* here after all. *Dammit.*

"But I like it," Kirby said, feeling his hackles rise at the sound of his own voice whining. *Like a baby! You're just like a baby*, he said to himself.

174

"Do you like going to jail, too?" her voice jangled his nerves, twisting his heart into turbulence.

"No, Momma," he answered. "I smashed the phone. I didn't use it."

"Do you love that lady?" she demanded. "More than your Momma?"

Kirby didn't answer. He was confused again; his mind felt full of puddles he couldn't jump. He did love the lady in the picture. Stephanie Kramer. She was *alive*. And Momma? Well, she wasn't.

"Did you fuck that lady in the picture?" his mother's tone was edging toward frenzy now. Kirby could feel the air was charged.

"DID YOU?"

His heart took off in double time, banging out an errant rhythm, merging with the faucet.

DRIP POUND DRIP POUND DRIP POUND.

"I love her, though," Kirby felt the corners of his mouth turn down in a pout. *BABY!* He chastised himself.

BABY BABY BABY BABY!

"You BURN UP those things, Kirby," she warned, her voice a shriek now, whizzing through the air. "YOU BURN UP THOSE THINGS AND YOU FORGET ALL ABOUT THE FILTHY SLUT IN THE PICTURE!"

DRIP POUND DRIP POUND DRIP POUND.

"NO, Momma," he tried to keep the tremble out of his voice. Kirby thought he might shake into pieces. He had never said no to Momma before, no matter where she was in the world.

175

"What?" she asked, incredulous, a whisper.

Kirby flipped over the driver's license and looked at Stephanie again. *She was so pretty.* And he was so alone. He held the photo up, shaking it in the air.

"I said NO MOMMA!" Kirby shouted into the room so loudly that it hurt his throat. "I SAID NO!" He gripped the license, feeling the sweat in his palm against the plastic.

Then he sat back on his haunches and waited.

His heart began to slow. His breathing evened. The dripping was steady.

And Momma stayed quiet.

Chapter 20

It was so fucking quiet. Mark was tired of the silence in the ICU, punctuated only by the soft whisper of voices and the quiet buzzing of the machinery monitoring heart rates and keeping them steady. He wanted Diane's heart to start beating on its own; wanted her brain to start sending messages to her body. A sense of impatience and anticipation followed him everywhere now. He couldn't shake the nervous feeling. She *had* to recover.

"Move," he demanded, staring down at her form. He squeezed her hand, willing just a tiny squeeze back. Anything.

"I'll take anything," he whispered to her.

He got nothing.

Mark let go of her hand, running his own along the base of his chin, thinking. There was a raspy layer of stubble there; he'd forgotten to shave again. He picked Diane's hand back up and bringing his face close, rubbed the palm of her hand along the sharp whiskers of his face.

"Wake up," he told her. "Wake up and feel me, Diane. I'm waiting for you."

He ran his free hand along the side of her face, caressing the soft, warm skin. The hair on her head was stubble, too, growing back from where the surgery had required it be shaved. He reached up, feeling the prickle of it while continuing to rub her hand along his jaw line.

177

"C'mon, girl," he urged. "C'mon, baby." He rubbed harder, faster, feeling the lump in the back of his throat start to form.

Diane was still.

Mark stopped rubbing. He stood back up, looking down on Diane. She was a shadow: her face slack and dreaming. There was no tone to her, no life force.

What if this was it? What if Diane never came back?

He swallowed. The lump rose up again.

What if she came back, but not to him?

Mark stood there a minute, contemplating that possibility. Half the hospital thought he was insane. They whispered things - *"I didn't even know he was seeing anyone." "How long has he been in there?" "It's not like she's his wife or anything."* - about him as if he couldn't hear them. And Mark did nothing about it. He just sat there without a defense. All he thought about, all he cared about, was Diane. He'd used up almost all his personal days sitting here in her room.

Was he crazy?

Mark reached out to Diane again, tracing the outline of her eyelids with his fingers. "What do you think, huh? Am I nuts?"

"It's a distinct possibility," the voice behind him made him jump. Mark spun around, taking in the woman in the doorway. She was matronly, small but buxom with a no nonsense look about her. Until she smiled, which she did then; her eyes lighting up her face and two huge dimples appearing in her cheeks.

"I'm Ruby Claire," she said, extending her hand. Her smile faded. "And I'm pretty sure I know exactly who you are."

"Mark Lawson," he said, clearing his throat. He shook her hand, amazed at how tiny it felt in his own.

"Ah, as I suspected. The man of the hour," she breathed and seeing him open his mouth to speak, she interrupted. "Never mind. I know the story," she waved her hand around as if a fly were circling her head. "Stephanie told me everything."

"There's two sides..." he began.

"You can trust I am a neutral party," she bustled past him, straight over to Diane. Leaning over to kiss her she said, "I just want my girls to be well again."

Mark saw the shine of tears in her eyes, felt his own start to well.

"I love her," he said as he watched Ruby fuss over Diane, fixing the bedclothes, pulling out a brush to pull through what was left of her hair.

"Hmmm," she said, "She needs a lot more than love right now. Hell, they both do." She continued brushing Diane's hair, humming softly. "Her favorite song," she told him. "I wanted to bring a radio, but they said no. Can you imagine? Diane's world without music? She loves it, all of it. Country, jazz, rock and roll," she sighed. "You name it, she liked it." She stopped brushing Diane's hair, turning to face him.

"Did you know that about her?" She asked him, eyes beating a hole into his face.

"No," Mark started. "No, we were just getting to know each other," he said, then added. "Well."

"I see," she said and Mark felt injured. She was suggesting that he didn't know Diane - that he hardly belonged here.

"Your point is made," he said softly. "And you'll forgive me if I say you don't sound like a neutral party."

She didn't answer him, talking to Diane instead.

"Just look at your hands!" she exclaimed. "I'm going to have to file this old polish right off of here with a power drill," she started digging around in her bag. "I don't even want to know how your feet look under those covers," she continued. "That's a job for our next visit."

"Ms. Claire, with all due respect. Diane and I were falling in love before this…"

"Right," she said. "Maybe your deep love will bring her right on out of this coma, then?" she asked. "Come on over. See what you can do." She gestured along the length of Diane's body.

Mark's heart hurt. *Neutral, my ass*, he thought, excusing himself, letting Ruby have her time with her adopted "daughter." His feelings stung but a part of him was happy that Diane, his Diane, had this mama bear to protect her.

He'd win Ruby over. When it was time. Until then, let her protect all she needed to. Diane had two of them on her side now.

What should he say? He wondered, his stomach a mass of wrestling tension. *After all these years, what am I supposed to say?*

Steve pushed open the door to Stephanie's room, peering into the gloom of it. It had taken him over two weeks to get here and he felt ashamed. He'd been afraid... of everything. What she might say. What she might look like. What he might, or might not, feel about all of it. He knew bits and pieces of what had happened to her; from the news, and from Dan, but he hadn't put them all together in his mind yet. He couldn't: not until he saw her himself.

And here he was.

Shaking in his damn boots.

His eyes found the bed and the lump that was in it. That was Stephanie. *Stephanie was the lump in the bed.* Only this Stephanie was unrecognizable.

Steve gasped. *Her face!*

Her face was a crude puzzle. The stitches took a jagged turn around her mouth and down along her jaw line. And her cheek, once high and sculpted, sagged to the left, another line of stitching holding it in place. It appeared that tissue around her nose was missing, but Steve couldn't tell, not in this light. It was distended, out of place. Wrong. The whole thing was just *wrong*.

A brief flash of him loving her, of the way she looked when she

181

closed her eyes to meet his mouth appeared before him. The contrast was shockingly cruel and heart wrenching. He pushed it away.

"Steve?" she asked in a hushed tone, hardly moving her mouth. She lifted herself up on her elbows to get a better look. "It is you," she said, letting her body fall back into place, a soft sigh, a sigh of defeat, escaped her.

"Hi," he said, forcing his lips up into a half hearted smile, feeling it fall as soon as he'd managed it. "It's me."

It smelled like sweat in the room, stale and acrid. Steve tried to block the smell, to keep the nausea from crawling into his belly. It wasn't just the light mist of old perspiration in the air, it was the smell of sickness and the look of devastation that danced all around her. It was like dust swirling in the air: an aura of ruin emanating straight from Stephanie. It was an offense to everything that was supposed to be a part of living.

The pain of seeing her that way, no matter what she had done to hurt him, sat square in the pit of Steve's stomach. It felt like an ache rising there and pulling at his insides. His knee started its familiar throb bouncing alongside the grief he felt for her in that long-standing moment.

Looking at her now made Steve forget about seeing her with Mark.

Or maybe it helped him to accept it.

"Can I sit?" he asked, holding up his cane to show her he really *needed* the chair.

She nodded and he lowered himself into the seat next to her bed.

Closer now, he could really see the damage. It screamed at him. *Unfair! Unfair! Unfair!*

Steve understood all about inequity in life.

He'd lost his girl. He'd lost his basketball. He'd lost his athleticism. He'd lost all of the things he used to define himself by.

Steve knew loss.

"I can relate," he said as if she should be expected to read his thoughts.

Stephanie nodded again, looking away into the distance. She knew what he meant.

A thoughtful silence fell over them both. It was stiff at first, but it smoothed the way to something else, something more familiar. Steve felt himself relax. He could feel Stephanie's breathing, at first ragged and labored, relax next to him as well.

He couldn't smell her anymore.

After a long while, she spoke again. "You picked a good day to come," she told him, unable to hide the grimace of discomfort at moving her mouth freely. She continued anyway, despite it. "It was my unveiling." Stephanie started to cry then, big shiny tears that rolled down her cheeks, wetting the stitches as they dropped.

Steve didn't know what to say. His eyes found hers.

"Don't pity me," she said.

"Okay," Steve got up, using the cane to support his knee, and went to her.

When he left her room, she was sleeping. A nurse had come in and put something in her intravenous bag, telling him it was time to go. Steve had climbed out of the bed where he'd lain for an hour just holding her, watching as the medicine helped her to slip away.

"See you, Steph," he said quietly, making his way into the hall.

His knee was on fire, having been curled up in the bed for so long and he needed a few steps to really get going. *Damn this*, he started to think, beginning to let those feelings of pity for himself run loose again.

Then he thought of Stephanie back *there,* left with a face and a body and a life that no longer belonged to her.

He could live with just the bum knee. But he couldn't walk very well with it. He kept his eyes on the ground, making sure he kept the cane from tripping himself up until the blood flow in his leg was going good again. Which didn't happen until he ran straight into his brother.

Whom he hadn't seen coming.

Chapter 21

She didn't see it coming, the crash back into the world, but here she was. Jesus, she'd just been floating, quietly, peacefully floating and then she'd been thrust forward full force; speeding past everything that was gentle and even and tumbling abruptly into... *where was she now? Real life?*

That sounded right although her thoughts dragged along cloudy and listless. But it wasn't quiet anymore, she wasn't drifting softly along, and it sounded like all hell had broken loose around her.

Diane sucked in air and choked as if she was drowning. Her eyes flew open like they were on pulleys and she took another breath, pushing at the mask on her face. It was suffocating her.

"Oh my God! Oh MY GOD!" A voice. Familiar.

Then rushing feet, hands, faces, someone pulling at the mask.

Who is that? Diane turned her head from side to side, trying to see and to take in everything. There were noises, blips and beeps, whooshing sounds. Voices. More now.

Whose voices?

Diane wanted to cry out, to speak, to ask what the hell was going on, but her own voice wasn't working. Air rushed in and out of her mouth, but words wouldn't come. She coughed.

A face flashed by her, big, round, red-cheeked, and there was tight pulsing at the top of her arm. She couldn't make out what was being said, but a stream of hushed voices in urgent conversation wafted all around her.

"Diane?" *Her name!*

She opened her mouth again, trying to focus on the voice that had said her name. "Whhh……" she stuttered. "Whhha……"

"Diane, I'm Dr. Patros. I'm here, can you see me here?"

Her eyes caught the tail end of movement, someone's hand, waving in front of her, but she couldn't focus. *She couldn't see where the fuck the hand went!* Panic flooded her and she started to thrash wildly. More chaos erupted around her.

"Diane, calm down! We need you to LAY STILL!" Someone held her arms and she let them, falling back into her thoughts.

Doctors meant hospitals and that must be where she was.

And then it all came flooding back…

Chapter 22

Mark saw Steve when he was about eight feet in front ahead and a hoard of emotion immediately overwhelmed him. Steve was looking down at his feet, maneuvering his cane one step at a time and Mark's first impulse was to flee before Steve saw him; to just turn the other way and make like a ghost. Just the sight of Steve, hobbled as he was with his leg, was like a quick jab to the chin and Mark was torn between reaching out to him in an embrace and reaching out to hit him back.

Dammit! Steve had turned on him, no questions asked. Mark's face felt flushed. The brothers hadn't spoken, hadn't looked each other in the eyes, since that night.

Stephanie seduced him. It was she that had come to Mark, promising him the moon, professing her love, making him believe they belonged together.

"Steve beats me," she told him, taking off her blouse to show him bruises, asking him, as a medical student, to heal her with his hands and then asking him, as a man, to heal her heart.

You never ever substantiated that those bruises were from Steve. You just wanted to believe! Mark told himself, shaking his head slowly back and forth at the memory, feeling sick in his gut.

She had looked so beautiful- her skin so tawny and smooth, her breasts, full and heaving- and her eyes so sad, as if she was lost in the world.

187

Mark couldn't resist her. And he couldn't resist the idea of having what was his brother's; of taking it right out from under Steve.

Steve, who always seemed to win at everything: basketball star, lady's man, big guy on campus.

Now look at him, Mark thought, watching his brother struggle, pain like a permanent wrinkle etched cruelly into his face. *Now what does Steve have left?*

Mark walked forward, increasing his pace. "Steve," he said as he approached and Steve's head jerked upwards. Mark didn't know what to expect. *Anger? Resentment? Forgiveness? Tears?* He felt his jaw lock in anticipation.

"Mark?" Steve's eyes narrowed and then widened as he realized he was, in fact, face to face with his brother. "I – I didn't expect… I mean, that's stupid. Of course, you'd be here. I just wasn't ready…" he trailed off again, stumbling over his words and Mark was struck again how unsteady Steve seemed, how unsure of himself. The polar opposite of all he had been. His heart bucked forward nervously and regret rushed in.

"No, no, please don't explain. I get it. Me either," Mark said unsure what to do with his hands.

"I was here to see Stephanie," Steve explained and fresh pain crossed his face: a look that was not lost on Mark.

"It's a nightmare what's happened to her," Mark's voice was sincere but the sound of her name between them was hollow, rough-edged. Mark longed to bury it. "Let's talk," he suggested swallowing hard, looking Steve straight in the eye.

Did Steve want to try to talk this out or didn't he? Mark's eyes searched his face.

"Do you think we could...?" Mark asked again, hopeful, but guarded. Steve might balance on his good leg and haul off and hit him. Or he might just turn and walk away.

And Mark would still probably deserve it. He'd only been with Stephanie a handful of times before Steve found them. He'd already begun doubting that what he was doing was right; doubting that Stephanie was a woman he could love. But *wanting* her all the same; and wanting Steve to *know*...

Steve didn't answer; his eyes were far away. But then he met Mark's eyes and nodded. "Yeah," he said.

Mark could almost hear Steve's heart racing, *could* hear his breath sharp and uneven. *He's scared. I'm scared.* Mark had to let his feelings out, "I'm sorry, Steve. I'm sorry for what I did. It was a terrible mistake, the biggest mistake of my life,"

That was what they needed to break the iciness between them, to make progress. Mark needed to say he was sorry. And mean it. And he did.

The life came back into Steve's eyes. The lines in his face softened. "I'd like to talk it out," he concurred. "It's time."

Mark jumped at the opportunity, relief melting whatever was left of the tension in his body. "Where? When?"

"My bar," Steve said, visibly relaxed now, too. The hand that held his cane in place was no longer shaking and his voice was stronger, more confident. "Bases Loaded on 5th and Maple. Come by for a beer, tonight? Tomorrow? Whenever you want." He stood up a little straighter and Mark could hear the pride in his tone.

Dan had been right. Steve did have something good. There was something good left beyond the affair, beyond his injury after all. They needed good to heal. Mark felt another surge of hopefulness.

"Later today?"

"Sure, that's fine. I am on my way now."

"Dr. Lawson?" Mark turned at the voice, saw a nurse rushing toward him. *One of Diane's nurses! Any hope he felt sunk immediately. What had happened to Diane?* Mark forgot all about Steve, all about anything but what the nurse was about to tell him.

"What's wrong?" He closed the gap between them.

"I thought you'd want to know, Doctor," she said, looking disheveled. "Diane Harper is awake."

Mark felt the room spin. He looked over at Steve who appeared puzzled but ready to come limping over to catch Mark should he start to fall.

"Mark, you're white as a sheet," Steve started to say, coming toward him.

"I have to go," Mark said, finding himself and making a beeline

190

toward ICU with the nurse trailing after him, going faster even as she was telling him he couldn't see her yet.

Steve stood in the hallway, confused, feeling his knee start to protest at having stood for too damn long already. He took one last glance toward Mark's back and another toward Stephanie's room and then he started making his way out of the hospital. He felt in his pocket, pulling out a pack of cigarettes and his lighter preparing to light one the minute he stepped outside. Maybe later today, all of the leftover pieces of his past would finally start falling into place.

Or maybe tomorrow.

Chapter 23

This week. This was the week he had to put some kind of plan into action. Kirby was a ticking time bomb and he needed to be stopped; to self implode would be ideal. Marty sat in his office, listening to the ruckus outside the door, trying to think. For the moment he was thankful to even have an office, a place to close the door against his coworkers and their fumbling attempts at saving the world.

How to convince a person to destroy themselves so that your own hands remained clean? That was the order of the day. *You should know this, he told himself,* cursing Kirby again for his stupidity. It was fucking up his brain, interfering with his ordinarily clever thinking.

Marty leaned back in his chair, letting his feet rest on the desk. A spray of papers lay across the desktop and he pushed them off the edge with his foot, watching as they fluttered to the floor. The papers were scrawled with graphs and numbers, notes to himself. *Chicken scratch*, as his grandmother would have called it. Bullshit, nothing, meaningless fodder.

What meant something now was getting rid of Kirby, thereby preserving himself. *And your lifestyle*, he reminded himself. *Don't forget that little recreational sex thing you've got going on.* Marty smirked, then grimaced, pulled away by the sounds bouncing just beyond the walls.

"Shut up!" he said to the people on the other side of the door, the ones making all the distracting noises. "I am trying to think!" He pounded his fist on the desk, knocking over a cup of pencils that clattered and rolled away from him. He caught one as it rolled off the side of the desk and in one swift motion, slammed the point down into his palm.

There, that would clear his head. Blood welled up thickly around the wound as he yanked the tip of the instrument out again. Marty watched it with satisfaction, a warm glow climbing up from the pit of his stomach. *Ahhhh, blessed relief.*

The clouds in his head parted.

"The angels sang hallelujah!" he said aloud, clapping his hands in mock prayer, spreading the blood, and laughing, a growling sound that issued from deep in the back of his throat.

He lifted his hand to his mouth, sucking out the blood like poison from a snake bite. It ebbed onto his tongue and he lapped at it absentmindedly until there was just a leftover trickle; his blood vessels were working overtime to squelch the flow.

Now he could think despite the activity outside. Now, all was right with the world again.

The more he thought, the more he was sure. Just a few simple steps, a few carefully planned measures and the deed would be done. It would be easy to convince Kirby that the police were hot on their tails. That running would do no good.

And that being dead was better. *Hell, they could do it together!*

Marty laughed again. *Watching Kirby die would be fun. Watching him realize that Marty wasn't coming along for the ride? Now that would be a thrill. What did those commercials say?*

Priceless, right! That would be priceless.

Marty could deal with work now. He cleaned up the papers, smearing them with rusty streaks and tossing them into the trash for the night cleaners. By the time they emptied the garbage, he would have forgotten the mess he'd made, would have forgotten how he injured his hand in the first place. Marty dropped to his hands and knees, crawling around, gathering up the pencils and neatening up his desk.

Perfect. Everything was in order. Just one last thing.

Marty rubbed a dollop of hand sanitizer into his wound, cleaning the last of the blood away. The sting from the alcohol was sharp and welcome. He poured another dribble directly onto the cut. *Nice and clean.*

Now it was time. Time to face life; time to move forward. He threw open the doors to his office, jumping right into his work again.   A broad grin spread across his face as he surveyed the scene, hopping to it. He was needed here, almost a damn hero.

It was so nice to be Superman.

It would definitely be this week. Stephanie had decided. No sense putting it off.   This week would bring just as good an exit day as any other.

She felt a little guilty leaving Ruby and Diane behind like that. And a little like a coward, too. *But Jesus, have you seen my face?* She asked herself.

She'd almost accepted her face, almost allowed the doctors to convince her that they could fix most of the damage that had been done to her face AND her body.

"Get me a mirror please," she'd asked Ruby the day after the bandages had come off and she had; a plastic purple hand mirror that cast a bit of a fuzzy, skewed reflection. Stephanie imagined Ruby had scoured store upon store to find just the right one: one that would cast the least cruel image of herself. And Ruby had brought it only *after* a heated argument between the two of them. And only then after the final stamp of approval from her new psychiatrist who, in Stephanie's humble opinion, was an easy target, ripe for manipulation. All Stephanie had to do was *say* that she was feeling stronger, better, more accepting and the shrink bought it, hook, line, and sinker. She'd had that bitch eating out of her hand after the second session.

Once she'd gotten her hands on the mirror, she hadn't let it go, keeping it under her pillow and bringing it out four, eight, a dozen times a day to go over her face again and again. She tried to watch television or write in the damn journal the psychiatrist had given her (bullshit, bullshit, bullshit. Stephanie was good at it, though, letting the words flow out in inky, brutal relief). She'd tried to do everything to pass the time but the mirror was a beacon and she was drawn to its truth.

At first, it was like seeing an intruder looking back at her: some alien life form wearing the mask of a bad dream. Stephanie pushed herself to keep looking, bringing the mirror closer and closer to her face and her body until she knew every stitch, every rip, every break and bruise as if they'd always been there.

It was her. This was her now.

Stephanie held it down between her legs too, staring at the angry red gashes there, counting the staples that held her together, cursing the stinging every time she urinated over the raw skin. The doctors had recreated her nipple and it was a pucker of brown now with no tip, just an ugly, wrinkly misshapen mound. She could feel no pleasure from it but no pain either so she guessed that equated to fairness in this new world perspective she'd been forced to accept.

Stephanie knew her battle scars and she loathed them. But she thought she could have lived with them; could live with them after the doctors were done with all the healing they promised her anyway.

But then she got the letter. And that had clipped in two the tenuous threads of hope that had started to form between her heart and her mind.

Ruby read it to her over breakfast this morning, both of them thinking it was a note from some well-intentioned stranger. Stephanie had gotten dozens of them; cards and flowers and get-well balloons all from

196

people who felt badly about what had happened to her and thought that slapping a stamp onto a get well card would fix all that lay before her now. They put them in the mail, then traipsed off to their jobs or their families or their un-raped lives and thought they'd done their good deed for the day. Stephanie hated the well wishes almost as much as she hated the scars, but Ruby thought they were good therapy; good for her thoughts and her spirits. She insisted on reading Stephanie every one.

"How nice!" Ruby would say after she'd rattled off the contents and Stephanie would roll her eyes. No additional response necessary.

This letter was different, though, arriving in a plain white envelope with her name scrawled thinly over the top. Inside was white paper, type set letters. No smiling puppy dog or bunch of flowers on the cover. No giggling greeting of wellness on the inside. This letter was the killer of all things that might have been. And it was from her own husband.

Ruby tried to stop reading it after the first line or two, threatening to rip it to shreds, to rip *him* to shreds. But Stephanie insisted on hearing every painful word. It wasn't a surprise really. For God's sake he hadn't been in to see her since that first night and she had almost grown tired of dancing around the issue with all of them: Ruby, the doctors and counselors, even with Steve. But she *had* danced, had made up excuses to cover for her husband's absenteeism; had made up lies to tell her own heart.

It was a shock.

He needed time.

197

Work was forcing him to visit during the late night hours, while she was fast asleep.

Twice she had awaken feeling watched, touched even. She *almost* believed that one herself.

It was easy enough to protect herself with little words of deception. But in the end, all she got was the letter. And it obliterated all those lies. She watched them blow up one by one, tiny bombs shooting out puffs of acrid smoke. A very poor fireworks show.

Stephanie wanted her money back.

It was straightforward, she'd give Paul that much. No beating around the bush for Mr. Kramer. He laid out the whole ugly truth and he didn't try to make it sound any better than it was. In that sense, he was better than all the doctors and the nurses, all the well-wishers, even Ruby. Stephanie didn't want positive spins or rainbows. She wanted the cold, hard facts. That was the only way she could be sure of making the right decisions...

"Stephanie –

My head is in my hands as I write this to you. My heart is in pieces. It seems an easy way to escape a terrible situation but please know this is not easy. Not by a long shot.

I think we both know our marriage was hanging in the balance. We were living a lie, hoping for a miracle but really looking for an excuse. I'm simply not built for this kind of thing. And this is my reason to move on. I hope you'll find a reason of your own someday and I know, without a doubt,

198

that you will come to agree with me.

Love passed us by, Stephanie, and there is nothing either of us can do to find it again. We can only move forward, enjoy life and find love again. I know that we both will find happiness for ourselves.

I will not begin any divorce proceedings until your immediate medical needs are met. Until that time, your medical bills will be covered by my insurance.

Please stay in touch, let me know how you are doing. You will remain in my heart and tears for eternity.

With loving regret,

Paul"

Ruby was crying when she finished, choking out the last words with all of her strength. "Bastard," she'd said, over and over, pacing the floor, shaking the letter in her hand. "I'm going to kill the bastard."

Stephanie let her rant, watching Ruby with dry eyes from her bed as she covered the floor of her room. "That's not necessary," Stephanie told her finally, realizing that it wasn't the end of her marriage that loomed in front of her like a dark, endless shadow. It was something much worse.

This week for sure.

And Stephanie knew exactly how she would be able to pull it off.

Thursday. Kirby thought that Thursday would be a good day to go see Stephanie. He could feel agitation rolling in his gut. He could feel

199

it rattling inside his brain, too, telling him it was time. Time to claim his woman.

You should ask Marty. Just in case.

But Kirby knew he wouldn't understand. He was afraid of Marty now: afraid of his anger and what he could do.

Marty might try to take her from me.

No, he could never tell him.

Kirby was lonely and had spent the past few weeks fumbling around his apartment, riding his bike, and looking at Stephanie. He was lonely now that his Momma had gone. The quiet was as thick as fog and syrup. Even his television couldn't cut it.

The telephone did, though, jangling in the back room like a fire alarm and making Kirby pee his pants a little.

Don't let Momma see, he started to think, and then stopped himself. Momma wasn't talking to him anymore. Momma was GONE. Kirby felt like crying. It was his own fault. He had sent her away.

Kirby hurried to the phone, picking it up from its cradle, nervous. No one called him but Marty. Sometimes a salesman, but most of the time, it was Marty.

"Hello?" His voice was soft, tentative.

"Kirby, my man!" It *was* Marty. And he sounded happy. Jovial and ready to play. Kirby felt himself relax a little. This was not scary Marty on the other end of the phone. This was his friend, the person who had killed for him. And Kirby sure could use a friend.

"Hi, Marty," he said, brightening at the prospect of having someone to talk to. "I missed you!"

"Hey, listen, Kirb, I'm sorry I was so tough on you the other day. Sorry I yelled at you, too, buddy. Let me make it up to you? How about we go out for some beers, just you and me? Like old times?"

"Yeah? Really?" Kirby was ready to go.

"Yeah, sure, buddy. How about Thursday?"

Kirby frowned. No, Thursday wouldn't do. Thursday was for Stephanie.

"I'm kinda busy then, Marty. Thursday? No, that's no good."

"What do you mean no good? Too busy for your old friend, Marty? I'm hurt!"

Kirby listened hard, trying to find the edge in Marty's voice. *Was Marty just yanking his chain? Pretending to be nice?* And then he thought of Stephanie.

"Ahh, Marty, I got something to do then. How 'bout the next day? Friday then?"

He could hear Marty breathing on the other end of the line. It sounded faster and more annoyed. Kirby shifted from foot to foot. He *really* had to go to the bathroom now. But he couldn't hang up and make Marty mad.

When Marty did speak again, his voice was controlled and even.

It didn't sound angry, but it sounded worried. That may have even been worse. Kirby had never heard Marty sound troubled.

Marty took a deep breath before he started talking again. "I didn't want to mention this Kirby," he began, his voice low. "But I'm kind of concerned. I really really need to talk to you about some things I've been hearing."

High alert! High alert! Kirby felt his heart drop into his toes. *Marty knew about Stephanie!*

"What are you hearing?" he whispered, closing his eyes, afraid to hear.

"Things the police are saying, Kirby. They know more now. We have to watch our backs. We have to be very *careful.*" Marty enunciated the word, dragging it out.

Kirby almost jumped for joy. *He didn't know about Stephanie!* And then he realized what Marty had said.

"Police?" he asked, immediately thinking of prison. He couldn't go back there. No way. Bad things happened in there in the middle of the night, hell, even in the middle of the day, and no one did anything to stop them. Marty had. But Marty wouldn't be there anymore.

Kirby swallowed hard and squeezed his eyes shut again. *Please no police. Please no jail cell.*

"What are we gonna do, Marty?" he asked, his voice trembling. "What are we gonna do?"

"I can come over to talk to you about that, Kirby. I think I might know a way."

"Okay, okay," Kirby stuttered, shivering now. He looked out the window, out along the street. *Nothing. No cops. No sirens. They weren't coming, not yet.*

"You're safe for now, Kirby," Marty promised, and there was a chuckle hidden in his voice. "I promise. I'm keeping things under control for now."

Kirby didn't answer. He scanned the street, listening hard for anything unusual. He'd stay there all night if he had to, standing watch. He didn't have Momma to do it for him anymore. He didn't have anyone.

"Kirby?" Marty asked, on the other end.

"Yeah?" Kirby asked reluctantly.

"Thursday then?"

"Thursday," he agreed, as he begrudgingly dropped the phone back into the receiver.

Chapter 24

They told him he could see her tomorrow, once she was stable, and Mark had no option but to agree. His insides were a mass of turbulence, the kind that stuck with you no matter what you did until you had your own matters settled, whatever those may be. Mark had two matters to settle: Diane and Steve. No sense staying at University.

He had been there, *(what three days straight now?)* wandering the halls, visiting Diane, looking in on Stephanie. He'd even managed to put the rumor mill to rest and set the record straight. He explained to anyone who would listen that he had been seriously dating Diane (*a little white lie, but hell, the truth was harder to explain*), that he was friends with both girls, and that the impact of their tragedy had really broadsided him. Once that little seed was in place, with the nurse corps in particular, the news traveled quickly around to the rest of the staff. And Mark had noticed a lot less whispering behind his back and a little less suspicion in everyone's eyes.

Good doctors, *doctor*. They don't mourn. They don't waiver.

His co-workers had either thought he was crazy, or that he'd hurt the women himself. But thinking that he was still suspect, that people *believed* he was capable of such a crime, was beyond his consideration at the moment.

"People are talking," Dan had told him, "because you were one of the last to see them together. Oakmont's gone overboard, pointing fingers at their own neighbors. We're all a little shaken."

And Dan was right. There'd been pickets at every police station in the city. Citizens were demanding answers. Mark could see the strain on the faces of Detectives Pranther and Avery. He could hear in their voices that they were grasping at straws as they went over the same, sticky details with him, with Leah, and assorted hospital staff time and time again.

"You'd think a group of educated people – doctors and nurses for God's sake – would know better than to give in to hysteria." Mark knew he was pouting and feeling sorry for himself, but it came through to the surface anyway.

"It'll pass," Dan assured him, as he clapped him on the shoulder. "Anyone who tries that kind of talk with me, I'll cut them off at the knees." He gave Mark a sympathetic look.

For now Mark was free to come and go as he pleased, so he left the hospital and headed to Steve's bar. A beer would do him good. Hell, two or three would be even better.

It was quiet there in that pocket of time between three in the afternoon and six at night. Mark counted just five at the bar, and they were a low-key bunch. In fact, only two of them actually appeared to know one another; the rest sat idly drinking and staring off into space. The televisions were on, casting a warm glow around the room, but no one was watching whatever mid-afternoon games that were playing, and the volume was turned down.

Just a beer or two, and then he'd go back to the hospital. Diane might need him, might ask for him. And her attending may decide it would be okay for Mark to go in and see her a day early.

"Quiet crowd," Mark said, standing at the bar as he tried to make conversation.

"It gets crazy around here," Steve told him. "Later on anyway." Their conversation was stilted, mainly because neither of them had any idea of where to begin. Steve's business partner was hanging around anyway, showing off the place to Mark and pointing out the details of how he had gotten the place going.

A bit of an egotist, Mark thought. But he had the right. The place was nice, really nice. He could see the draw.

"I thought I'd never meet Steve's younger brother." Gregory studied Mark up and down, and Mark felt awkward under his eyes.

Gay maybe? Mark wondered.

"Mark's a doctor," Steve jumped in, balancing himself between his cane and the bar. "He's busy." He shot Gregory a look imploring him to shut up. A surge of regret at having slipped, at having told Greg anything about Mark, haunted him now.

"Ah yes. Have you worked on that woman who was attacked?" Gregory asked, "The one Steve dated?"

Gregory smiled, and it looked out of place. Mark's eyes fell, and he wondered just how much Greg knew about him and Steve anyway. Steve shot Greg another steely glance as he felt the veins in his neck start to pulse.

"No," Mark said hesitantly, looking from his brother to Greg, and back again. "No, doctors don't *work on* people they know."

"Right," Greg pushed. "That would be *unethical*."

"How about that beer?" Steve interjected, his voice unnaturally loud. It cut the weird vibe between them all and thankfully, the conversation about hospitals and Stephanie and brothers diminished as quickly as it had started.

Gregory shut up, and Steve sighed relief as he expertly poured Mark a beer, handing him a chilly mug with a perfect frosty head. He brushed Mark's hand as he handed him the glass, and again Mark was struck by the thought that Greg was flirting with him.

"Belgian," Gregory told him, as he crinkled his eyes into an – *invitation?* - smile.

Was this guy coming on to him? What the fuck?

"That's the best beer we have." He looked at Mark again, holding his eyes for just a touch longer than was comfortable. "Drink up. You sure look like you could use one." He kept watching Mark and waiting for him to try the beer, so Mark did, letting the cold suds wash away the bad taste in his mouth.

"Superb," he said. "Great beer. Probably the best I've ever had." He nodded, and Gregory's face lit up.

"Well, if you'll excuse us, Greg," Steve interrupted sensing the exchange was lumbering. "We're going to go do some catching up in my office."

"Yeah, sure, Steve. Nice to meet you, Mark. I hope you'll come around here again with Dan and some of the old gang." It was another strange thing to say. Greg hadn't known them in college; he didn't spend social time with them now.

Now he was part of the gang? Mark was confused.

"He's fairly new in town. A guy's guy, you know," Steve whispered to Mark as they walked away. "He likes to know what's going on in his place, and he likes to hang out with the people who come in." He shrugged, trying to cover up his own part in the gossip. "Dan must have said something. About us."

Steve felt like a cad trying to lay the blame on Dan. But hell, he was just patching it up with his brother. It wasn't a good time to add insult to injury.

"He's not gay?" Mark asked as they cleared the bar area, feeling slightly ashamed and a little dirty for asking.

"Hell, no!" Steve almost laughed aloud. "The girls line up for that one." He made a movement between his thumb and forefinger. "Money. Women can smell it."

Mark let it go, settling into a chair in Steve's office, a messy corner with a door.

"I've got a desk here somewhere." Steve tried to break the ice a bit by joking about the mess of papers and wrappers that lined his workspace.

"Some things never change." Mark replied, remembering Steve's room at home and at college. Bombs could have done less damage.

"I'm glad you decided to come."

"Well, it's time to lay this to rest."

"Let's not rehash the dirty details," Steve said. "I mean, I don't want to. We both know what happened and why it happened isn't an issue anymore. The bottom line is that we all fucked up. You, me, and Steph included. We all crossed lines."

Mark nodded. "I crossed a big one. Jealousy I guess. But we're grown men now." He paused. "I'm just – well… like I told you - I'm sorry, brother. It wasn't right doing what I did."

"I beat her," Steve blurted. *So Stephanie hadn't lied after all.* "We fought, and I beat her, and then we'd have sex. It was a vicious cycle, craziness. I was addicted to it. The power of it. And I cheated on her. All the time when the team was on the road."

A dozen images flew threw Mark's mind then. Steve jumping into the stands at a basketball game to pop some big mouth in the face. Steve berating him in front of the other guys when they were kids, making Mark carry his sports equipment and walk two steps behind them. Steve's face when he found Mark with Stephanie, his hand coming back to deliver a blow.

But Steve had always been wild - always prone to fight and live on the edge. People seemed to admire that in him. Mark had known it all of his life and accepted it. It was just the way his brother was and had been since childhood. Steve led, and everyone seemed to follow.

"Not anymore, Mark. I'm done with all that. I'm a different guy. After Stephanie got raped, I even threw out the percocets. They made me… woozy or something, like I could pass out, but still be walking around. Weird, huh?"

"That's not a drug you want to take long term, Steve," Mark advised. He hadn't known his brother was abusing painkillers. *Of course not. How could he have known?* "Are you sure you are okay? Going cold turkey, there could be complications."

"I've got to learn to live with this leg and the past, to not cover up the pain. I wouldn't hurt a fly now," he insisted, and Mark could hear in his tone that it was very, very important to Steve that he believe him.

"That's great, Steve. I mean, that's a great attitude to have. I'm happy for you. And for your success," Mark gestured around the office. "The bar is terrific."

Steve smiled, a sheepish, grateful grin that Mark had never expected to see cross his brother's face. The whole situation felt just a little off to him. Steve being so composed and mature, it wasn't *natural. And the things Steve was confessing…*

"I'm sorry, too, Mark," Steve continued. "For holding a grudge so long. I mean, I wanted to kill you. I dreamed about it. And then the injury. Man, that ended it all for me. That's how I felt. Just pissed on. And heavily, totally raging about it."

"Raging," Mark repeated, his mind working over time, trying to

210

take in all the things Steve was saying.

"Nothing like a fucking tragedy to put things in perspective," Steve said. "I mean, I totally get what's going on in Stephanie's head right now. You get pissed on, things happen that are totally out of your control, and it's like you fight back or you give in, you know? Or you keep flipping. One minute, you're fighting to take back what was yours, the next you just cave under the pressure, and you want to throw in the towel. Man, I caved for so long, Mark. It was nuts. I sat on the toilet with a gun in my mouth one day, and the next, I was going to win back my girl." He laughed sarcastically. "I didn't know if I was coming or going. Getting the bar helped, right, but still, there was this void. Some of my days were just missing. Do you get that?"

He looked at Mark, wide-eyed and expectant, and Mark could see the loss in his face. First Steve found his brother balling the woman he loved, and the woman he loved reciprocating with her heart and soul and body. And then, just a few short months later, he falls on the basketball court, shattering his knee against the shiny, acrylic finish, which severed any hope for a professional career.

Steve lost his athletic scholarship. Dropped out of college. All were very bitter pills to swallow. And yet, not quite enough for Mark to understand what Steve was trying to tell him.

Was his brother a rapist? Was this some strange confession? Why the hell was he thinking this anyway?

Mark opened his mouth to answer, forming his lips around words but finding none.

"I feel saved or something." Steve had continued talking. "Clean again. I just want a fresh start. Let bygones be bygones." He was smiling again, and Mark saw a light in Steve's face that he supposed had been missing for a long time. He felt a flash of guilt at having suspected something as ridiculous as Steve having something to do with the terror in their community.

Outlandish! Mark told himself. *Stephanie would have recognized him for sure!*

"I'm glad," Mark managed. "It seems like everything has started to repair itself. I want you to have a happy life, Steve. I want to be a part of it."

Right?

"I missed you. Brother," Steve was saying, trying on the word. "I didn't realize how much I missed you until just this minute. I'm sorry I hated you for so long. I wanted to *kill* you, Mark. Do you get that? I mean, that's sick. Is that sick?"

I don't know! Mark thought. *Is it?* He looked at his brother. "I crossed a line that wasn't meant to be crossed. I broke "man" code. Brothers don't go there."

Don't tell him about Diane. Not yet.

"I'm sorry I blamed you for everything that happened. I'm not innocent, not by a long shot." He looked earnest and thoughtful, not like a bad guy at all. Not like someone filled with rage. Steve gestured at Mark's empty glass. "Another?

Mark swallowed. "Stronger?" he asked. "Got anything a little stronger?"

"Yeah," Steve said, pulling out a bottle of bourbon from the top drawer of his desk. "My reserve," he said, blowing into a shot glass he pulled, seemingly out of nowhere. "A little dusty," he said, shrugging. "But the alcohol will kill it." He handed Mark a shot.

To hell with germs. Mark tipped it back and then placed the empty shot glass on the edge of the desk.

Steve lit a cigarette. "My last bad habit," he explained. Mark watched the smoke drift aimlessly toward the ceiling while Steve poured himself a shot and poured Mark another.

"To the future," Steve said, toasting his brother.

"Cheers," Mark answered, letting the alcohol swallow up all of his niggling doubt.

"I feel better," she told everyone. "Like there's a light at the end of the tunnel." And in general, that was true. Stephanie felt like a weight had lifted from her shoulders over the past two days. Diane was awake and that was, in her mind, the last thing she really needed to know. Stephanie checked off that block on her list of "Things To Do."

Diane's going to live? Check.

It was a short list, and that was good because time was of the essence. She'd wasted enough of it already.

Make amends with Steve? Done. Check that box.

They hadn't really talked about it, but an unspoken understanding had passed between them, of that she was sure. The transgressions of the past were going to stay in the past.

She was whistling to herself when Leah came by. It was a stupid commercial that kept sticking to the insides of her head.   She'd asked for Leah, despite the exaggerated display of horror and sympathy she knew was coming. *Hey, to get some sunshine you had to go through some rain, right?* And here she was, standing reluctantly at the door, trying to get a good look at Stephanie before Stephanie saw her.

Getting Leah into her room? Check.

"Stephanie, MY GOD!" Leah said, as she rushed forward, and Stephanie could read the shock and horror in her face. It was one thing to hear about someone's injuries and quite another to see them up close and personal like this. "I knew it was bad, I mean, I heard." Leah stumbled over her words. "But, MY GOD," she repeated, shaking her head as if to clear it from some awful vision.

Stephanie nodded. *Yeah, sucks to be me*, she thought, but she said nothing.

Wouldn't that be what Leah was thinking right about now? How

214

much it would suck to be her? And how lucky she was to have her pretty, little face and body and mind all intact and glowing and healthy?

Leah came closer to inspect the stitches. "They look like they're healing, though," she said, giving Stephanie a quick hug before pulling back again.

At least she didn't go overboard pretending, Stephanie gave her that much. She was getting used to living with this brutal truth and honesty. It sure did illuminate things for her.

"I'm faint just looking at you, poor thing," Leah said, as she sat on the very edge of the bed. "How are you? Really? I mean I just can't imagine." She shook her head slowly back and forth.

Stephanie steeled herself. Like hell would she tell Leah how she *really* was.

"A little better," she said. "The cop outside my door keeps the nightmares away." Stephanie smiled a little, and Leah sighed.

"It's just a matter of time before they…"

"Catch those bad guys?" Stephanie finished, her sarcasm floating right over Leah's head.

"Right!" she said, as she grabbed hold of Stephanie's hand. "The whole place is running scared. Security is walking us to our cars every night. I'm afraid to go to the grocery store alone! I mean, it's time! I keep telling the detectives every time they try to talk to me about seeing you and your friend that night,"

215

"Diane," Stephanie interrupted. "Her name is Diane."

"Right, Diane. I keep telling them to stop wasting time talking to me, and start searching for the people that did this. I mean, Jesus already!"

"Sure, yeah, I can see the frustration there."

"Well, I'm so happy you wanted to see me. Really, Steph. It's been so hard thinking about you lying in here and not knowing if I should come in after my shift or just leave you alone, or what you wanted me to do, you know? If it was me, you know, I might not have wanted to see anybody I knew for awhile, least of all someone from that *night*! I mean, the memory has to be just horrible."

"Horrible. Yes. You could definitely say that."

"I just can't even go there. I don't know what to say or ask or anything."

"I don't remember much," Stephanie lied. "It was dark and confusing. Everything just rushed up at once and happened. And they knocked me unconscious for a while. A lot probably happened that I won't ever remember."

"That's probably better," Leah said. She leaned in closer and bobbed her head up and down, as if to convince Stephanie. "There are some things that it's better not to remember."

"Yes, of course. Most definitely. So why don't you fill me in on your life then. What's new in Leah's world?"

It turned out there was plenty. Leah told Stephanie everything. All about her new manicurist, their old cheerleading squad, the latest hospital gossip - Mark and Diane included. Stephanie's stomach curdled a bit at that, but she let it go, concentrating instead on Leah's mouth as she talked on, taking in the perfect lines that made up her lips. It hurt, looking at her face that way and remembering the way her own used to be. Stephanie fought the urge to touch her own lips, to *compare and contrast*.

"I've just been reading a lot, doing crosswords. Oh, and scrap booking," Stephanie told her all of a sudden. "I've really gotten into it. Making memory books of better times. My psychiatrist suggested it." It was such a stupid thing to say, such a ridiculous therapy technique, that Stephanie had to control giggles.

"What a good idea!" Leah exclaimed. "So therapeutic!"

Stephanie almost burst out laughing again.

"Yeah, I think it's working," she choked. She hadn't felt like laughing for so long, she was taken slightly aback.

"Oh, Stephanie, I'm so glad." Leah told her, and Stephanie was unable to read if there was sincerity in her words. Then Leah lowered her voice, whispering conspiratorially. "Will they be able to fix your face?" she asked.

Stephanie didn't miss a beat. "That's what they tell me," she said, almost finishing it up with a wink but then knowing that would be taking it a bit too far. This had to be seamless.

"Where's Paul?" *Leah had to go there. Of course.* "I haven't seen him around the hospital."

"Oh, he's been in a lot. Early mornings. Long before your shift starts," Stephanie told her. "He works days you know."

"Sure, of course!" Leah slapped her forehead.

She'd been thinking about it, the little bitch. Probably spreading rumors all over University that Stephanie Kramer's husband hadn't been in to see her. I hope she gets whatever she deserves after this.

"So listen, Leah, I'm getting a little tired now," Stephanie said, motioning toward the IV bag hanging next to her bed. "Pain meds."

"Oh, sure, oh, right. Yeah, I'll let you get some rest."

"Come back to see me?" Stephanie asked, hiding the smirk.

"Of course!" Leah said. "Okay, see you later then." She started to leave.

"Oh, Leah?"

'Yes?" She spun back around, her long dark hair flowing lazily around her head. Stephanie was reminded again of how much she hated everything.

"Could you bring me some scissors?"

Leah looked confused. "Scissors?"

"For my scrap booking. Sometimes I can't sleep, and I might want to work on that later. I hate to bug the night nurses. They're always so busy." She smiled broadly, ignoring the pull on her stitches when she stretched her mouth that way.

"Oh, sure, sure. I bet I can dig some up for you somewhere."

"Thanks, Leah. I really appreciate it."

Leah smiled, turning to go again.

"Leah?"

"Yes?"

"Please don't forget."

"Forget my old friend? No way!"

"Thanks." She let Leah go then.

Then Stephanie just lay back on her pillow and waited. The rain was over, and she was ready for some damn sunshine.

Chapter 25

The sun was shining today, at least that was what they told her. Her room was windowless, sterile, and dry, so she had to ask what the day is like. Spring-like, they said. The first warm day they'd had. Winter was over. Just hearing that made her long for the sun on her skin.

When can I leave? Diane wanted to ask, but she was afraid of the answer. She was afraid of the truth, really. There were parts of her that weren't working right. Her head, for instance, was clear one minute and garbled the next, and her resulting speech fluctuated from steady to slurred. Even a word that sounded right in her mind might come out as if she were drunk.

What kind of attorney would she be now? How could she defend someone when half her words were meaningless? The worry poked at her.

Don't ask, she told herself. *Don't ask and they won't tell.*

There were moments when her left hand felt numb, and she had to open and close her fingers to get it working again. It hadn't woken up with the rest of her.

Disconnects. That's what the doctors were calling the numb hand and the mumbled speech. They behaved as if these were minor annoyances and that she should just be happy to be *here* again. They told her the disjointed connections between her brain and her body were very likely just temporary, that her operation had been a success, and that there was a great chance she would be whole again.

They just weren't sure when.

And then they told her about Stephanie. What had happened to Stephanie was not even in the same category as what had happened to her.

"I have to see her." Diane managed those words with firm resolution. The memory of their last discussion sat on her shoulder like a vulture waiting to feed.

"In time."

"As soon as possible."

That's all the doctors would promise. Diane had to stay in bed, monitored every minute, and there were a lot of good reasons why her getting up and walking around was a danger. Blood clots. Increased pressure to her brain. Potential drops in blood pressure.

For now, there was no escaping this bed, this room, and this situation. Nurses came in every hour, on the hour, taking pressures, taking blood, asking her how she was feeling.

"Any changes in vision?" they asked, heads over her medical chart, their pens poised in their hands to document everything she told them. *No.*

"Headache? Drowsiness?" *No. No again.*

"Trouble sleeping?" Definitely not. *That was a joke, wasn't it?* She'd been sleeping for six weeks.

Although last night, sleep was impossible, despite the drugs that pumped through her veins, and despite the clogged brain and foggy thought processes.

She couldn't rest last night because she knew Mark would be coming to see her soon. Diane had no earthly idea what she was going to say to him. She'd dreamed of him right before she'd awakened from the coma, and now Diane found herself yearning for him despite his deception and the fact that he had been intimate with her best friend.

She wasn't going to try to understand her need. Blame it on the brain fog or some strange emotional weakness stemming from her injuries. Vulnerability. Whatever. But she couldn't help how she felt. It was what it was. Inexplicable.

She wanted to fix things with Mark.

She at least wanted to *see* him again.

She'd forgotten most of what had happened to her that night in the alley. Up until the time she saw the foot (*Stephanie's foot. God, she still couldn't believe it was Stephanie's foot*), she'd lost the memory. The only reminders she had left were the physical ones. But she remembered the dream she'd had before waking, as if she had lived it. The one about her parents. And the one about Mark. That dream was one of the few memories ringing clear and true in her head.

Diane was still a child, and her parents were still very much alive. She was sitting on the couch, dressed up in a pink party dress, and her mother was braiding her hair, tying on all the colored ribbons that Diane had loved as a young girl.

"You're going to be the prettiest girl there!" her mother exclaimed, hugging Diane close and then pushing her back to get a good look at her. "If only I could do something with this hair." Her mother's look turned from joy to concern and a frown crossed her face.

"Her hair looks just fine, Emma, stop fretting over the silly things." Her father appeared in the doorway, leaning against the frame and pushing his hands into his pockets. "Leave her alone. She's just perfect. Everyone's going to love her." He beamed at Diane, and she beamed back, crossing her legs like a little lady and laying her hands in her lap. She was wearing tiny, white gloves and looked like she was ready to go to church services on Easter.

"Time to go!" her mother announced, in a sing-song voice, all the joy returning to her face. She pulled Diane up from the couch, and both parents walked her to the door, each of them with a hand on her shoulder.

"Where are we going?" Diane asked, feeling excited. It must be somewhere important for her to be dressed in this fancy outfit.

"Time to go!" her mother said again, and this time, she had tears in her eyes.

"I don't want to go," Diane said, starting to feel frantic as she realized she was going somewhere alone. "I want to stay here with you!"

She was terrified. She pushed against them both, struggling to free herself from their grip.

"We love you! Time to go! We love you! Time to go!" Her parents kept chanting in unison, as they pushed her out the door and into a stand of trees.

For a moment, the dream grew hazy again and when Diane's eyes cleared, she found herself in some kind of forest. There were trees and bushes everywhere, and the air was heavy with dew. It felt like sunrise was just about to occur. Looking down, Diane realized she was a grown woman now, and that she was naked. Feeling more frantic than ever, she began pulling off leaves from the trees, trying to cover herself, but they kept tearing to shreds in her hands.

She started running blindly, holding her hands over her breasts and trying to protect them from the scratching branches to every side of her.

"I have to get out of here!" It's all that she can think.

"I have to get back home!" She cried out, running wildly. Her thighs and hands were covered with scratch marks, red and welling. Diane began to cry. Where the hell was she? How could she get home?

As she came into a clearing, there was a man standing with his back to her. He had his head down, and it sounded as if he was sobbing. Diane was afraid of him, but at the same time, she moved forward until she was so close she could actually feel his chest moving up and down and hear his quiet tears and sniffling. She put one hand on his shoulder before she could

224

stop herself, holding her breath. She can't back away now. The man is going to turn around. She knows who she is.

Instinctively, she brought one arm across her chest, and with the other hand covered herself between her legs.

The man turned around, and it was Mark. His eyes were haunted. He looked her up and down, tears falling silently down his cheeks. Diane felt her face grow hot from embarrassment as his eyes explored her exposed body. She felt herself take a step back because he was looking at her with a mixture of desire and love. His face was pale, and his eyes were surrounded in black as if he hadn't slept in days.

She felt unprepared as he opened his arms, welcoming her into a hug. Diane stumbled backward again just as he said, "Don't cover yourself. You're so beautiful. Please, come to me." He motioned again for her to fold herself into the circle of his arms.

The dream was obvious in its symbolism. Even as she lay in an unconscious state, she had been thinking of him. She felt her grip on the past loosen just the slightest bit. It was time to move forward, wherever that may lead.

What should she say when Mark came in, when she saw his face for the first time since before all of this? Where should she start?

Diane shifted in her bed, taking deep breaths in and out as she tried to stop her heart from beating like a jackhammer through the monitor. That would bring the nurses for sure, and she didn't want anything to interfere with Mark's visit.

Mark.

I think I am ready to see you now.

Chapter 26

The bitch was back. Damn her, busting in here during the busiest time of the day and making his patrons nervous. He thought back on their first meeting, mulling over every word in the back of his mind. Why the hell was she back?

He tapped his fingers nervously on the counter top and reached in his pocket for his cigarettes. He had been trying to quit, tired of waking up with a heavy chest and a loose cough every morning. But shit like *this* was making it impossible.

He watched the detective exit her car, wearing her uniform, the light shining off the badge on her chest. Couldn't she at least do him the favor of showing up in plainclothes this time? She had that fancy pants uniform on the last time she was here, and it had bothered him just as much.

A woman had no right trying to do a man's job. He narrowed his eyes. He could think of a lot better things he and Miss - *what the hell was her name again?* - should be doing to pass the time today. He thought back again to their first meeting.

"Sheryl Avery, City of Oakmont Police," she'd introduced herself.

There it was. Avery. That was her name.

"Yeah, I see your badge, lady," he'd answered condescendingly. "My name's Goodwin. I'm the owner of Java, if you didn't already know," *he told her, puffing up at the word owner.*

Paying him no real respect, she continued. "I have the dubious honor of collecting information in a recent rape case you may have heard about."

"Yeah, yeah, it's the talk of the campus, lady," he pouted again. "Listen, can we talk in my office, back here? You're reminding my patrons that they got something to worry about. It's bad for business," he said, leading the way toward a crowded back room that served as storage and office space.

Mr. Goodwin had sat at the desk, pushing some papers around and trying to look as official as Officer Avery. God, how he hated a woman who acted as high and mighty as this one.

"You may also have heard," Sheryl began immediately, leaving him little time to collect himself. "That the two women who were attacked a few evenings ago were actually here in your esteemed establishment prior to the attack."

He fidgeted nervously. "I may have heard something like that," he answered.

"Do you know the actual women to whom I am referring?" she pressed on.

"Yeah, I know who they are. I seen their names in the paper," he said, knowing how stupid it would be to lie. "Took one of their orders for tea that night," he added.

"Yes, that's right," she said, trying to open up the floodgates. "Did you have any conversation with Diane?" she said. "By the grace of God, they're both still alive. But I was hoping you could fill in some blanks for me."

"I just took her order is all. We didn't have no real conversation." No sense telling her what he'd thought when he took Diane's order. That wouldn't look good, and he didn't want any trouble.

"I see a lot of kids in here every day," he added. "These two come in a lot, though, that's how I know who they are."

Sheryl cleared her throat, giving him a disapproving look, one that dismissed him as unimportant.

Bitch. He toyed with a pencil on his desk.

"Were you here all evening, sir?"

"Yeah, I stayed around here," he admitted. "They was sitting near the toilets. I seen them talking to a man, but I don't know his name. He comes in here sometimes, looks like a pretty boy," he figured that was as good a description as any. "He left, and then they left. I don't know where they went after that, or who they talked to, or what happened next." That should satisfy her, he thought.

He didn't want any more bad press surrounding this place.

He leaned back in his chair and tried to look imposing so that she might give up and leave.

"What time would you say it was when the man left? Did the girls leave right afterwards, or did they wait a bit?" She began peppering him *with questions.*

"Look, lady, I don't sit around picking my ass and staring at a clock all night. I am a busy man, and on that night this was a busy place. If I knew I was supposed to be watching over these three, I wish you had told me before now," he smirked, thinking he would intimidate her with his great wit and sarcasm.

"Mr. Goodwin, sir," she said, emphasizing the sir with a heavy dose of distaste in her voice. "I highly suggest that you lose your sardonic comments. And would you mind referring to me as Detective Avery from here on out?"

Shit, he thought. She wasn't going to leave yet. He noticed some of the students pointing and staring into his office, and he got up and quickly shut the door. This wasn't good, and it was getting worse.

"Look, la- I mean, Miss Avery," he said. "I'm telling you what I know. The one girl, the tall one, had some tea, but the little one didn't order nothing. The pretty boy left right before them, but I didn't see anyone follow them out. I'm telling you, I don't know anything more than that." He sounded almost as if he was pleading with her now.

"Was there anyone else you recognized that night?"

"A lot of the kids come in here, like regulars, you know"

"So who else was here that you know as a regular?" she asked, pen poised and ready to catch any names he threw at her.

"Look, there was a lot of familiar faces hanging around here that

230

night, but I don't always know their names," he hoped she realized he was actually telling the truth. He rattled off a half-ass list, first names, last names, a few he maybe guessed and didn't really know. Too bad. Let the bitch figure out who was real and who wasn't. Then he told her, "I can't think of any other names that I may know. You gotta understand, I see hundreds of university students and professors every day come through this place," he finished, leaning back again and looking a little drained.

"I'd like to talk to your staff from last night."

"Oh, shit, lady," he said, forgetting the formalities again. "You ain't coming back in here again to scare off more of my clientele, now are you?" he looked like he might cry.

"I'm afraid so, sweetheart," she answered sarcastically, with a wink. "This thing is bigger than the both of us."

She *had* come back and interviewed his staff and some of the patrons who had been there that night for hours, but he was sure she had gone away empty handed. No one had seen anything. He listened to their conversations intently as he brewed their coffees and rang up their purchases. The talk was rattled and frightened, but it was naïve. He knew everything around here. And he intended to keep it that way.

Still, he hadn't known she was coming, not this time.

But here she was again, busting her big ass through the door and headed right for him. He stood there coolly, trying to stop himself from sweating through his shirt.

"Cigarette?" he asked her as she reached him.

She smiled, and if he didn't know any better, he'd think it was genuine.

"No, thanks." She coughed a little *just to be a bitch*, he figured, and fluttered her hands in the air to wave away his smoke.

"What can I do for you, Detective Avery?" He smiled back, a smirk of distaste.

"DNA," she said. "A spit sample, if you would."

He froze, his cigarette halfway up to his lips.

"DNA? Why? Am I a suspect?" He felt the sneer on his face, but he couldn't hold it back.

"Everybody's a suspect, Mr. Goodwin. I'm just trying to clear your good name." Her smile was bigger now. She was the black widow crossing her web to look her victim in the eye. Right before she devoured him.

She didn't know who she was dealing with.

"Name your poison," he said, changing the subject and pointing at the menu. "Coffee is on the house."

"I'm here on official business," she said, dismissing his offer and thrusting a card at him. "This is the address of the lab. We'd appreciate your reporting within the next 48 hours. They'll give you instructions there, but it's a simple procedure. It will only take up a few minutes of your time. I know time is important to a busy man like you." He didn't take the card from her and she laid it on the counter in front of him.

"Yeah, I'll chat with my lawyer and get back to you," he told her.

Settle down, man, he told himself. *There's nothing there. Nothing.*

His voice was calm and even, betraying nothing out of the ordinary. "Sure you wouldn't like that coffee?"

"No time," she said, as she prepared to go. "I highly suggest you consider the test," she said. "You have nothing to hide, right?" She was baiting him.

But he wouldn't bite.

He held up his hands. "Nothing," he agreed, shrugging innocently.

That promise would be all she would get from him.

Chapter 27

He was going to promise her the world. A good life. A happy future. That was all he could do. Mark was a bundle of nerves as he paced the hall, waiting to see Diane.

He knew what he was going to say. He just had no idea how Diane would react to it.

The most important thing was that she was awake, alive, and well.

She was coherent, Dan had promised him. Perfectly capable of thinking and speaking. There were some residual effect, but nothing alarming, nothing that promised to be a lifelong hindrance. *Thank God.*

Mark swallowed hard and checked his watch. Ten a.m. Visiting hours had officially started at University. It was time. Mark started up the stairs.

Diane checked the clock on the wall, trying not to count the minutes. *Would Mark show up right away? Or would he wait until the mid-afternoon lull so they would have more time alone to talk?*

She'd already been poked and prodded this morning, her vitals carefully charted, and all of the pertinent questions asked. Light-headedness? Hallucinations? Nothing unusual?

She was happy to report that none of those symptoms plagued her. The only problem was this deep, gnawing feeling in her gut, the anticipation

of what she hoped would be reconciliation with the man that she - *thought?*
believed? knew? – she loved. She would hardly report that to the nurses,
though.

What could they do about it, anyway?

They were all curious, asking sly questions about her relationship
with the handsome doctor that had kept coming in to sit by her side over
the past six weeks. That's how Diane knew he had been there, *really knew*
with her head and not just her heart. She suspected some of the nurses,
the younger ones in particular who knew Mark from working there, were
disappointed and jealous. She had caught one or two of them casting sliding
glances at her, trying to see what she had that they didn't.

It seemed ridiculous that they could feel jealous of the half bald
coma patient they were charged with caring for. But it *felt* as if some of
them were.

The hardest questions they asked her weren't about her relationship
with Mark, though. They were about her parents and her family.

"Where were they?" The nurses asked, referring to her parents, as
they checked her stitches, washed her hair gently on one side, and bathed
her with a small plastic tub and a sponge. Diane knew they were just trying
to make conversation, but they were curious, too. Trying to see what she
was all about. The medical staff wasn't used to seeing bright, beautiful
young women receiving a minimal number of visitors. People like Diane
were *loved.*

235

Did she really have no one but Ruby and Mark to some see her?

She told them the truth. Her parents were dead. Killed in a car crash nine years ago. No siblings. No grandparents. Her small extended family was lost to her, in different states, people she never spoke to.

Ruby and Mark and Stephanie were really all she had. Diane had been so busy beating the odds, excelling, and making a career that she really hadn't noticed how small her circle was. Now, it was glaringly, painfully obvious.

Diane wiped a drizzle of tears from her eyes and looked around the room. There were flowers here, along with balloons and well wishes from the staff at Hazleton and Horowitz. *Your job is still here when you are ready!* The card read in big, curvy, *happy* letters. The company secretary had written it out, for sure. Someone she had never met. To her, to them, Diane was a potential employee who'd had a terrible, regrettable accident. That was all.

There was a plant from an old professor and a giant teddy bear from a few friends in her apartment complex. These were people she knew, people she liked. But they weren't people who would come sit at her bedside every chance they got, hold her hand and will her to get well.

Her parents were gone. They may be looking over her from above, but they wouldn't be here for her wedding or Christmas. Or for the birth of her first child. *That was the reality.* For the second time in the past twenty-four hours, Diane felt herself looking forward and not back.

Maybe it was time to think about starting her own little family unit. Diane shook her head. *Where the hell did that come from?*

It was just that life seemed so damn precious right now.

Diane thought of Stephanie then, of the horrors that she had faced alone after they left the bar that night. *How was she holding up? What was she thinking?* Diane had asked every medical person who passed through here and received only pat answers. Medical mumbo jumbo, she liked to call it. Ruby filled in some of the blanks, but Diane guessed she was holding back too. Everyone seemed to want to protect her from the reality of Stephanie's situation. Everyone seemed to think they had Stephanie and Diane's best interests at heart, but it was demeaning, insulting really, to be kept from the truth.

It must be bad. Stephanie must be really bad for them to hide the details from her like they were. Diane's heart ached to see her.

How much did Stephanie know about her?

Diane didn't think, no, she knew, that none of them could begin healing until they forgave each other.

Mark's face appeared at the door, looking pale and shaky. Nervous energy. It was cute on him. Diane smiled gently, beckoning him in with her eyes. She was still worried about speaking, worried her words would not make sense. But she was determined to get the message to him.

Forgiving begins now. She was most assuredly ready.

"Diane," he started, as he rushed toward her…

237

"Bitch! Stupid, Fucking Cunt!" Marty spat on the girl, leaving a glistening line of spittle in the back of her beautiful red hair. She was curled in a ball in his basement, sobbing, her back heaving with the effort and the outline of her spine showing through her taut skin. He couldn't remember how she got here.

"All he knew was how fucking pissed he was right now.

"She was a beauty. Well, she had been. All full hips and curvy features and long, powerful legs. Big pink lips against pale, unblemished skin with a light spattering of freckles everywhere. Eyes as green as an island. Now she was a little wacked up.

But she deserved it, dammit.

She'd come home with him willingly, that much Marty recalled, and they'd been going at it pretty good. He'd been ready to enter, spreading her legs wide to receive him, as he looked down on her. She had her head thrown back, and her breasts were trembling. Yeah, he'd been ready to bring it home, pushing the tip of his penis into her, her hips coming up to meet him.

That's when she screwed up, though. As he thrust himself forward, her eyes flew open.

And she'd laughed.

THE SLUT HAD LAUGHED AT HIM!

"Is that all you got?" she said, bucking up into his thrust. "Is that all you got for me?"

That's all he remembered. Marty wasn't sure how they'd gotten from upstairs in his bedroom to down here in the cellar, but here they were. He was completely dressed. And she was a naked, trembling mess.

"Get up," he said, kicking at her rib.

"Please," she sobbed at him, not moving, not lifting her head from the ground. "Please leave me alone."

Begging. He hated begging.

"Get up," he repeated. "Get your fucking, jiggly ass up off that floor and look at me." It was a rumble, a command, and he felt her stiffen against his foot, but she didn't do as he told her. She just kept weeping, an inane snivel that Marty would only tolerate for another second or so.

He kicked her in the perineum, a place where she'd only hours earlier displayed a piercing, and she moaned, curling herself tighter into a ball.

"Aagg... please." Her voice was wavering.

Marty grabbed her by her hair, ready to pull her to her feet, but she came up with him on her own. Her eyes were black, streaks of mascara and pink lipstick melting into a rabid clown's mask. She couldn't stop crying, and she kept her shoulders hunched and her eyes down.

"Look," Marty said, chucking her under the chin, almost good-naturedly. Her eyes were forced to meet his.

He was hard, raging, and he wrapped his hands around his penis, pointing it at the sky. "This isn't enough for you? Huh, pussy?"

239

He could see her face crumble in on itself.   She didn't answer.

"Not so funny anymore, is it?" he asked her. She hadn't known her mistake, and now he would show her the error of her ways.

"Suck it," he said, poking her in the leg with his member and rubbing it against her.

She let out another moan, this one of protest.

"You're sick," she managed, and he slapped her hard across the face, pushing her to her knees.

What if she bites? The thought blazed across his mind, and he quickly pushed it away. No, she looked too scared. He could see her shaking. But just in case, he slid his gun from the holster he wore on his back and pressed it against her temple, watching her eyes widen in terror. Tears sprang immediately.

Lessons were in still in session. Marty snorted at the rhyme, enjoying his creativity.

She was on her knees, looking up at him with huge, dripping eyes.

"I thought you were a nice guy," she stuttered.

Marty laughed. She was going to die, and she didn't even know it.

"Nice guys have needs, too," he told her.

He pushed his penis against her lips, forcing them apart. She gagged, and he pushed harder, forcing himself in.

"You be good now," he told her, as he touched the top of her head and rubbed her hair. "You be a good girl, and you may get to go home soon."

He knew this wasn't true, but he had to make her believe that it was.

When it was over, he pushed her down again, but she didn't return to her ball on the floor. She lay flat on her back, her head to the side, spitting what she could out of her mouth. She gagged again, but held things down.

"There's a girl," he told her, leaning over and patting her head again, and she rolled her eyes to him.

"Can I have something," she choked. "Something to cover myself?" Her eyes were dry, but a mix of makeup and black blood was everywhere. Bruises were starting to show against her fair skin. The angry red and blue marks were welling. Marty looked down at her, shaking his head as he pulled on his pants and stuffed himself inside, feeling satisfied that she had been properly schooled.

Maybe he'd keep this one around for a little while. One last hurrah before she had to go. Marty looked down at her, glancing at his watch and considering. Did he want to come home to a live body? Or a dead one?

Her teeth were chattering. "The floor is cold," she told him.

Marty got her a towel, a bar of soap and a robe. He pointed at the utility sink in the corner.

"Clean yourself up," he told her. "I'll be back later."

He left her there, turning out the cellar light and double-locking the door behind him. He would most definitely be back.

He touched her face and ran his fingers gently down her cheek.

"Don't cry," he told her. "Please don't cry."

Diane opened her eyes. "It's just… so overwhelming to see you," she told him, carefully choosing her words as she tried with all her might not to slur them. She covered the hand on her cheek with her own, *her good hand, numb but without a cast*, and let it travel along with his.

"I love you, Diane," Mark told her. "I want to take care of you forever." He began kissing her face all over. Her forehead, her cheeks, her chin, the tip of her nose. And finally, her lips, gently at first, like the flutter of wings.

Her own lips quivered at the lightness of his touch, and Diane couldn't stop shaking until he pressed his mouth tenderly, firmly down against hers. She moved her mouth against his, hesitantly, and then with vigor. Mark reciprocated, running his hands along her arms and thighs. It was as if he was checking to see if she was real.

Is this really happening? She asked herself. It felt deliriously imagined.

But she could taste the light flavor of mint from his toothpaste and smell the cologne, something spicy, that lingered on his cheeks. She could feel his chest heave against hers, their hearts beating in tandem.

It was real.

They stayed that way for a long time, touching and kissing and staring into each other's eyes. Diane hadn't intended this. She thought they would talk, straighten out the bad things and then, maybe…

But here they were. For the first time since she'd met him, Diane felt almost free.

"Where do we go from here?" She asked him first, measuring her words. She talked slowly, happy when she heard them come back at her making perfect sense.

"Forward," Mark told her, not missing a beat. "Always forward."

He took her hand, and they sat that way, figuring things out. He'd brought her an I-Pod with her favorite songs (*Ruby relented, giving him a list of music*), and he'd written a speech, declaring the sun and moon in her honor. They both laughed at that until he got to the serious part. The part that begged her forgiveness and in which they went over the deception that had meant so much to her a few weeks ago, but seemed so small and unimportant now.

Let go of the past. It was the only way.

And then he gave her the promise ring. It wasn't an engagement (*that would be too crazy, too fast*), but it was a promise for the future.

That was what she had been waiting for, had been *needing*, all along.

"I need you. Back in my life." Diane was in her room, telling *her* how sorry she was.

Shouldn't it be me that's sorry? Stephanie thought to herself. "I'm sorry, too, Diane," she said, but her words felt false and empty. It was like Stephanie couldn't feel much of anything anymore, in her heart, anyway. Her damn privates were still sore and thick and draining, and the stitches on her face were itching like hell, but emotionally, there was just nothing. There was just nothing, and she figured she should at least be feeling guilty about *that*. Except that she wasn't.

You are such a fuck up, she told herself.

Diane kept talking as if she didn't know Stephanie was a shell, holding her hand, reassuring her that the line of surgeries filling her calendar for the next several months would make everything okay again. That the counselors and psychiatrists would make her mind well.

"My heart is lost though. Everything I looked forward to just evaporated." Stephanie said, throwing her hands over her face as soon as she realized she'd said it out loud.

"We'll mend that together," Diane said, not missing a beat. "We'll mend each other." She took Stephanie's hands away from her face and squeezed them. "You and me against the world, right?"

That's what they used to say when they were back in school together - that it was just the two of them against the world. Sometimes, it had really felt like that was true.

How had she kept the truth about Mark from Diane? And then she'd dumped her, running off to be with Paul and leaving Diane in the dust, just a second thought. What kind of friend had she really been anyway?

"I've been thinking," Diane started. "A lot. And this bad thing, this horrible thing that's happened to you, and this kind of horrible thing that has happened to me…"

"Equally horrible," Stephanie interrupted. "Being beaten into a coma is equally horrible." It was a statement that defied argument.

A look of understanding crossed Diane's face. "These horrible things that happened to us, well, we can let them destroy us and who we were. Or we can fight back hard. And overcome them."

Stephanie nodded. She *wanted* to believe what Diane was saying. She just couldn't cross the bridge to it.

"That whole thing with Mark, it's back there," Diane pointed her thumb behind her. "It's behind us."

Stephanie nodded again. "Yeah, yeah, I'd like to forget all about that."

"I'd like to know what's ahead for us instead. Wouldn't you?"

Stephanie shrugged. *She knew what lay ahead.* She tried to push her own self-pity and loathing away, but it ate its way into her soul anyway. *Sure, it's easy for Diane to move on. Her face is normal. She has a man who adores her. She has a career waiting in the wings to sweep her up in its glory.*

What about me? Stephanie wanted to ask. *What about me?* Instead, she apologized again. "I'm sorry, Diane," her empty words pinging off the walls. "Really sorry."

"I told you, it's over, done."

"How can you just let it go like that?" Stephanie asked, meaning everything. *How could Diane just forget ALL that had happened to her as if it was no big deal? Not just the lies but ALL of it. The dead parents, the lonely childhood, the attack she'd endured. How do you just drop all of that out of your heart?*

"It's called forgiveness, Steph," Diane told her, reaching forward and hugging Stephanie.

She tried to hug back, but she felt like a limp dishrag in Diane's arms. Diane gently eased Stephanie back toward the bed.

"They're letting me out of the hospital," Diane said, breaking the news with difficulty.

"When?"

"Today. I just had to see you before I left."

Come back, Stephanie thought. *I don't want to be alone.* But of course, she didn't.

"I'll come and see you tomorrow," Diane said.

"Sure. You know I'll be here."

"I'll come every day." Diane leaned forward and kissed Stephanie's forehead.

And then she was gone.

Chapter 28

Mark was there to take her home. It was just her and Mark, exactly as they had planned. It was bittersweet relief, leaving University Hospital behind. Aside from having to leave Stephanie there, leaving University meant leaving her injuries behind, too – at least leaving the worst of them. She still had a speech therapist and a physical therapist, too. They promised miracles. Diane chose to believe them.

The alternative was too depressing.

"How are you feeling?" Mark asked her, as they made the drive to her old apartment. It wasn't safe to stay there, she knew, but she wanted her things at least. Diane wanted her baby album and her parents' photos, her old teddy bear, and the knit cap her grandmother had made her when she was twelve: the kinds of things that meant something to her.

She didn't answer Mark for a few minutes. He didn't push the issue, and Diane was learning, much to her pleasure, that Mark wasn't that kind of person. He let people think about what they wanted to say, and he didn't pressure them to hurry up and say it. He let people be who they were, she guessed. And being quiet with him was okay. They didn't need to fill up the spaces with a bunch of meaningless chitchat.

So how did she feel? Really?

"Lucky, I think," she finally said. "I'm not in that wheelchair anymore. And I can talk clearly. Most of the time, anyway." She slid a sideways glance his way, watching him watch the road. "And I have you."

That got him to smile, a big, broad, light-up-his-face kind of grin. Mark reached over and rubbed her shoulder. "That you do," he agreed.

She spent the rest of the ride looking at his profile and thinking how handsome and thoughtful and loyal he had been to her. She'd give him his one mistake. Everybody deserved at least that in this life, didn't they? What he was now was more important than what he had been years ago.

He helped her out of the car, and together, they walked into her apartment building. Her mail slot was overflowing. "Bills," she smiled sheepishly. "And junk mail."

"Story of my life," Mark said. He was still paying off medical school himself, and he probably would be for years to come.

"It's so dusty in here," she said, running her hands over the coffee table. "Like time stopped." She wandered around, looking at everything, thinking about the last time she had been there. *That night.* She had been rushing around to meet Stephanie in time and had knocked over her plant, a big draping ivy that she had lovingly cared for for years now. It was still toppled over, dirt drifting out in a dune around the pot as brown leaves sagged along beside it.

She turned and looked at Mark, erasing the memory of *before* from her now.

"I killed this plant," she said. And then she broke down in tears.

Mark came to her, held her close, and let her cry into his shirt. They sat together like that, in the warm, sooty heat of a late spring day in Diane's old apartment, mourning what shouldn't have happened. But had.

When she was done crying, Mark lifted her face in his hands, kissing away the last of the wetness there. She gave him a gentle smile, her lips curving just the slightest bit at the ends. "I guess I needed that," she told him.

"It was time," he agreed, holding her tight again. "Time for a good cry."

He made them tea from a box of bags he found in the kitchen while she gathered up her stuff. "I'd rather have coffee," he told her, carrying the mugs into the living room where he had left her packing a box. Diane stood up to meet him.

"I'll be your cream and sugar," she said, stopping several feet from him. "That was so cheesy!" she said, chuckling a little. Then, almost immediately turning serious, "I meant to say, I'm ready, Mark. I want you to love me."

Mark's mouth dropped open. He had no intentions on rushing Diane into anything. He also had no intentions of refusing her offer. He stood there, holding the steaming mugs of tea and staring at her in disbelief and desire.

"Diane," he said, finally, his voice husky. "Are you sure?"

"Put down the mugs, Mark," she said, motioning with her eyes at the dining room table. Mark did as he was told.

She was shaking as her hands found the buttons of her blouse and she began to loosen each one, allowing the garment to fall to each side and expose her bra. Mark looked thrilled, the edges of his mouth trembling slightly, but he didn't come any closer. He just watched.

Diane felt nervous again at the feel of cool air against her skin.

Was this how she imagined it would happen? Her seducing him?

She didn't pause, though. To do so would be terrifying. Sliding the blouse off her shoulders, Diane unhooked her bra for him and let that fall away with her blouse. Mark paused, watching as she pulled her pants and panties as one over her hips, let everything fall to the carpet, and stepped out of the leg holes. He stood just looking at her beauty, unable to move.

Hurry up! She thought. *Hurry up and get over here before I chicken out!*

Diane's body was pure perfection, and her skin was like warm honey. Her breasts jutted out, proud, full, and bouncing as the fabric fell away, her dark, hard nipples begging to be sucked. Mark finally took the five steps across the room, stopping directly in front of her.

There was no going back now.

They didn't speak, but Diane heard a groan escape from Mark, from somewhere deep inside him. He reached out and fondled each breast tenderly at first, and as she responded, with more urgency. She closed her eyes, enjoying his hands on her. Her waist was slim and smooth, and it curved around at her hips. Mark's eyes trailed down between her legs as his hands moved from her breasts, to her stomach, and across her hips to her thighs. This was the first time he had seen all of her, and she was magnificent.

"You're more than I imagined," he whispered, his voice hoarse from desire. "I promise to take my time and be gentle."

Diane let out a small gasp as he fell to his knees. His fingers spread her lips, and he began gliding his tongue up and down her labia. For a moment, she was lost in the sensation, and then Diane grabbed his head, pushing his tongue into her.

"Oh God," she began, moaning as his tongue found her clitoris, licked around it and sucked it gently between his teeth. He reached behind her and pulled her cheeks apart as he lightly tickled, exploring with his fingers.

"Oh…" She moaned even more loudly as she circled her hips against him, pressing his head tighter to her body.

Diane felt as if she was riding unbuckled in a roller coaster. Her head was spinning. She was in dangerous territory.

As he felt her nearing orgasm, Mark stopped, pulling back and looking up at her. Her expression was filled with lust.

"Can I do something for you?" she asked. Her voice sounded gruff and coated with longing. He nodded up at her with hooded eyes, and then stood up to face her. She wasn't sure what to do then, and a flood of fear and inexperience filled her for a moment.

Mark sensed her uncertainty. "Here," he said, taking her hand and guiding it down his chest and toward his penis. She took her cues from him, unbuttoning his shirt, rolling it over his shoulders, and then lightly trailing her hands down over his stomach and across the front of his pants. She let her lips linger on his chest, planting a dozen soft kisses around his torso, and stopping when she got to the top of his jeans.

What would he look like naked? she thought, as she tried awkwardly to pull the zipper down. Another moan came from somewhere in the back of his throat, and Mark's hands guided her own again, freeing his penis from his jeans. They slid his pants down together, and she saw the tip of his penis push over the waistband of his underpants.

"Mmm…" she said, looking at it, gingerly touching the top, not sure what to do.

"You can lick it," he told her. "Suck the head." He gave her direction, and she dropped to her knees, licking the tip of it as he pulled his underwear down. The top was smooth and bulging, and she took it between her lips, sucking softly and then adding more pressure. It throbbed in response. It seemed to have a life of its own.

"Like a lollipop," he told her. "There, you can take a little more." Mark pushed a bit more of his penis into the tight O of her mouth.

It tasted salty, and Diane wasn't sure she was doing this right at all. But she sucked harder, and when she heard the sounds he was making, she knew she was making him feel good. She clasped his ass cheeks, pulling

253

them slightly open, and this made him slide in and out of her mouth faster. She felt his balls, heavy and hanging near her chin, and she realized she had taken most of him into her mouth.

How was she doing this without choking? She asked herself.

Without warning, he pulled back, and his penis came out of her mouth with a loud, wet pop. She was frightened for a moment when she saw his eyes. They looked so *hungry*.

"I want to take you now," he told her, pulling her from the floor as he took her by the arm and brought her to the couch. He brought her to the edge of it and pushed her gently backwards so she landed on her ass. Diane was trembling.

This was it.

"Don't hurt me," she managed to say, as he leaned forward.

"Never, baby. I'll never do anything to hurt you." His mouth closed on hers. Their tongues met, and he sucked at her lips, touching her breasts again, and rubbing the nipples between his fingertips. She touched back, letting her hands run over the length of his penis again, over his balls, and along the insides of his thighs as she got to know his body.

He stopped kissing her then, gathered up her breasts in both of his hands, and took one tip, then the other, into his mouth. She watched him nurse and felt something well up inside her, stirring inside her vagina. She spread her legs, leaning back into the sofa, and Mark followed along with her, keeping his mouth at her breast.

"I'm ready, Mark," she breathed his name, and the heady feeling of longing engulfed her as she did so. At this he climbed forward, pulling her under him in one quick movement. He had one hand on her breast as he prepared himself to enter her, guiding the tip of his penis to her.

"I need to be inside you," he said, hoping she was lubricated and ready to accept him. Her eyes, shiny and glazed, told him she was, and she brought her hips up to meet him.

"Tell me what to do," she said, again confirming she was ready. He fingered her tenderly, testing. She felt wet, but he took his time, trying to control himself and not push in all at once. There would be time for that later, and Mark fought the urge to take her quickly.

Mark slid into her slowly, an inch at a time. She was tight and unyielding at first, but anxiously pushing against him as she helped him to enter. He moaned as he began to slide in further with each lunge forward.

Diane bit her lip. "Aaahhh…" She said. This was a mix of pain and pleasure she had never known. She pressed her hips forward and up, accepting Mark's penis, ignoring the muscles inside that were fighting against being impaled.

She wanted him so much. She wanted *this* so much.

And then something gave, the muscles relaxed, and he was all the way inside of her. His free hand began fondling her breasts again as he sucked her nipples, and she responded, arching her back and throwing her hips toward him wildly.

She never dreamed it would feel like this. She ached. It hurt and tingled all at once. She was acutely aware that he was taking her virginity. She had given herself fully to this man.

Her head turned from side to side, and she moaned loudly, incoherently.

So this was what it was like to have a man love you and desire you and take you. Almost indescribable.

As they neared orgasm, he rose on his arms to look down on her. She was lovely and sexy and perfect to him in every way. They found each other's eyes, their hands meeting as well.

"I love you," he told her, overcome.

"I love you, too," she said, freely and unabashedly.

And then they were bucking wildly against each other, moaning and writhing as one, their tongues and mouths and bodies pressed together frantically. They came almost together, Mark first, and they both spent several minutes lost in the throb and drum of its aftermath.

When the last shades of passion fell away, and the day turned to evening, they slept in each other's arms, crammed together on Diane's sofa. When Diane opened her eyes again, Mark was on his elbow, staring down at her and tracing his fingertips along her cheekbones, her eyelids, her chin.

She smiled up at him, realizing that now she was his. And he, hers.

"Are you ready to go home now?" Mark asked her.

Diane looked around her apartment. At the empty walls where she'd taken down photos just hours before. At the dead plant in the corner that had made her cry. At the mugs of tea they had abandoned right before they had shared their love for one another.

Diane wiped the last bits of sleep from her eyes. She was wide awake, on the verge of renewed life.

"I'm definitely ready," she told him.

What had she been thinking, asking for scissors? This wasn't going to work the way she had intended at all. First off, they were dull. She'd be lucky to cut paper with them. The shears themselves had warped and didn't close properly, so it was a struggle to hold them together just right to make a cut. Jesus, she'd be clipping at herself for hours and still be alive and full of blood when they found her the next morning.

She knew because she had pulled up a thin layer of skin along the inside of the wrist and had made a snip there, watching her flesh pinch and wrinkle as she wrestled with the blades, finally managing to close them. What was left was a thin, open slice, but not much more. It had hardly bled. But it had hurt like a bitch.

Shit. This was NOT going to work.

"Happy Scrap booking!" Leah had said when she dropped them off, and Stephanie had had to hold her own hands down in order to keep from slapping her. Leah deserved whatever she got when the hospital administration found out she had been the one to provide their *suicidal* patient with scissors. Stephanie could hear the rumors rushing through the hospital like a growing wave. A tsunami.

"Leah Sanchez did what? NO! Not to the girl that got raped? You're kidding!!"

That's what they'd all be saying. Or something like that.

Yes, Stephanie would make damn sure they all knew where the scissors had come from.

How's that for a big "fuck you," Leah, she whispered, as she turned the scissors around and around in her fingers, studying them. There was a speck of rust on the upper shear. Maybe some grievous infection was coursing its way through her bloodstream right now. By the time they caught it, it would be too late.

One could only hope, she sighed.

She put down the scissors and picked up the mirror. The fucking thing was acrylic, not glass. Stephanie had figured that out when she slammed it against the floor and it didn't break. Ruby knew exactly what she was doing when she bought the thing, and so did the counselor. *Foiled again.* Stephanie felt like she was the main character in a very bad cartoon.

She looked at herself, tracing the red network of scars with her fingers. It looked better without the stitches, but still not good. Stephanie squinted her eyes. She looked just like a doll that had been broken and glued back together by a careless owner. Distorted.

They can fix that.

Stephanie shook her head. It didn't matter. They couldn't fix her soul.

She looked around her room. It smelled like a funeral parlor. All those flowers! All those 'Get Better Soons!' She didn't even know who they were from.

Stephanie was really all alone in the world. She hadn't realized it until now, but she was a castaway. Stephanie had ridden the coat tails of everyone who would let her, just to get farther away from her mother and the projects where she'd grown up. And here is where the winds of fate had dropped her.

Hell, there was no escaping destiny.

You should talk to Diane about it. At least she loves you. Ruby loves you.

Snip. Snip. Snip. Stephanie opened and shut the scissors in her hands.

Maybe… even Steve loves you.

She snipped again, listening to the sound of the sheers biting at the air.

The damn things were so warped, it was starting to hurt her fingers to open and close them. She switched hands.

She wasn't going to manage to get any more weapons in here anytime soon. No razors or belts or ropes or sharp objects. No bottles of pills or jugs of poison. There was only one way.

Stephanie stretched over the side of the bed, making a little mound with her pillow on the floor and standing the scissors straight up between it.

She was going to have to fall onto the scissors. Just the right way. She didn't want to injure an arm or a knee or anything else that could be corrected. The points had to enter somewhere vital. An artery, her heart, intestinal walls.

It was the only way.

Chapter 29

Kirby was so tired. Tired of standing watch at the window. Tired of jumping out of his skin every time he heard a siren. Tired of keeping his mother's voice out of his room. The past few days had been tough.

And he was hungry, too. Starving. He'd run out of cereal this morning, and that he had to eat with the last of the milk, which had soured. If he hadn't been so hungry, he might have dumped it right down the drain. But as it was, he just closed his eyes and swallowed. Good thing that cereal had been chocolate. It covered up most of the *yuck*.

He couldn't very well leave, could he? Who would be the lookout now that danger was close? Who would keep an eye on his treasures?

But he was going to have to leave. By lunchtime, he was going to be hungry again, and there was nothing left to eat.

The only thing that had gotten him through was his television. And Stephanie. Stephanie's face, so pretty and serene, stared back at him and calmed his soul. Kirby was sure of it now. She was meant to be his.

That's why he'd met her that night.

He was still in his clothes from two days ago. They felt stiff, and his own body odor was as spoiled and sour as the milk. Stephanie would not want to see him like *this*.

Kirby took one last, fleeing glance out of the window. Nothing. The street was empty except for a few pedestrians and a cat in the alleyway.

"Here kitty, kitty," Kirby said, tapping on the window. The cat ran away, scared at the sound, and Kirby laughed. It made him feel a little better to remember he was bigger than something else.

He'd just closed the bathroom door and stripped his clothes off when he heard the knocking. Noises carried in this old building, and at first, Kirby didn't realize it was someone at his door until it got louder. Someone was saying his name.

Kirby's insides turned to ice. His stomach turned nauseous all at once.

The fuzz! He thought, remembering the term from some old movie he had seen as a youngster. Kirby pressed himself against the shower wall, wishing he could blend into the tile there.

The window! He'd crawl out the window. Kirby tiptoed out of the bathroom and crossed the hall in a sprint, holding his testicles in place.

Lord Jesus, help me!

He yanked the top drawer in his dresser, and it clattered to the floor, falling on his foot and spewing clothing. Kirby jumped up and down on one foot, trying not to cry out from the pain. *Shhhh shhhh shhhh!* He told himself.

"Kirby! Open up!" The voice was sharp. Familiar.

It was Marty. Kirby wiped at his brow, pulled on a pair of pants, and hurried to the door.

"Marty!" He threw it open, forgetting their last conversation and the fear attached to it. "My main man!" Relief thrummed in his veins.

"Quick, let me in." Marty pushed past him, shutting the door. "I don't know if I was followed." He lowered his head conspiratorially, and all the worry came flooding back.

"Shit!" Kirby began, bouncing up and down on the balls of his feet and chewing at his thumbnail. "Shit shit shit shit shit shit," he chanted.

Marty was wearing a suit, and he looked official.

"It's gonna be okay," Marty said. He kept his voice low as if someone may hear them, and Kirby's eyes darted around. Looking for spy stuff. *The place could be bugged!*

"What are the police saying now, Marty? Did they ask you questions about the ladies?"

Marty nodded. "They've been sniffing around at work," he told him. "I've seen people following me home, too. People I know. It's just a matter of time."

Kirby's face blanched, a gray, deathly pale. His lips quivered perceptively.

Marty would know. He must be telling the truth.

"I gotta pack," Kirby said, racing back into his bedroom. He began frantically picking clothes off the floor, pushing them into a pile, and searching for his knap sack. Marty followed him.

"What's this?" Marty said, lifting something from Kirby's dresser.

Something flat and plastic. Marty stood there staring at it, and Kirby watched his face start to redden.

Stephanie! He had the picture of Stephanie!

"That's mine!" Kirby said, snatching it away and holding it behind his back. "It's not yours, it's mine!"

"That's the girl," Marty said. "The one you hurt!" He pointed his finger at Kirby. "The one that the police know about."

Kirby stopped for a second, thinking. *That wasn't fair, that wasn't fair! He loved her! They were meant to be together!*

"You hurt her, too, Marty!" He accused. "You hurt her worse!"

"I didn't put my thing in her," Marty's tone was soft. "I didn't do the nasty, dirty thing to her. The one like your Momma did to you, Kirby. You didn't like it when your Momma did those things to you, did you?"

Kirby hung his head. His face was a burning fire. *How did Marty know that? How did he know?*

"She loves me," Kirby mumbled, feeling sick again. "My Momma loved me, and Stephanie loves me, too." He put his hands around his tummy. He could feel it churning.

"It's okay, Kirby," Marty was saying. "I'm scared, too."

Kirby's head shot up. "You are?"

"I know all about jail, remember? I was there, too."

"But not locked in, Marty. That's the worst."

"I know a way," Marty continued. "It will take away the pain

264

forever. I brought some for both of us." Marty's hand went to his pocket and he produced a small bottle.

"These are happy pills. I got them from work. They make you forget all the bad things. Do you want to forget, Kirby?" He held the bottle up and then showed Kirby a pill. It was blue, like an egg he saw once in a bird's nest. It had been so beautiful that he'd picked it up and run home with it to show his Momma.

"You touched this egg? You stole it from the Momma bird's nest?" she asked him, hands on her hips, a look of disgust crossing her face.

"Yes, Momma, I brought it for you," he told her.

"This egg ain't no good to me, and now it ain't no good to the momma bird either. They won't warm an egg that's been touched by a human!" She'd smashed it into the sink, and Kirby had closed his eyes at the thing that was inside.

He cried then, and he started to cry now, just thinking about it.

Puddles again. Puddles in his brain. Muddy, cloudy, deep puddles with piranha swimming inside. Yes, he wanted to forget them.

"Yes," he said, sitting down on the bed. He felt as if someone had knocked the breath out of him. Kirby's stomach rumbled again, moving in different directions. He felt so sick inside. "I want to forget," he said quietly, laying down and clutching his stomach.

"Open up," Marty said, and Kirby held out his tongue. Marty placed the pills there, three, four, maybe five of them, Kirby didn't know. He had to swallow back bile to get them down. But he did it.

"Good job, Kirby," Marty said, as he sat on the edge of the bed and patted his hand. "I want you to be so happy that I gave them all to you."

"Thanks, Marty," Kirby said, closing his eyes. The pain in his stomach was subsiding. And Marty was right. He was forgetting all about the bad things. It felt like he was floating away. Kirby's eyes closed, and all he saw was blackness. There was nothing bad there, nothing scary.

This was so nice.

When he woke up again, it was dark outside, and Kirby was covered in vomit. It stuck in his hair, big chunks of cocoa puffs and curdled milk and blue pills. The discharge trailed down the side of his bed, leaking into a stiffening puddle on the floor. His throat was a desert.

That milk had been so bad. It spoiled his forgetting.

Kirby remembered everything.

He pulled himself from the bed, testing his stomach. He was shaky, but okay, and he climbed into the shower, sitting on the floor and letting the water course over his body. Kirby opened his mouth wide, letting the water flow in to soften the scratchy, dry edges of his throat.

Marty was gone. *Where had he taken his happy pills?* Not here, definitely not here. Kirby was all alone again, but he didn't want to be alone anymore.

Kirby decided. He'd clean himself up. And then he was going to see Stephanie.

Chapter 30

They had nothing. *How the hell had they been through all this time and still had nothing?* Sheryl sat on the bleachers of the University track field, pensively tapping a pen back and forth on the notebook in front of her. It was quiet here. Only one lone soul was running the track below, and the weather was magnificent. It was their best day yet after an endless, gray winter. Sheryl could smell the lilacs, and she breathed in deeply. As cliché as it sounded, she hoped the new birth of spring would bring new perspectives, new clues, and an end to the rapes that had plagued them all.

She could still feel the sting from comments she overheard last night. Things about the Oakmont police buying their badges at the dime store. Things about how they weren't even trying to solve the case. Sheryl had stopped reading the paper and watching the news. But could she blame people for thinking it? To the outside world, it looked as if the detectives were floundering.

Sheryl concentrated on the victims, going over each of them and trying to reconnect with their memories. They had all given her parts of what had happened to them, but none of them could recall everything. Maybe she could fit all of their pieces into one big answer.

How many times had she been down this path now? Not enough, she answered herself. *Not enough.*

Sheryl sighed, absentmindedly chewing on her nails.

"You're not going to have fingers left at the rate you are going," Jim teased, as he sat down next to her with the heavy thud of someone who was exhausted. "What's eating at your brain today, partner?"

He *looked* tired. Ragged. And he had been different lately. Distant from her somehow.

"I'm just thinking about the women. Trying to add up their stories. There are so many little bits…"

"That's your department," he said. "Women talk to women." And this was true. Sheryl interviewed the victims, painstakingly listening to whatever they would tell her, gently coercing all the mortifying, embarrassing details from their memories. It was horrible work, and it made her insides shrivel every time she had to do it.

Worse still, she'd made a promise to all of the women. And she had yet to come through. Why should they trust her?

"The perpetrators wore masks in all of the attacks but one. And Stephanie Kramer remembers nothing. Okay, it was dark, she'd been drinking, and they took her by surprise. How could they have known she was going to be there? Do they know her? Does she know them? Did they follow her?" Sheryl thought out loud.

Jim shrugged. "Opportunity? That attack wasn't planned. That's most likely. Or they were pushing their luck. Trying to see how far they could go. That's appealing to criminals or anyone who likes to test their limits. To you and me, even. We go beyond the rules sometimes, you know? When it's necessary. She was in the wrong place at the wrong time, and so was her friend. The odds of that are low, but that doesn't mean they are impossible. They were a potluck supper."

Sheryl frowned at the bad description and at the implications of the comments.

"So what do you think they'll do next? Start sending clues in the mail? Start attacking women in broad daylight? How far is too far, Jim?"

"That's when they get caught," Jim said. "That's when they fuck up. The thrill of the hunt takes over their fear. They get careless. Take more chances."

"So you think we'll have to wait until they make more mistakes to solve this? I can't allow another woman to get attacked. That's out of the question." She slammed closed the notebook. "It can't happen."

"I got Lawson covered. Him and his brother. There's no way Mark did this. But his brother, Steve… I think we need to take a closer look at him." Jim looked bored, an unlit cigarette hanging lazily from his mouth. Sheryl plucked it out, and Jim didn't protest.

"I've got a bad feeling about that Goodwin," she told Jim. "He's not going to show up for the test. He's going to hide behind his squirrelly little lawyers and make us waste time *forcing* him to provide a sample of his spit, for God's sake."

"So what do we got? Shoe tracks, a couple cigarette butts, and a handful of confused and terrified women?"

"That's about it," Sheryl told him.

"Not good." Jim said, stoic as usual. He never betrayed an emotion, never seemed to lose control. Strong. Confident. Jim was all the things she admired in an officer.

And here she was, coming out of her skin. Sheryl looked at the ends of her nails, cracked and shredded from all the chewing.

Why couldn't she keep it together? What kind of cop was she anyway?

"It's a girl thing," Jim told her as if reading her mind. "Girls emote."

"A whole hell of a lot of good that does us," she said, standing to go. She vowed to toughen up. "See you at the station?"

Jim nodded, and they walked back their cars together. Sheryl turned on her radio to listen with sinking hope for any bulletin, any news from headquarters that would break her losing streak.

Just something little. Something that fits, she thought. There were little tidbits about a convenience store robbery, a shooting, and a carjacking. But nothing that would help her solve her crime. Nothing that could help the women feel just a tiny bit of justice had been served.

When she looked up again, Jim was gone. Sheryl started her engine and headed back to the station.

She was gone. The bitch was gone!

How the hell had she managed it?

Marty stood in the middle of the hallway, shock holding him in

271

place. The front door had been closed and latched when he'd gotten there. Everything looked *normal.* He'd even started to call out to her. Depending on how this went, he'd decide what to do with her *after*.

"Ready or not…" He'd gotten that far when he noticed the basement door.

It was standing wide open. The frame wasn't broken. It looked like she'd just opened it up and waltzed away.

He should have fucking killed her when he had the chance.

Panic settled in his chest. *How long had she been gone? How far had she gotten?*

She was injured, but he didn't think anything had been broken. A good-hearted neighbor, a passerby, anyone could have stopped to help her.

Shit. Shit Shit Shit.

He had to get the fuck out of here.

Marty dug through his desk. His credit cards, his passport. New identification. Screw his clothes. He could buy new clothes. A movement caught the corner of his eye right before he left the room, a red, blinking flash in the corner of his vision. Marty was so frenzied, so desperate that at first, he didn't know what it was.

The answering machine. There was a message.

Don't listen, he thought at first. *Just get going.* The minutes were ticking away behind him, and he was pushing it now.

But he had to know. Whatever was on that machine might tell him how close they were on his tail. He pushed the button, bracing himself.

The message was from Kirby. *But Kirby was dead!* He had watched his breathing slow, then stop with his own damn eyes. Marty was sure of it!

He didn't stop again for anything. Marty grabbed the documents he needed, and then he was gone.

Sheryl was at her desk when the woman stumbled into the station. She looked like she had been run over. Her hair was hanging in her face, but Sheryl could see she'd been beaten. There was a trail of blood dribbling from a rough, black scab on the corner of her mouth. She was limping. She had no shoes on, and the bottom half of her legs were covered with bruises.

Domestic violence. It was her first thought as she rushed forward to meet her, letting the women lean on her for support.

"You're safe now," Sheryl assured her, putting her arm around the woman's shoulder. "You're safe."

The woman looked at her then, a mass of tears and blood and makeup trailing down her cheeks. "I've been raped," she said, and the words cut a hole in Sheryl's stomach. "He left me in the basement." she looked crazily into Sheryl's eyes, grabbing her by the arms so hard she left pressure prints there. "But I know where he lives," the girl finished, as she collapsed in sobs.

The world turned fuzzy for a second, and Sheryl steadied herself against the wall.

"What?" She whispered unbelieving. "Where? Who?" And then she yelled behind her. "JIM! JIM, GET THE HELL OVER HERE!"

Chapter 31

The halls were dim and confusing. The overhead lights cast a strange flicker on the walls, and all of the doors looked the same. Kirby had been wandering here for what seemed like forever. His stomach still felt queasy, and he'd had to stop in the bathroom where he vomited a burning stream of bile into the toilet. He hugged the cool sides of the toilet and then laid his face on the rim before he could move again. When he'd come out of the bathroom, he'd felt more turned around, more *lost*, than he had been when he entered.

But at least he was done with all the puking. He wiped the light sheen of sweat from his forehead and kept moving.

Marty had tried to kill him. He knew that now. Those weren't happy pills. They were killing pills.

Marty wanted to kill him so that he could get away. That's why he called his house. And let the lady out of the basement. That poor lady. She wanted a ride, but Kirby only had his bike. And he had needed to get to the hospital. He hoped she found her way to the police.

The police could have Marty. But they wouldn't get Kirby. Kirby and Stephanie were going to heaven together.

A lady had stopped him on the second floor. She was wearing a doctor's coat, and she looked very stern and official.

"Can I help you?" she asked, stopping him by putting her hand against his chest.

Kirby hadn't known what to say. He stared at her, ready to run if she said anything that sounded like she was calling security. Or, God forbid, the police. Instead she'd looked at her watch, guessing his intentions.

"Visiting hours are over," she said. "You'll have to come back tomorrow."

"Visiting hours?" Kirby had asked. *What did that mean?*

She looked annoyed, tapping her foot but taking her hand off his chest. "Are you here to see someone? A patient here at the hospital?

Kirby's brow unfurled. *Ah!*

"Yes," he said. "Yes!"

She pointed down the hall, at a bright red exit sign.

"Visiting time is over." It sounded like she was talking to a child. "You have to *leave* and come back tomorrow at ten in the morning. You can't see any patients now."

Dammit! Kirby smacked his hand across his forehead. *Now he understood.* He nodded at the lady, but he wasn't leaving. He *pretended* to leave, lumbering down the hall where the lady had pointed and disappearing around the corner. He waited, counting to one hundred, just like he was playing hide and seek. When he peeked back around the corner, the lady was gone, and the hallway was all emptiness and flickering lights again. Kirby breathed relief.

"You need to look official, too." It was his Momma talking! *How*

276

had she gotten here, to University Hospital? Kirby thought of his bike outside, leaning against the side of the building, resting in the shadows. He knew how *he* had gotten here. Momma must have followed.

He swallowed hard. "Momma?" he said quietly, testing the air.

Nothing.

He started to walk again, listening to the squeak his sneakers made against the dull, waxed floor. The sound made his teeth hurt, and he tried walking by picking up his feet and laying them down instead of dragging them along.

"KIRBY!" It was a hiss, sharp and insistent, and it came from behind him. He wheeled around. There was a man there. A man in a coat, but it wasn't his voice that Kirby had heard. The man was looking down, not at him, and he was carrying a container by the handles. It had little bottles inside, vials of blood. Kirby wrinkled his nose. But he knew what he had to do.

The man was close, still looking down. Kirby moved his body, blocking his way. The man saw his feet first, and by the time he looked up, Kirby had clocked him, knocking him out cold.

The poor man! He hadn't even had time to look surprised. Kirby stared at the figure slumped on the floor and felt bad for hitting him like that. His carrying case had tumbled over, but only a few vials had spilled out. Nothing had broken.

"Hurry!" It was the voice again, and Kirby gathered up the ampoules,

277

laying them haphazardly in the bottom of his plastic case. *But where was he supposed to put the man?* His eye scanned the hallway.

All the doors looked the same. He jogged down the length of the hallway, searching for something that looked safe and familiar. They had different signs on them: *hazardous materials, OT/X-ray clinic, Laboratory.* Kirby had no idea what these were or if any people were lurking on the other side, waiting to ask who he was and what he was doing.

Because visiting hours were over.

The bathroom, he decided. Kirby began dragging the man by his arms down the hallway, back to where he'd gotten sick. But what if someone was in *there*?

Kirby's own arms were getting tired. The man was heavy, and the case was tipping again in his free hand. Someone could come down the hall at any time.

JANITOR. That sign stopped him. That would be better than the public bathroom.

It was like a closet in there, dark and small with rows of linens and bottles of cleaning fluid. He left the door open, only a crack so that he could see, but the corners were still black, scary looking and full of ghosts.

There were industrial-sized buckets on wheels, and Kirby kicked one out of the way, watching it roll to the far end of the tiny space. *They had those in prison!* Kirby had tripped over a bucket just like these when those men, the ones that worked in the prison laundry, had come after him.

278

The day he met Marty. The day Marty had saved him.

"Don't think about them buckets," his Momma said. "Don't even look at them."

"Okay, Momma," he answered. "Okay, okay, okay, okay!"

Kirby laid the man on the floor, trying to be careful, but dropping him anyway, and the man's head bounced on the hard surface.

"Sorry," Kirby whispered, pulling the jacket from the man as gently as he could and pulling it over his own arms. A little tight, but it would do.

Don't forget the blood box, Kirby told himself, reaching down for it. He heard the bottles rattle against each other. That would make him look very *official.* He gritted his teeth. *And don't break anything, stupid!*

Kirby left the closet, closing the door behind him and wishing he could lock it. There was no one around. *This was his lucky day!* But the hall was bright compared to the room, and he just stood there, squinting as he tried to decide how to find Stephanie.

The dark was calming. She didn't have to worry about anyone seeing her face. She didn't have to worry about answering questions or pretending to be okay. She could just *be.* But that, just like everything else, was only temporary.

She thought about leaving a note. A big, long diatribe explaining to everyone - *as if they wouldn't know* - why life just wasn't worth the effort. But when she tried to write it, scribbling out words and then whole lines, she felt selfish and shallow.

There were a million people in the world who had suffered more than she had, and who were suffering at this very minute. Stephanie scrapped the note idea.

Just do it, she told herself. *Quit thinking and start doing.*

She sat there, not moving.

Okay, just one little note. Stephanie clicked on the nightlight above her bed and started writing.

The floor was cold. Cold, hard, and unyielding. *How on earth?* There was something in her nose and faces in a circle above her, murmuring excitedly. She could sense action taking place behind them. Feet running, sirens blaring. She tried to pick her head up off the floor, but a hand pressed it gently down again.

"Stay still, don't move. You hit your head pretty hard."

Who was that? And more importantly, *what the hell was going on? Where was she?*

He found her. He found her! Momma had helped him, of course, helped him to read the signs. *Without her, he would have walked right by! He might have been wandering this hospital until morning!*

But the chart, the big one behind the nurse's station had her name on it. *Kramer.* In big black letters. And so Kirby knew where Stephanie was now.

He just didn't know how to get to her. There was a policeman sitting in front of her door. That was why he was standing on the fringe of the hall, staring down there, waiting for something to happen. His heart was a frantic drum.

"Be still and quiet! And watch," his Momma told him. Kirby did as he was told.

It seemed like forever that he had to stand there. From his hiding place, he watched nurses come and go, their feet making soft *whoosh*ing sounds against the floor. Kirby's own foot was asleep, and he longed to jump up and down on it to wake it up, but he knew better than that. He was to be quiet as a mouse. That's what his Momma used to say when he was a boy and he wanted to run and play outside with other children. But he had to play inside instead and be a good boy, *quiet as a mouse*. It had been hard then, and it was hard now. But he did it anyway.

And no one even noticed him.

His eyes were growing weary when the policeman left. Kirby felt a poke on his shoulder, something waking him up. He'd been falling asleep on his feet, but he wasn't dreaming. *The policeman really was leaving.* Kirby watched him take a call on the phone that was on his belt and watched him begin talking, fast and furious. And then the officer had just left, rushing down the hall in the opposite direction like a jet. Kirby heard him tell a nurse at the desk that someone would be there to cover him.

This was his chance. And he took it.

He had to hurry.

Her room was dark, except for a tiny light by the bed, and it was hard to see. She wasn't in her bed. Kirby let the door close behind him, and he was swallowed up by the inky light. He was still carrying the case of blood tubes, and he set it on the floor. He wasn't here to take her blood. He was here to save her, to take her to heaven with him where it was safe.

"Stephanie?" he whispered.

No answer. Kirby moved in, closer to the bed.

"I'm fine, I'm fine," Sheryl struggled to her elbows, letting one of the young recruits, Officer McCarron, pull her up the rest of the way. "Please!" She was on her feet, pulling her arm out of his grip then. *She needed some fucking space!*

"You took a tumble," the officer was telling her. "After the news and all. Chief says you gotta go in the ambulance, whether you like it or not. Can't take the chance of you suing the police department or nothing." He smiled at her. "You might have a concussion or something."

Sheryl struggled with his words. She had no idea what had just happened. *What news? Had she passed out?*

"Where's Jim?" she asked, looking around at the sea of activity in the precinct, trying to locate him. It was a madhouse in there!

Officer McCarron spat the mouthful of coffee he'd just taken straight into the air.

"Jim? That's who *we* are looking for, Avery. Funny stuff!" He shook his head.

That's all it took for her to remember. The girl. The address. The name.

James Martin Pranther. The girl said that was who had raped her.

Chapter 32

Stephanie opened her eyes, looking out into a sea of nothingness. *Was she dead? God, please let me be dead,* she thought. She moved a little, lifting her forehead off the floor.

She was lying face down on the floor, her leg folded under her and throbbing miserably, almost bad enough for her to cry out. She could smell disinfectant. And she could hear the interminable beeping of the hospital machinery. She was definitely *not* dead.

"Stephanie!"

Who the fuck? She stopped moving and turned her head to the voice.

"What on earth are you doing on the floor?" Hands, big hands, were pulling her up from behind, sending a fresh wave of searing pain pounding directly into her brain.

"My leg," she managed. "My leg," her breathing came out in heavy puffs of effort. *The pain was so bad!* "I think it might be broken."

The big man who was holding her propped her up gently - *almost lovingly?* -on the bed.

"Aaar," she moaned, as she came to a rest. "It hurts."

They looked down at her leg together. Not broken. Stabbed. The scissors, the stupid ass dull scissors, were sticking straight out from the middle of her thigh.

"Ouch," said the man, and Stephanie got a good look at him now.

As good a look as she could by the dim nightlight anyway. Black hair combed straight back from his face. Light eyes, although she couldn't tell the color. Heavy brow.

This was a new face. Someone who had never been in here before. She strained to see his name tag. *Henry Chavez.*

"What now?" Stephanie asked, getting more annoyed as it dawned on her that things hadn't gone like she had planned. Not even close. "Can you take it out, or what?" And then, trying to cover up her intentions, she added. "It was totally an accident. I must have fallen out of bed with them in my hand or something."

He seemed unfazed by the fact that she was in possession of scissors in the first place. "Sure." He smiled, grabbing the handle as he prepared to pull.

"Whoa, whoa, hold up there, Henry!" Stephanie tried to pull away, her heart seizing just slightly.

He looked confused, the smile fading first from his eyes and then from his lips.

"I'm not Henry, silly," he said, threading his fingers through the loop at the top of each shear. "But I don't want you to meet Momma with these in your leg." He shook his head. "Why'd you do this anyway?"

Stephanie's heart froze completely now, and she wasn't sure what to say. *This was just weird. Did he say he was taking her to meet Momma?* The first prickle of pure fear threaded its way down her belly.

Stephanie glanced around, ignoring the pain and his hands, which were tenderly poking at the scissors. She was looking for the remote with the call button. Stephanie nonchalantly let her fingers trail slowly under the sheets. She didn't want to piss him off or alert him to what she was doing. Something told her that was a very bad idea.

The damn remote was attached to the bed. How could she have lost it? She needed a new nurse.

But hey, it looks like this nurse is going to help you bleed to death. That's what you wanted isn't it?

Henry started to tug, pulling her skin up with it.

Where the hell were his gloves? Ever hear of possible infection, Henry?

"Please don't pull it," she said abruptly. His fingers paused, and he stopped, looking her straight in the eye. "Please," she said again, feeling the threat of tears.

"Okay, Stephanie. Okay, don't cry." He patted her arm, not letting his eyes leave hers.

Look away! Look away! She begged him with her mind. The guy was creeping her out, sending a new tingle of fear up the back of her neck.

"I'm sorry about your face," he said, looking at her hard. "It's different than the picture. Marty, he's not a nice guy all the time. He got me out of prison you know – when he worked upstate. He killed the guys who were trying to hurt me. But then he hurt you. And he gave me those pills!" He told her, shaking his head as if he just couldn't believe it himself. "He's definitely going to jail now. That lady in his basement, she's gonna tell. I let her out, you know."

Stephanie felt the world swim away. *What was this guy talking about?* He shook her back to him, pushing her shoulders back and forth as if she was a baby doll.

"But I still love you. It's not too bad, your face." He said simply, as he closed his eyes and pursed his lips.

He was preparing to kiss her! Stephanie hastily turned her head to the side, and he ended up kissing her temple, his lips skidding off at an angle with her movement.

He pulled back, grabbing her eyes again. "Don't you love me?" he asked, a frown pulling at his features. His entire face looked as if it had melted.

Where the fuck was the remote!

Stephanie's eyes widened, and she couldn't find her voice. Her hands frantically tugged at the bedclothes, feeling for the cylinder that would bring the night nurse. Anyone. She'd take anyone at this point.

This guy was dangerous.

He took her by the shoulders and closed his eyes again, coming toward her lips.

A flash of memory, a face, eyes closed, head thrown back in delirium, grunting, pounding at her body...This *face?* *WAS IT THIS FUCKING FACE?*

He smashed his lips against hers, crushing her mouth. She felt something pop (*the last of her stitches?*), and she could taste a trickle of blood in the back of her throat. Her chest was a fire pit, and she couldn't feel her heart beat anymore. It had raced away.

Stephanie wasn't even sure she had a heartbeat any longer.

His hands moved, away from the scissors, one closing over her breast and kneading it with his fingers. The other straddled her throat, testing her larynx. Stephanie felt vomit rise there. She curled her hand over the handle.

Don't think about it. Just do it.

And she did, yanking with all her might, feeling a knot of anguish and a surge of flowing liquid meld into one as she did so. The scissors stuck, tugging at her muscle, at whatever else they had pierced when she'd attempted to fall on them. She yanked again, feeling the pull, and then they were free.

Kirby sensed her movement, drew back and looked at her again, his hand still lingering on her breast.

"Don't worry," he said. I'm going to take us both where its safe..."

She lifted the scissors, a thin line of blood splattering across her face and into her eye. Holding them high, directly over her head, she plunged them into the side of Kirby's neck. His eyes widened, and his tongue came out of his mouth.

"Momma?" He was still looking into Stephanie's eyes, and she could see now that his were light blue, the color of the sky on a perfect day.

Such beautiful eyes, she thought, as she looked back at him, watching them glaze.

"Momma?" Kirby asked. Someone was coming toward him, holding out her arms. There was a light behind her, bright and blinding, and Kirby had to squint to see. "Momma, is that you?"

She had come for him after all. Pretending to let him take Stephanie with him, to have a real girl to love. But Momma had wanted him for herself all along. And now she had him.

Kirby looked up at the figure standing over him. Wooly hair, turning gray. Round, soft body. It was his Momma all right. She had come for him.

And now she would have him forever.

Kirby's world blinked out.

His eyes never closed. He looked like he was daydreaming far away somewhere. The man was still warm, but the weight of his body was heavy, threatening to fall against her. Stephanie was holding him at arm's length, afraid to let him fall and slump away on the floor somewhere.

She needed to see that he wasn't coming back.

She opened her mouth, feeling the fresh clot of blood at the top corner crack open again while the throb in her leg reach high intensity. Her dressing gown was sticking to the blood on her thigh now, and her whole leg was a furnace.

Stephanie might have underestimated herself. She might not have been ready to die today after all. The man's body slid a little closer toward her. He was a lead weight. She let him slide, and he collapsed into a heap on the floor.

Her voice returned.

Stephanie started screaming.

Chapter 33

They left the hospital together, two women, two men, and an older lady. As of that day, that moment, they were all each other had. Stephanie and Diane had come in together, so it seemed only fitting that they would exit the same way. Diane had gone up to collect her best friend and brought her down to join Mark and Ruby and Steve in the lobby. And then they left University Hospital as a group, with their last member firmly intact.

"It smells like summer," Diane said slowly. She was now in the habit of pronouncing each word with the precision of a surgeon, even though her speech was almost perfect.

"That's because it is," Stephanie told, her thinking the last time they had crossed this road, it had frost clinging to it. Outside of the seasons, the world hadn't really changed that much.

"Mark and I are going to take a vacation, I think," Diane continued. "Somewhere quiet. The top of a mountain or something."

Who knew? Maybe they would go on vacation and never come back. Maybe they would erase this old, bad dream for good by starting fresh somewhere else. But most likely, they'd return. Oakmont would call them back. It was where they started, and it was where they belonged.

Mark pulled her to him, letting her lean against his side. Diane's gait was still shaky, her center just a hair off. Gravity may come back to her, and it may not. For now, she'd lean.

"That sounds good, Diane. Really nice." Stephanie tried to smile, and the hint of one felt like it might even have crossed her face. She let Ruby take her hand, feeling her squeeze it gently with reassurance. Stephanie squeezed back.

They got one of the bad guys, at least.

But one of them had escaped. Jim Pranther was probably out of the country by now, at least that's what Sheryl Avery told them the police were speculating. They didn't know everything about the beginning, except that "Marty" had been a prison guard when Kirby Donaldson was housed at Upstate Correctional. Kirby had been small time then, a peeping tom, really, with a few thefts under his belt. Just a kid with a mental problem and a low IQ. As far as Stephanie understood it, he'd been tormented, raped, and bullied by some of the other inmates in Upstate. So when Pranther took matters into his own hands by disposing of his tormentors, and blaming it on a prison gang, he was able to mold Kirby into whatever he wanted.

She didn't want to think of Kirby as a victim, but somehow Stephanie did. He was the man who had raped her, and had tried in the end to take whatever sad remnants were left of her life. She hated him, but she felt sorry for him, too. Mostly she was still struck by the fact that she had fought for

292

those sad remnants, however tattered they were. Maybe she wanted to live more than she thought she had.

Stephanie hoped they would track down Pranther. Sheryl promised they'd keep searching and following leads, but Stephanie wouldn't hold her breath. Instead, she would try not to live her life in fear that he would come back for her. She would try not to walk in the shadows and hide her face from the world.

She instinctively reached up, feeling the fresh, pink scars that etched lines in her face. There were a few more surgeries to come, ones that promised to fade most of the outside damage away. Here, in the light, she was self-conscious, already steeling herself for the stares and the questions from passers-by, the looks of sympathy and pity. If only they knew that the scars on the outside were only the tip of the iceberg.

But who saw those inside things, really? People didn't think about what lay just below what they could see.

"Let's hit Bases for a drink," Steve said, knowing there were people there waiting for them to return home. Not people who really knew them as they were now, emerging from whatever it was that they had each emerged from. But people who knew them before and who might get to know them again. Potential friends.

Steve looked over at Stephanie, wanting to hold her other hand, to put his arm around her waist and pull her close. Just looking at her made his heart swell with something. Steve didn't want to call it love. Not yet.

Admiration maybe?

Yeah, he *got* Stephanie now; he knew where she was coming from. And if she could come back from that, she had one hell of a spirit. Someone who could *get* him too, and be an understanding ear at the end of the day. That's all Steve wanted in life now. It was what the five of them hoped they had in each other, he guessed.

That was probably all anybody needed.

Even the bad guys had been good guys once. Life took people to funny places, and sometimes to places they didn't want to go. To the edge. To the brink. Sometimes they came back; sometimes they decided to stay lost.

And just because they were present today, doesn't mean they would be tomorrow.

But for now, for this moment, it meant there would be no time for tears.

HELP SUPPORT OUR TROOPS

In addition to being an author, Janice M. Turner or rather SGM Janice M. Turner supports our troops and her fellow comrades through the non-profit charity, RE-MASC.

RE-MASC: Reclaiming our members of the Armed Services through Counseling

RE-MASC is an organization dedicated to the treatment, education, research and testing of Post-Traumatic Stress Disorder and how it affects the soldier and their family. RE-MASC is a non-profit organization committed to giving our soldiers the care and recovery treatment to help combat war induced stress. They offer a wide variety of choices for an effective solution to this very serious threat to our military community. RE-MASC offers both a HOTLINE and live counselor. The RE-MASC family also provides the option of referrals to licensed psychological professionals for the diagnosis and treatment of PTSD, Suicide Prevention, Drug and Alcohol treatment, group and family counseling sessions and more.

PLEASE VISIT **RE-MASC** AT
HTTP://WWW.RE-MASC.ORG

QUICK ORDER FORM

QUANTITY DISCOUNTS ARE AVAILABLE ON BULK PURCHASES OF NO TIME FOR TEARS FOR EDUCATIONAL PURPOSES, FUND RAISING OR GIFT GIVING.

PLEASE CONTACT US FOR MORE INFORMATION

EMAIL ORDERS:JANICEMTURNER.COM
PHONE: (571) 312-6234
WEB PAGE: HTTP://WWW.PIRAASPUBLISHING.COM
        HTTP://WWW.INFONOTIMEFORTEARS.ORG

To order No Time for Tears, fill out the information below and mail it with your payment to:

PIRAAS PUBLISHING
PO BOX 3093
Alexandria, VA 22302

NAME: _____

ADDRESS: _____

CITY,STATE,ZIP: _____

COUNTRY: _____

Please send the following number of books:_____Qty
Price: $19.95 each

Shipping by Air:
US: $3.75 for the 1st book, $2.00 for each additional book.
Canada and Mexico: $5.00, Other countries $12.00

Credit Card Orders available through Paypal
NTFT@piraaspublishing.com